"You require proof," she said. "This is proof."

"A little black box?" It was worse than Nick had imagined. What the hell was it, anyway? A compact? Was she about to powder her nose?

Kia pointed it at a standing lamp he'd been using as a clothes catcher. It was drapped with T-shirts and shorts that he might be able to wear one more time before he forced himself to go down to the basement of the building and do a few loads of laundry.

So, what did she expect to prove?

A red beam shot out from the box. The floor lamp popped and then was gone, clothes and all.

He couldn't move. He just stared like an idiot at the spot where his lamp had once stood.

"Is that enough proof?"

KAREN KELLEY

Earth Guys Are Easy

KENSINGTON PUBLISHING CORP.
http://www.kensingtonbooks.com

BRAVA BOOKS are published by

Kensington Publishing Corp.
119 West 40th Street
New York, NY 10018

All Kensington Titles, Imprints, and Distributed Lines are available at special quantity discounts for bulk purchases for sales promotions, premiums, fund-raising, and educational or institutional use.

Special book excerpts or customized printings can also be created to fit specific needs. For details, write or phone the office of the Kensington special sales manager: Kensington Publishing Corp., 119 West 40th Street, New York, NY 10018, attn: Special Sales Department, Phone: 1-800-221-2647.

Brava and the B logo Reg. U.S. Pat. & TM Off.

ISBN-13: 978-0-7582-1768-4
ISBN-10: 0-7582-1768-4

First Trade Paperback Printing: February 2008
First Mass Market Printing: July 2009

10 9 8 7 6 5 4 3 2 1

Printed in the United States of America

To the slightly (Snort, that's an understatement!) off-balanced Sherry Spearman. Thanks for making me laugh until my sides ache.

To Connie Sughrue. It's great having you for a friend!

And because he twisted my arm, this book is also dedicated to Tom Griffin. Okay, okay, he's a good friend, too.

Chapter 1

Kia hoped one day her cousin stumbled across her charred remains and felt remorse!

The craft tilted.

Hang on!

Oh, nooooooooo!

She scrambled to flip the lever that would switch her to manual control, then gripped the guidance bar with both hands. This wasn't good! Her teeth rattled and her body shook from the violent vibrations that overtook the craft. She was going to crash into Earth and her life cycle would extinguish!

It was all Mala's fault. If her cousin hadn't decided she just had to go to Earth in search of something more than their perfect world, then Kia wouldn't be in this predicament.

Her concentration switched back to the orb she raced toward. It grew bigger and bigger. Her anxiety level mounted higher and higher.

The craft began to spin as it entered Earth's atmospheric pull. Clouds rushed past, then mountains, blurs of colors.

Oh Great One in all your infinite wisdom—Help!

The craft suddenly began to slow. Okay, this was better. Some measure of control returned.

Until she crashed into an immobile object and came to an abrupt stop. It was all she could do to keep from slamming her head into the control panel.

She swallowed past the sick feeling in her stomach. Not even one millisecond on Earth and already she felt ill. The planet was probably rife with disease and pestilence.

Okay, she could do this. She drew in a deep breath, raising her chin. After all, she was a warrior—brave and true of spirit.

And queasy.

Oh Great One, creator of every living, breathing Nerakian, the contents of her stomach were about to depart her body. Not good. She'd never been sick a day in her life.

Deep breath. Slow inhale, now exhale.

Better.

When the world stopped spinning, she stood, waving her hand in front of the door.

Nothing.

She raised her foot and executed a perfect kick, connecting with the metal. It groaned and creaked, then trembled open.

Her craft would not be safe to travel in again. Not that she wanted to return the same way. No, she would face the Elders' wrath and ask them to transport her and Mala back to Nerak in a tube transporter—a much smoother way to travel. There was a lot to be said about newer models.

Freezing air swirled inside the craft. She shivered. Earth was a cold planet. Why would Mala want to stay here? She'd said it was because she'd wanted imperfection. That no one could survive in their perfect world.

Mala had gotten *her* wish, it would seem. Earth did

not look at all perfect. And what was wrong with perfect? It certainly hadn't done *her* any harm.

No, she had a feeling it was more than that. Her cousin had been stuck on the idea of being with a real man rather than a machine since finding their grandmother's secret diaries and her video of interplanetary space travels to Earth.

Kia had never seen the attraction of having a man, Nerakian or otherwise. Not that there were any men left on her planet.

Now that she thought about it, Mala had been particularly interested in the documentary Grandmother had stashed away: *Debbie Does the Sheriff*. Her cousin had been extremely excited with her found treasure. Kia hadn't cared to view it. She'd been quite content with her life.

She grabbed her satchel and jumped down. Her feet landed with a thump.

Solid.

Good. She would've hated to be sucked down into nothingness.

No, it didn't matter what Mala found so intriguing about Earth, Kia was here to take her back to Nerak by whatever means necessary.

Kia had been given the DNA of a warrior, not that she'd ever had the chance to actually use her skills since they were at peace. But if she had to use force, she would.

She removed her locator from her front pocket and flipped it open. After putting in the necessary data, she pushed a button.

Nothing.

She jiggled the instrument. The small screen remained black.

Broken. Now what?

Mala was living on a ranch. That was the only information Kia had. A ranch, possibly with herds of animals.

A loud rumbling vibrated the ground beneath her feet. An army of brutish men? She slipped behind a tree and waited to see if warriors would appear, but the rumbling faded.

Her gaze moved upward. A tree. But up close, it felt . . . different than she'd expected. The description in the archived books described it perfectly: brown, rough-textured bark.

Another loud rumble shook the ground. What could be making that horrible noise?

She was a warrior—she stood taller, one eyebrow quirked; she would investigate.

She touched a button, shrouding her craft in invisibility, then removed a black cape from her satchel and fastened it under her chin. She would look into the rumbling and maybe locate Mala in the process. Soon this nonsense of staying on Earth would be forgotten and they could return to Nerak.

An hour later she came to the realization that she might be going in the wrong direction when she came to a fence and beyond that was a road. It didn't look like a ranch.

Ranches were supposed to be dwellings with smelly cows and . . . and cow-men. Although she hoped she never came face-to-face with a half-cow, half-man. That might even test her beyond what she was prepared to encounter.

But the rumbling didn't come from animals. It came from the wheeled craft traveling on the road.

"Primitive." She shook her head and tossed her bag over the fence. A few seconds later, she stood on the other side. Now what?

Just when she thought her day couldn't get any worse, one of the large craft pulled close to her, swirling up a cloud of dust that made her cough.

"Need a lift?" a burly earthman asked as he leaned his head out the window.

"A lift?" Why would she want this overgrown beast of a man to lift her?

"Yeah, need a ride? I'm going to Dallas if you're headed that way."

"Do they have a ranch there?"

He nodded. "You must be talking about that one from the TV show—Southfork. Yep, it's still there and open to tourists."

Tourists? What was a tourist? No matter. She would soon be with Mala. "Good, then I will ride with you."

He leaned over, disappering. She wondered if he might have dissolved into a puddle. Adam-1, her companion unit, had gotten too close to an incinerating machine once and melted into a shiny blob of metal. Very messy.

A few seconds later, part of his craft opened and then he straightened.

"If you're goin' with me, then you'd better hurry. I gotta get this load on in."

"I'm . . . goin'." She hurried around the side of the conveyance and climbed inside.

She would observe this man while she searched for Mala. The language on this part of the planet was similar to her own, although he talked rather peculiar. She would learn his manner of speech so she would blend in.

She climbed up and into the front of his machine and tried to make herself comfortable on the lumpy seat. Her hover seat was much better. And her craft cleaner.

Her nose wrinkled. What was that odor? It was quite possibly the worst thing she'd ever smelled. The sooner she found Mala the better. Surely her cousin was ready to leave this awful, imperfect world by now.

She waved her arm, but the door didn't close. Apparently, the closing mechanism was broken. The man leaned across and pulled it shut. His body odor filled her nostrils. If he didn't move from her immediate vicinity she really would empty the contents of her stomach.

"You're a cutie." He moved back to his side.

She looked at the man. Part of his hair was missing. The top part. Only the side hair remained, and it stuck out at odd angles. His uniform consisted of a wrinkled orange shirt with the logo of his department: "I'm a Mother Trucker and Proud of It!."

He was disproportionate, too. His abdomen protruded over his pants to an alarming degree.

"Name's Hank. You got a name?" He wrestled with a stick that came up from the floor, then pulled onto the road.

The motion of his craft jerked her forward. She grabbed the door and held on. "Yes, I got a name. It's Kia." Her teeth felt as if they'd be jarred loose any second. "Does it go airborne?"

"That's what I like, a woman who likes speed." He grinned and she noticed the bouncing craft had already caused him to lose most of his teeth.

Hank shifted the stick, then pulled a cord above his head that set off a loud horn and left her wondering if the noise had damaged her eardrums.

"Yee-haaaaa! We're truckin' now!" he said as the dial jumped to ninety. "Yep, this eighteen-wheeler will dang sure get you where you're goin'."

No, they weren't going airborne. They were still

stuck on the road. When this horrendous episode was over, she would tell Mala how displeased she was about everything. She would probably tell her with each passing of the suns until their life cycle ended just so Mala wouldn't forget.

"We gotta have some tunes playin'." He turned a knob and pushed a button.

Screeching filled the craft, bouncing off the interior. It was a horrendous sound like nothing she'd ever been subjected to. Earth torture. It wouldn't work. She'd die before she revealed Nerakian secrets!

"That's my brother Elmo on the CD. He made it hisself. Danged if I know why he hasn't hit the big time."

Your taters are turnin' mushy in the fields and the infernal revenue service says you owe back taxes, but you gots the love of a good woman and . . .

"Enough!" Her ears were aching from the obnoxious noise. She turned the same knob and peaceful silence filled the interior. Hank's brother would make a good interrogator, but apparently he was harmless, except for his voice.

Hank frowned. "You got an attitude problem, don't ya?"

"You will take me to this Dallas and you will do it quietly."

His eyes narrowed. "And what if I just pull over and let you out? You can hoof it the rest of the way. I dang sure don't need a mean-spirited woman riding with me."

She raised an eyebrow. He backed down, turning his attention to the road once more. He mumbled something else but she couldn't understand what he said. It was for the best.

Soon her eyes drifted closed. Traveling to Earth

had drained her. If she slept for a few minutes, she would awaken refreshed.

"Hey, lady, wake up."

She roused slowly to that incredible stench again. Hank leaned into the conveyance on her side, the door open. When she turned her head away, she realized darkness surrounded her. Had the end of her life cycle started? Was her light fading away? The man was extinguishing her with his body odor.

Would she never see her sisters or Mala again?

"Boy, you slept like the dead. It's already night."

"Night?" It took a second for his words to sink in but when they did, she sighed with relief. She remembered now that Earth only had one sun. Nerak did not have night as the two suns rotated opposite each other.

"Yeah, you been sleepin' about four and a half hours. You didn't even stir when I stopped to fill up."

He already looked pretty full to her. Not that she cared as she peered through the front glass at the darkness that surrounded her.

"Is the ranch near?"

"I ain't goin' that far. You're on your own from here."

She climbed down, jumping the last part. She'd been sitting so long, her legs almost buckled. She grabbed the door until she felt steady.

The crisp night air seeped into her bones. Nerak was a comfortable temperature year-round. She hugged her arms around her middle as a cold shiver swept over her. Cold wasn't good. Mala must be ready to return by now.

"There's a bathroom inside that bar across the street there if you've a mind to use their facilities, but it's a biker bar so you best be watchin' yourself," Hank told her. "Someone in there can tell you where the ranch is. Not the best place to be hangin' around, though."

He shuffled his feet, then let out a deep breath that made her nose crinkle in distaste.

"Talk to the man behind the counter. Fred knows me and he'll help you out."

She nodded and started to walk away.

"Most people would at least say thank you seein' as how I gave you a lift."

She would have to remember that. "Thank you."

He muttered something about ungrateful women but she'd already started walking away. She stretched her sore muscles as she made her way toward the dark, squat building with the bright flashing light proclaiming it as Paw's Roadhouse. She watched until it was safe, then hurried across the road.

Other than the bar, there was little else on this strip of road. A flashing light declared the structure beside it as a motel, except the last letter didn't light up so it looked like Mote.

There was a row of small conveyances in front of the bar. She ran a hand over the sleek metal and leather of the nearest machine. It was nice. Maybe these vehicles went airborne.

As Kia started toward the door, a woman came out. Not like any woman she'd ever seen, though. Blazing bright red hair matched her bright red lips. She wore a tight pink top so low her voluptuous breasts almost spilled out, and skintight shiny pink pants that sparkled when she moved.

Kia frowned.

And she chewed something that made a smacking noise.

The woman's gaze ran over Kia. "Honey, you're in the wrong place."

Kia tested her new words. "I gotta see Fred."

The woman thumbed over her shoulder. "He's inside. Last I saw, he was cleaning off the counter. I never would've thought he was your type." She shrugged as she moved past Kia.

Not her type? Kia wondered what her type was.

Chapter 2

Nick Scericino sat in a back corner of the small, smoke-filled bar, baseball cap pulled low on his forehead and his elbows resting on the table. His back was to the wall as he hunkered over, nursing a longneck that he'd had in front of him for the last hour. It had already grown warm. Not that it mattered. He was on duty, the beer only a prop so he wouldn't look conspicuous.

He tensed as familiar warning signals sounded in his head.

Something was about to happen. Not the drug deal. This was different. A gut feeling that didn't have anything to do with the bust.

Slowly, his gaze scanned the room. Had someone slipped inside? He quickly discounted that idea. The way he'd positioned himself, he had a good view of the front and back entrances. He had a suspicion whatever was about to go down wouldn't be good.

The door opened, letting in a blast of cold air. His gaze swung in that direction.

Then *she* came into the bar.

Windswept coal black hair that hung past her shoulders, skin warmed to a deep golden tan, as if she spent a lot of time in the sun. Her black top molded to her delicious curves, inviting a man to look. Black pants fit her like a second skin, inviting a man to touch. A black cape reached almost to her boot-clad feet, warning him to stay the hell away.

She scanned the smoky room. Her gaze stopped and held his for the briefest amount of time before moving on.

She had the deepest blue eyes he'd ever seen. Or maybe they were black. She was too far away to know for sure. Either way, he'd been sucker punched by the burning heat from that one look.

Sweet.

And definitely trouble.

Why the hell was she here, in one of the roughest bars on the outskirts of Dallas? She didn't look like the usual biker bitches that trolled the bar for drugs or a cheap thrill with some badass gang member.

He let his gaze slide over her. No, she didn't look like her taste would run to cheap thrills or drugs, but then, it wouldn't be the first time he'd been fooled. It just didn't happen very often.

She glided over to the bar. He couldn't hear what she said to the bartender over the noise of a heavy metal song playing on the jukebox. Apparently, one of the bikers did because he sidled up to her, running his hand over her shoulder and squeezing her arm.

The heat from her eyes changed to a cold stare. The biker should've been frozen to the spot, but he didn't seem to be taking the hint the lady wanted to be left alone.

Nick raised his bottle to his lips, concealing what he was about to say. "We have a problem."

"No, we don't, Nick," came the voice of his partner into the earpiece Nick wore.

"You saw her?" He took a drink of the lukewarm beer.

"I couldn't miss her, but it doesn't matter. We're here for a drug bust. As soon as the mark comes in and makes his buy, we take him down. It's the only way we're going to get any info on the Russian mafia. We're not here to get you laid."

Yeah, yeah, he knew the drill. Get someone on the inside to talk—a stoolie. Sometimes they would do anything to stay out of prison. Hell, they'd rat out their own brother if it kept them out of the pen.

That's why they were staking out the bar. Doobie makes the buy and they have him. The street had it that he was on good terms with the Russians.

Except he hadn't shown. Nick glanced at his watch—after midnight. And he probably wouldn't. Had someone tipped him off? Hell, they were probably wasting their time.

He glanced up. There was still the girl. Man, she was a looker.

"We *are* talking about the same woman, aren't we?" he asked.

"Leave it alone, Nick," Sam warned.

"Do I have a choice? Some biker is hitting on her, and I don't think she's going to take much more of his pawing."

"Nick, think about it first. You're already in hot water because of Elizabeth."

"That wasn't my fault. How the hell could I have known she was the mayor's niece? Besides, the last time I checked, twenty-eight was legal."

"For Christ's sake, you talked her into stripping at a nightclub."

He closed his eyes for a moment, remembering. Man, Elizabeth had been so hot that night. Gone was the tight bun that held her pale blond hair in place, gone were the heavy glasses and restrictive clothing.

Sweet.

He sighed and reined in his wayward thoughts. "It wasn't a big deal. She kept her thong on. What she did lose were all those stuffy restrictions her family had weighted her down with."

"You'll never learn."

The lady in black shook off the biker's arm, but he grabbed her again.

Sam had once told Nick that he didn't have to look for trouble, it found him.

Maybe he was right.

"I can't let this slide. What the hell good are we if we don't protect everyone? Don't worry. I won't screw up the bust. Not that I think it'll be going down to-night."

Sam muttered something that sounded vaguely like a curse, but Nick blocked his words as he stood and made his way to the bar. All wasn't lost if he could convince the biker he'd be better off leaving the lady alone.

Nick drew close. "Hey, buddy, I don't think she cares for your attention. Maybe you should just back away. Give her a little breathing space."

The biker turned around to face Nick, looked him over, then grinned. Half his teeth were missing and the few that were left had already turned yellow. He was an ugly cuss: long, dirty hair, a single earring, and the foulest body odor Nick had ever had the misfortune to come across, and in his line of work, he'd come across a lot of reeking bodies. Hell, even the ones that had been dead a week smelled better than this creep.

"And what if I don't want to? What'cha going to do about it?" the creep asked.

The biker had taken his measure and found him lacking. Damn, now his feelings were hurt. Nick straightened to his full height of six-two, but the biker was still taller, still bigger.

Nick was a firm believer in the bigger they were, the harder they fell. What he had a problem with was getting the bigger ones to the point where they'd fall.

"If we're going to battle it out, then let's take it outside." All he had to do was get the big bruiser away from the bar, then maybe they could get him cuffed and out of the way.

"Battle?" The lady straightened.

Now she decides to open her mouth? He wanted to mention that it might not be the best time.

"I can fight my own battles," she continued. "I'm a warrior, trained to fight."

He'd figured there had to be something wrong with a woman who looked this good. Now he knew. She was crazy. Damn, she was going to get them both killed. She was going to . . .

"I'd like to battle you, baby." The biker rubbed his crotch.

"Then we shall battle." She slammed the heel of her hand up and into his nose, then shook her hand with a pained expression on her face. "Ow." Her frown deepened as she examined it.

The biker grunted and grabbed his face as blood poured out of his nose.

"That hurt!" She glared at the biker as if he'd been the one to ram his face into the heel of her hand.

She brought her knee up, landing it with a resounding thud right square in the man's groin. Nick grimaced when the biker groaned and doubled over, then crumpled in a heap on the scarred wooden floor and held his crotch a hell of a lot differently than he had a moment ago.

Man, that had to have hurt. The lady had good moves; he'd give her that. Maybe she wasn't crazy after all. "Remind me never to piss you off."

"Piss off? I don't know this." Excitement glittered in her eyes. "That was very exhilarating."

Damn, he could lose himself in her eyes. He forced himself to concentrate. "Who the hell are you?"

Before she had a chance to answer, chaos erupted. Someone threw a chair across the room, and two women started exchanging blows at the back of the bar.

A biker came toward them. "Hey, that was my friend you just took out."

Nick's fist connected with the biker's face. Blood spurted from his nose. He grunted, stumbled back a few steps and tripped over a chair, then landed with a splat on his ass.

"We'll battle some more?" the lady asked.

She bounced on her toes, ready to duke it out with anyone who came near. He didn't have any desire to get his head bashed in and there were three more bikers making their way toward them and looking like that was exactly what they had on their minds.

"Come on, let's get out of here," he yelled as he grabbed her arm. For a moment, she only looked at him. "Sometimes retreat is the best defense."

She nodded. "Of course."

But that didn't stop the look of disappointment crossing her face. He'd seen a lot of men who got an adrenaline rush when it came to fighting, but this was the first woman. Hell, he loved a good fight as well as the next man, but she . . . she . . .

Damn, she reminds me of myself.

Now, that was a scary thought.

Something crashed to the floor. He didn't look to see what, but instead tugged on her arm. "Come on!"

They hurried toward the front door, ducking and dodging like they were in the middle of a war zone, and right now that was exactly what it felt like. The captain was going to kill him for screwing this one up.

Sam was rushing toward the bar as they were running out. "This way," he called.

Sam didn't wait to see if Nick followed. That was pretty much a gimme. They'd been partners for seven years and knew what the other would do.

They jumped into the nondescript deep green, battle-weary Chevy they were using for the sting. Sam started it and peeled away, spraying loose gravel everywhere as a couple of the bikers ran out of the bar.

Sam didn't talk. Just wove in and out of back streets until he was positive they weren't being followed. He only took his attention off his driving once, and that was to cast a dark glare in Nick's direction. A look Nick had seen more times than he wanted to count.

"What the hell were you thinking?" Sam finally asked. His jaw had begun to twitch.

Sam's dark expression wasn't good. Nick had seen the twitch before, too. The twitch meant Sam was barely controlling his anger, and that didn't happen often.

"You're on probation," Sam continued before Nick could say anything. "We'll be lucky if the captain doesn't suspend us both."

"It was my call, not yours."

"Then why the hell do I catch as much flack as you? Why the hell is my ass always on the line the same as yours? Just answer me that."

Nick couldn't. Damn, he didn't mean to screw up. Shit just happened. What was he supposed to do? Let the woman fend for herself? That wasn't going to happen no matter who came down on him.

Sam stopped at a red light, took a deep breath, then turned to the woman who sat between them quietly listening to their discussion.

Sam's mouth turned down. "You shouldn't have been in that bar. It's bad news." He glanced at the light, then back at her. "Where's your place?"

"I don't have a place."

Sam and Nick exchanged questioning glances.

"You don't live here?" Nick asked.

"I'm searching for my cousin, Mala."

"Does she live here?" Sam asked.

"On a ranch."

"Does it have a name?"

"The man who brought me here said the ranch was called Southfork. You can take me there."

"Uh," Nick began, then looked at Sam. Sam let off the brake and drove under the light before he looked at Nick. Sam's expression told him the lady was Nick's problem, not his.

A lot of help he was.

"I think the guy who brought you this far might've misunderstood. Do you have any money? We could drop you off at a motel maybe?"

She looked at him. God, she had the most beautiful eyes, and his first assumption had been correct. They were a deep blue.

His brain quit functioning. He couldn't think, couldn't say a word as he lost himself in those fathomless orbs. He'd never been this fascinated by a woman. What was it about her that reeled him in like a starving fish?

"What's money?" she asked in a voice that was soft and sultry. Her words caressed him, sliding down his body, promising more than just a touch.

Sam's laughter filled the car's interior, bringing him out of his daze. He glared at his soon-to-be ex-friend, then softened his look when he met the lady's confused expression.

Okay, so she didn't know what money was. Big deal. She was probably from another country.

"Where are you from?"

"I'm from Nerak," she said with pride.

Sounded foreign. "Is that in Russia?" Nick asked.

"I don't know this Russia you speak about. I'm from Nerak. I must find Mala."

Nick caught the full force of those magnificent eyes once more when a streetlight illuminated the car's interior.

"You'll help me?" she beseeched.

"Yeah, I'll help." His mouth had gone so dry he could barely get the words out.

She looked down at her hands, then back up at him as if she remembered something she was supposed to say.

"Thank you."

The words were spoken so softly that he barely heard them. No woman had affected him the way this one was doing right now. He wanted to wrap her in his arms, protect her, keep her safe . . . kiss those pouting lips, caress every inch of her body, have hot, wild sex with her all night long.

Ah, God, he was in deep shit.

Sam's chuckles didn't make him feel any better.

Chapter 3

Kia didn't understand Sam's laughter. "I don't think your friend is . . ." She sought the word she wanted. "I think your friend's . . . crazy. Am I correct?"

The one called Sam abruptly stopped laughing, but then Nick started. When Sam glared at Nick, he stopped. They were very odd men. No wonder the Elders had genetically altered the DNA so only females would be born on Nerak.

"What are you going to do?" Sam asked.

"I don't know." Nick's forehead furrowed into tiny lines.

Was something wrong? She couldn't imagine what. They had won their war. At least, they had until Nick said they should retreat. But it had seemed their only choice at the time. He was wise to suggest it. He must be a great warrior.

Why wouldn't he be great, though? He probably used his skills every day while she'd only practiced with companion units. Certainly not the same.

The Elders were correct about men fighting all the time, though. Even Hank had been argumentative. It was exactly as was stored in the archives. Not that there was a lot of information, and most of it was dated, since the Elders had forbidden interplanetary travel.

"We could always take her to the station," Sam suggested.

"You know damn well they'd . . ." He cast a quick glance in her direction. "You know where they'd send her. Can you see her staying in a homeless shelter?"

She had no idea what Nick spoke about, but she liked his voice. It was deeper than her sisters', and deeper than that of Adam-4. Nick's words sounded raspy, rough, and they sent tingles over her body. Very unlike the man who'd brought her to this area. She was almost certain Hank's dialect wasn't the right one to use after all.

She continued to study Nick. He didn't look perfect. He had a thin scar near his ear that ran down his jawline, and his nose was a little crooked. He had very black, thick, windblown hair. As if he needed to brush it, but she liked it better this way. Nothing about him seemed to fit, but everything seemed to come together quite nicely.

She inhaled a deep breath. And he smelled good. She didn't know this scent, but it stirred something pleasant inside her.

When he looked at her, he met her stare unflinchingly. Since she had a tendency to intimidate people on her planet, this was quite a unique experience.

And meeting his gaze wasn't difficult. He had beautiful eyes. Deep brown. They made her feel . . . strange. The burst of adrenaline running through her veins abruptly changed to liquid heat. Her nipples tightened and were suddenly sensitive to the material rubbing against them.

"I'll take her to my apartment," Nick finally said.

"Are you sure?" Sam turned his gaze from the road for a second to stare at Nick.

"Yeah, I'm sure."

Sam gave Nick a funny look.

"We're not going to the ranch?" she asked. She really wanted to see Mala and tell her it was time they left. She frowned. But then she would have to find her craft.

"I think the guy who brought you here was a little confused about where you wanted to go," Nick said. "There are a lot of ranches in Texas, but your cousin isn't on that one."

Oh. This wasn't good. How would she ever find Mala? Worse, what if she was stuck on Earth? She glanced Nick's way. That might not be so bad. She would like to interact with the human for a short time. Purely for research, of course.

"Your apartment?" Sam asked once more.

"I'll be safe enough." Nick cleared his throat. "Sorry about tonight."

Sam sighed heavily. "Who could say I wouldn't have done the same."

"Thanks. For backing me up. For everything."

Too much talking—and riding. She only wished they would get to their destination. Their vehicle apparently couldn't fly. Her body felt bruised and sore, especially her hand after hitting the man who was being obnoxious. If only Lara were here to mix one of her healing smoothies. Her sister had many talents to make one feel better.

But Lara wasn't, so she'd have to suffer. At least she didn't feel quite so alienated now. She watched the one called Nick. It was good that she would meet one of her own kind—a warrior. He would no doubt be able to help her find Mala.

Maybe they would have sex later. Excitement from the battle still ran through her veins. Sex would help to slow her heart rate. Who would have thought using her skills would be so exhilarating?

Sam finally stopped in front of a building and

Nick got out. Kia scooted out right behind him. It was good to be able to stand on solid ground again.

Nick leaned into the car and spoke to Sam, talking low enough that she couldn't hear what he said, not that she was really listening. She was too absorbed in looking around.

A long row of two- and three-story buildings lined the concrete walkway. On the other side of the street were buildings with glass fronts. One displayed clothing. She would've liked to walk closer for a better look but Nick straightened and Sam drove off.

"You can stay the night on my sofa. Tomorrow, we'll find out more about this cousin of yours."

She nodded and followed him inside the building. This was good. She knew he would not harm her. He'd been in protective mode when he told the man at the bar he should leave her alone. Only the very best warriors had the protective mode.

Besides, she could always zap him with her phazer.

They went inside a small box that shook, then ascended. When the door opened again, they were on another floor.

Ah, a very primitive beaming station of sorts, except it didn't disrupt one's cellular structure.

"This way," Nick said and led her to a door.

She stepped from the station, then watched as the door shut behind her. At least this one wasn't broken. It had swished shut without even waving her arm. Maybe some things on Earth weren't as backward as she'd thought.

When she turned around, Nick stood in front of an open door. She hurried to catch up. He motioned for her to go ahead of him, into another room.

"Welcome to my home, such as it is."

She stepped inside at the same time Nick came in

behind her. There was a click, then light flooded the room.

Her gaze moved slowly around the littered space. Articles of clothing hung from every piece of furniture, and he had quite a lot. She sniffed; at least it didn't smell too bad. Not like Hank or the man in the bar.

She raised her eyebrows at him. Warriors should set an example.

"The maid had the week off," he murmured. He kicked the door shut and moved around the dwelling picking up his discarded clothing.

"Maid?" Maid, she'd heard of this word. It was someone who took care of you. Companion unit? Did men have companion units on Earth? If his had been gone for a while, then maybe he would have sex with her. She still felt the need to expel energy.

"Yeah, a figure of speech." He tossed clothes into a corner of the room, then straightened and looked at her. "I don't even know your name."

"Kia." She removed her cape and folded it neatly before placing it inside her satchel and setting it on the floor. When she straightened, his gaze slowly moved over her. Her body tingled with pleasure.

"The couch lets out into a bed," he mumbled.

"Then you would like to have sex now?" She separated the material of her top and let it fall to the floor, baring herself to the waist.

He started coughing and sputtering. It was as she had thought. Earth was full of disease. Nick suffered from some sort of malady.

"No, I mean, well, hell." He strode to her and scooped up her top.

"You have moisture on your face," she observed.

"No, shit."

She peered closer at his skin, then frowned. "No, I believe it's just moisture."

"Funny," he grumbled, shoving the top at her, concealing her breasts.

She glanced down. "You don't like my body?"

"I like it just fine." He placed her hands over her top so it didn't slip down again.

"But you don't want to have sex."

"Who wouldn't want to go to bed with you?"

"Then we can have sex and relieve our excess energy." Earthmen were very strange. She only hoped whatever he had wasn't catching.

"Damn, lady, are you always this forward?"

"Yes. When I'm ready for sex. I haven't had sex for a few months. There has been no reason, but I would like to have sex now."

"You just don't . . . I mean . . . oh, screw it." He took her into his arms, his mouth lowered to hers. Her hands were caught between them.

She hadn't expected his lips on hers. She assumed they would have intercourse and that would be the end of it. But this unexpected turn was rather nice.

Had this been what Lara meant when she said companion units were cold? Nick didn't feel cold. Not at all. Maybe she'd been too quick to judge.

His tongue slipped inside her mouth.

Oh! She stepped back, still holding her top. "You stuck your tongue in my mouth."

He frowned again. "Haven't you ever French kissed?"

"I've never had anyone stick his tongue in my mouth."

His eyes narrowed. "You have had sex before—with a man?"

"Of course."

There was such a small technical difference between a companion unit and a human that she didn't think it important enough to mention.

She'd had sex plenty of times since reaching the age of discovery, just not with an earthman. Maybe she wouldn't tell him that. Learning she was from another planet might shock him, and she wanted to experience sex first. A comparison with her Adam-4, nothing more.

Not that she expected to get much out of the union, but she would at least be able to tell Lara that men were nothing special.

She would explain she came from another planet later.

"You may stick your tongue in my mouth again." She opened wide and closed her eyes. He'd closed his when they'd joined lips and she wanted to blend in while she was here.

But he didn't stick his tongue in her mouth. Instead, he slipped his hand behind her neck and lightly massaged. Oh, that was nice. She closed her mouth. A moan slipped from between her lips. Maybe he was part healer? He massaged very well.

His lips brushed across hers, followed by a sweep of his tongue. Tremors swept over her. Oh, yes! Her lips automatically parted and when his tongue caressed hers, her knees almost buckled. She really liked this French kiss.

He moved back all too soon. She dropped her top. Something much like a gurgle escaped from him. She glanced down at her naked breasts. He really had a problem looking at her nudity.

"Do you want me to put my top back on?"

He shook his head. "No, I just want to look. My God, you're beautiful."

For some reason, his words pleased her. Maybe

he'd like to see more. Then she would have him un-
dress so she could compare him to Adam-4. After she
studied his body, they would do more of this French
kiss.

She tugged on her pants and they came away from
her body.

He swallowed hard. "Boots and a thong. You're
every man's fantasy."

She tugged on the thong and it too was gone,
then she sat on his lounging sofa and raised one leg.
"Would you pull off my boot?"

He shook his head. "No, I think I want you to
leave them on. They're kind of sexy."

He knelt in front of her, nudged her knees apart,
slipping between them. "Sweet." He leaned forward,
taking her breasts in his hands and massaging, tugging on her nipples.

She gasped. Adam-4 had never . . . but then, he
wasn't programmed to . . . A flush of heat stole over
her. His hands created tingles of pleasure inside her.

Nick leaned closer, taking one breast into his mouth,
sucking, and running his tongue over the nipple. She
melted into the lounging sofa. He cupped her other
breast, giving it equal attention.

The lights flickered. He moved back and glanced
up, then at her. "Power surge."

Who cared? She just didn't want him to stop. She
arched toward him, wanting more.

"Kia, that's a pretty name," he whispered. His gaze
slowly moved down, leaving a trail of heat behind,
stopping at the thatch of curls between her legs.

"You want to discuss names? Now?" She didn't
think so!

She leaned forward, pulling his mouth against hers,
needing to feel his tongue caressing hers again. And
while they kissed, she tugged the front of his shirt

apart. There were several pinging noises as buttons hit the hard surfaces of the furniture.

He laughed. "Slow down, sweetheart. We have all night."

She leaned back with a frown. Never had Adam-4 laughed while they had intercourse.

"No woman has ever ripped off my clothes. I think I like it."

He was forgiven for laughing. She hadn't intended to tear his shirt. It didn't come apart like her clothes but she was glad it gave him pleasure. "I wanted to see you naked."

"If nothing else, I'm obliging." He stood and removed his shirt the rest of the way but his gaze stayed on her.

Her eyes drank in the sight of hard, tanned flesh. She stood, needing to touch. Reaching forward, she ran her hands lightly over his chest, trailing through the dark hairs.

"I've never had sex with a man who had hair on his chest. It feels strange to my touch." She moved downward, to a jagged scar. "What's this?"

"Knife wound."

She looked up as he unfastened his pants. "Someone attacked you with a knife?"

"I'm a cop." He shrugged as he kicked out of his pants. "Sometimes there are risks."

"What's a cop?"

He frowned again. "I protect the city from the bad guys."

"A code enforcer. I knew we were of the same breed."

He grinned. A lopsided grin that made her toes curl into the fibers of the carpeted floor.

"No, I'd say we're different."

He shoved his underclothes down and kicked out

of them. He was right. They *were* different. She hadn't made Adam-4 nearly big enough. She suddenly looked up. "Do you vibrate?"

He stepped closer, running his tongue around her ear before dipping inside. "No, but I bet I can make you tremble."

As she swayed toward him, she had no doubt he would make her tremble and much more. Maybe this was why Mala had looked for more than what Nerak could offer.

There had been something on the documentary, *Debbie Does the Sheriff,* that had made her want to explore Earth. Now that Kia was experiencing her first earthman, maybe she didn't blame her so much.

Enough thinking. She didn't want to think—only feel.

Her arms came up and wrapped around his neck, her lips brushing his jaw. His face had a rough texture, but nice. She ran her hands through his dark hair, liking the thickness, wanting to touch, to explore every inch of him. She'd never really examined Adam-4. She'd made him. There was no reason to assess what she'd created.

But Nick was different. She liked the way he felt. The different planes of his body. The sinewy muscles, the hard ridges—she wanted to check out every inch.

His teeth tugged on her earlobe. She tilted her head so he would have better access.

"I like that," she told him.

"I know," he murmured, kissing her neck.

"How?"

"How what?" He continued to kiss her neck.

"How can you tell I like what you're doing?"

He leaned back and looked into her eyes. "You're serious?"

"Yes." She'd programmed Adam-4, and the unit

had performed exactly to her desires. But with Nick, she didn't know what was coming next. It was a little disconcerting to realize he knew what she wanted without her asking him to perform a certain task.

"It's not difficult knowing what you want," he said as he brushed his hand across her nipples.

She closed her eyes and bit her bottom lip as heat spread through her. When he stopped, she thrust her chest forward, wanting more of his touch, but nothing happened.

"Why did you stop?" She opened her eyes, frowning at him.

"You asked how I knew what you wanted. I showed you." He lightly rubbed her shoulders. She swayed toward him. "Your body language tells me that you want more. The little moans that escape between your lips—all that tells me how excited you are."

"I should have known. Warriors are trained to be observant. You are a great warrior with much experience, I think."

"My captain might disagree."

She moved closer, her nipples brushing across his chest, the hairs tickling, arousing, unleashing emotions dormant all her life and ready to explode free. "Then I think your captain doesn't know you very well."

"I'll tell him you said that."

"I'm glad we're going to share our bodies." She ran the tips of her fingers across his nipples before flicking her tongue over one. He tasted salty, not unpleasant.

She moved behind him, running her hands over his back, cupping his butt. Firm, nice. He groaned, his hands coming around to capture her waist and press her closer.

It was strange the way he reacted to her touch.

Adam-4 hadn't been programmed to respond, only to give her basic pleasure. Nick's response heightened hers.

She leaned into his back, her body molded against his. They fit together very nicely. She wondered how he would react if she touched his erection.

Sliding her hands down his front, she grasped him. He jerked forward, gasping for breath. His reaction made her itch to do more, to give him more pleasure.

She slipped from his hold and moved to stand in front of him. There was so much that she wanted to see, and she'd never once denied herself. What she wanted right now was in front of her.

His erection stood tall, thick. She trailed her fingers downward and encircled his penis, sliding his foreskin down, then back up. He sucked in a deep breath when she ran her thumb over the tip. It was soft, pliable, while the rest of him was hard.

Her gaze met his. His eyes were glazed, his breathing ragged, as if he were in pain, but the look of rapture on his face told her differently. She slid the skin downward again, then back up.

"Enough," he growled.

"Why?"

He raised her chin with one finger.

"Who are you?"

She ran her hand down the side of his face. "Does it matter? Have you not had intercourse just to release pent-up emotions?"

"Yeah, I have, but, I don't know, this is different."

"How?"

"Call it another gut instinct."

"Do you want to stop?" She tilted her head and looked up at him.

"Stop?" He slowly shook his head. "No, I don't want

to stop. Hell, baby, I'm just getting started." He scooped her up in his arms.

She gasped, her arms tightening around his neck as he carried her into the other room and laid her on his bed. Not as soft as hers, but the way her body was growing warmer by the minute, she didn't really mind. She'd never wanted Adam-4 the way she wanted Nick. Hunger filled her and she knew if she didn't get release soon she might be driven insane.

As soon as he lay beside her, she pushed him onto his back and straddled him. Closing her eyes, she rubbed against him, feeling the heat of his hard length against her sex. For a brief moment, she forgot he was beneath her, but then his hands cupped her breasts, letting the weight fill his palms.

She drew in a sharp breath. Never would she have thought to program a companion unit to do two things at once. This alone was worth the trip to Earth.

Nick's rough hands rubbed against her nipples, sending spasms of pleasure through her. She leaned forward, wanting more, needing more. Nice. This was so nice. Maybe she'd been too closed-minded about interplanetary travel.

She was so lost in the pleasure Nick's body was giving her that she didn't protest when he rolled her onto her back, but when he fumbled in a drawer beside his bed, she wondered what he was doing and watched closely. If this was some sort of Earth ceremony, then he'd picked a most inopportune time.

He tore open a packet, then covered himself with an odd-looking sheath. He must've realized she was staring at him because he looked up.

"Protection. Never leave home without it."

"Protection?"

He shrugged. "I take chances with a lot of stuff, this isn't one of them."

She touched the sheath. His erection quivered. "You can still have pleasure?"

"More than I knew existed."

The sheath was slick and fit snugly. "Are we going to have sex now?"

He chuckled. "Oh, yeah."

Then she didn't care what he put on. He entered her body. She closed her eyes, taking pleasure in his length as he slid inside her moist heat. He filled her, she contracted against him, he moaned.

"Ahh . . . just like that." He sank deeper inside her.

She grabbed the bedcover, fisting it in her hands. "This is . . . good," she breathed.

Slowly, he moved inside her. Dipping deep, then sliding back out. Her body ached for more. She wrapped her legs around his waist, moving her body to his motion. She watched him, just as he watched her. His pupils dilated. His breathing became more ragged.

Her own breathing became difficult. When she was able to draw in air, his scent filled her: masculine, sex . . . raw need. She'd never smelled the scent of sex from a male but it touched each of her senses. A kaleidoscope of sensual bliss.

As he increased his motions, she grabbed his shoulders. The friction inside her intensified. Their strained breathing filled the room.

Other noises penetrated the clouds of ecstasy as lights danced above her, but she paid only a second's attention to the odd occurrences. She didn't want to lose the momentum of what she felt at this very moment.

When the first wave of her orgasm crashed over her, she caught it close to her, the ripples sliding down her body.

"Oh, God, this is so frigging fantastic!" His body

jerked right before he groaned, collapsing on top of her.

As her world came back into focus, she realized he'd had an orgasm. She'd given him pleasure. A thrill she couldn't describe filled her. She liked knowing she could give as well as receive.

A few seconds passed before he rolled to his side. "Damn, I can't even take a deep breath. That was incredible. I know this sounds crazy, but for a minute I thought I saw flashing lights and it sounded like every appliance in the kitchen was going on at once. Fuck! I feel so damned electrically charged up right now." He laughed. "I know, that sounds pretty weird."

That's what the noises were. They must have created an electrical current. It would explain the odd lights, too. She wondered if that might be a problem.

And that wasn't the only one.

She looked at him. He'd said sex with her had been incredible. He was right. She'd never experienced anything like it. That's what scared her. She'd never been afraid before tonight. Her life had been perfect, her world had been perfect.

"What are you thinking?" He lightly brushed a hand over her breast.

Thinking? How could she think when he touched her like that? This wasn't good.

"I'm thinking that I'd better find my cousin soon. Otherwise, it will be hard to leave."

He moved his hand to her other breast, brushing his fingers across her puckered nipple. She arched toward him. How could this be happening? Sex always relieved her tension for months, but already the heat began to flame inside her.

"Who says you have to leave right away?"

She turned on her side, running her hand over his hip. "I swore on the promise stones."

He nuzzled her neck. "What are promise stones?"

Maybe it was time she told him more about where she was from. He seemed ready to listen. "The stones I brought with me from my planet."

His hand stilled on her breast. "Your what?"

"Planet. I'm not from Earth. My planet is many galaxies away. It's called Nerak."

"Well, hell!" He swung his legs off the bed.

Maybe this hadn't been a good time to tell him she was an alien.

Chapter 4

Nick should've known there was something wrong with Kia. He could count on one finger the number of times he'd had sex this incredible, and that time didn't count because he'd been a virgin.

He dropped his head to his hands. Man, this really sucked.

"You're upset."

He laughed without mirth. "An observant alien."

"Your laughter holds no warmth." She sat up in the bed.

"Ya think?" He turned to look at her at the same time the sheet fell around her waist. *Ah, God, have mercy.* He squeezed his eyes shut.

Don't think about those luscious breasts and the way it felt to touch and squeeze them.

He opened his eyes, then groaned. She sat without making any kind of move to cover herself. He'd had wet dreams about moments like this. She was killing him.

That was it! She'd been sent here to torture him. Drive him crazy with lust.

"Can you"—he waved his arm—"cover yourself or something?"

"You don't find me attractive?"

"You know I do, but I damn well won't take advantage of . . . of . . . someone who isn't all there." Why did shit always happen to him? It never happened to Sam. Only him.

"What do you mean by 'not all there'? I assure you that I lost nothing of myself when I entered the atmospheric pull of your planet."

Amen to that! Kia was all there physically. Man, was she all there!

Ah, crap, this wasn't good. He'd been twelve the last time he'd cried. He would not fall apart now . . . but he *really* felt like crying. Or downing a six-pack. Or maybe both.

When he looked at her again, she'd covered herself with the sheet. "What I meant is that you can't be from another planet, and since you can't be from another planet there's only one explanation left."

She raised a sardonic eyebrow. Even that gesture looked tempting. He wanted to crawl beneath the covers and tell her it would be okay, that he would help her, that he wouldn't leave her until he'd figured everything out.

Except that she had the sheet and if he crawled beneath it, he damn sure wouldn't be thinking about saving her.

"Do you think Earth is the only planet?" she asked. "That's very presumptuous of you. Your race is actually inferior to mine."

He combed his hand through his hair. Sam was never going to let him live this one down. Just like he hadn't let him forget that Elizabeth was the mayor's niece.

Or the time he'd gotten so plastered he'd awakened the morning after an all-night binge to find himself in bed with the butt-ugliest woman he'd ever seen.

It'd scared the hell out of him when he'd rolled over thinking he was waking up next to Angelina Jolie and discovered Sandra Bernhard.

Damn, she hadn't looked half bad the night before. Sam wouldn't have even known about her except he'd dropped by Nick's apartment before Nick could get rid of her. That was the last time he'd drunk that much. He was pretty sure Sam was going to have a field day with this, too.

He stood and yanked on a pair of shorts that were draped over the back of a brown leather chair. Wrinkled, but they looked clean. "Do you remember anything about the last place you were at? I mean before you got to Dallas."

Maybe if she gave him a little information, he could take her back where she belonged. Damn, there was probably some law against having sex with an . . . an . . .

Hell, he didn't know what she was. He did know what she wasn't. She wasn't an alien.

"Is this a test?"

"No, it's not a test. I'm just trying to get you back to where you belong."

Both eyebrows shot up. "You are advanced enough that you travel in space?"

"No, I don't go around flying in outer space, but then, neither do you. I'm sure there's a state hospital somewhere out there missing a patient." That's it, he'd have Sam check to see if there was an APB out for her or something.

As he reached for a shirt, she stood and went to the other room. He couldn't move, couldn't ask what she was doing. He was frozen to the spot, his eyes practically falling out of his head.

He could only stare at her fantastic body. It should be a crime for a woman to be built that damn perfect. Luscious breasts and a killer ass. What more could any living, breathing man ask for out of life?

He forced his mouth to close and took off after her.

"Hey, where are you going?"

For all he knew, she was going to open the door and walk out of his apartment. Yeah, and if Mr. Jenkins happened to be in the hall the old man would have a heart attack. He'd damn sure die happy, though.

Nick came to an abrupt halt when he walked into the living room. Kia had picked up her bag and was reaching inside. He could feel the blood drain from his face.

"Okay, now hold on a minute. Put the bag down. Move nice and slow."

She pulled out a small square box. He breathed a sigh of relief. Damn, he'd just aged ten years. He'd thought she was going after a gun.

"You require proof," she said. "This is proof."

"A little black box?" It was worse than he'd imagined. What the hell was it, anyway? A compact? Was she about to powder her nose?

She pointed it at a standing lamp he'd been using as a clothes catcher. It was draped with T-shirts and shorts that he might be able to wear one more time before he forced himself to go down to the basement of the building and do a few loads of laundry.

So, what did she expect to prove?

A red beam shot out from the box. The floor lamp popped and then was gone, clothes and all.

He couldn't move. He just stared like an idiot at the spot where his lamp had once stood.

"Is that enough proof?"

He dragged his gaze back to Kia. God, she was magnificent as she stood there bare-assed naked and holding a . . . a . . . box that had . . . had . . . disintegrated the hell out of his clothes-draped lamp.

Fuck!

No, this couldn't be happening. He drew in a deep breath and tried to rationalize the problem. No answers, nothing. He was drawing a blank. He wasn't the rational one. Sam always figured everything out, thought ahead . . .

Sam!

That was it. Sam had set him up. Damn, why hadn't he thought of that earlier? Sam was trying to get back at him for the prank he'd pulled last week. Sam had fallen for it hook, line, and sinker.

He started laughing. "Sam put you up to this, didn't he? What are you supposed to do? Call him up and tell him I fell for your alien story?" He strode behind the bar and into the kitchen and opened the fridge.

"I didn't know Sam before tonight."

He grabbed a beer and twisted the cap off, tossing it into the trash as he turned back around. "Okay, there for a minute I did start to wonder. You had me going with the disappearing lamp. How'd you do that?"

He raised the longneck to his lips. There was a light thump on the bottom and the beer disappeared. He was left with puckered lips but no bottle.

Okay, now that wasn't funny. It'd been his last one. There was an unwritten law you didn't mess with a man's last beer.

His eyes narrowed at her.

Sam had really outdone himself. This was no local magician. Nope, she was damn good—in more ways than one.

"I'm not sure when your things will return, but

they will. This is a phazer. It's not meant to harm, only to give someone time to get control of her emotions. On Nerak, where I'm from, we no longer have weapons that destroy."

"So why didn't you use it on the biker in the bar?" *Answer that one, babe!*

"There were too many people around. It's not wise that others know I'm from another planet."

He frowned. Good answer. But he still wasn't buying that she was some sort of alien from another planet.

"Sorry, lady, you'll have to give me more proof than a little black box."

"Your penis will also fall off in the morning because we had sex."

He grabbed his crotch, the color draining from his face. "You're joking, right?"

She smiled. "My sisters say I don't have a sense of humor. I think I have a very good one."

She sighed. "Of course it won't fall off. But don't you find it strange that you refuse to believe my weapon is from another planet yet you'll accept that your penis will fall off?"

He frowned. "That's not what I was thinking." He quickly moved his hands.

She raised an eyebrow.

Okay, so maybe he had been thinking that, but hell, his dick meant a lot to him and he damn sure didn't want it falling off. It wasn't that he thought she could actually make it disappear, it was just the idea that it could happen.

"Sorry, lady, I'm not buying into your parlor tricks."

"I told you. I don't disintegrate objects. I just make them go away for a while."

"Whatever." Sam must've really shelled out the

cash for this little joke. Too bad it was money wasted. He opened the refrigerator again and looked around, finally grabbed a soda, then remembered he had a guest—sort of. "Want one?" He held up the bottle.

"What is it?"

"Oh, yeah, I forgot you're from another planet." The lady was carrying this all the way. "This is called a soda. It quenches your thirst."

"I'd like to try your drink," she said.

For now, he'd just play along. See if she'd come clean about Sam hiring her. He handed the soda to her. She looked at it as if she was wondering what she was supposed to do now so he took it from her and untwisted the top before giving it back.

Yeah, she was real good. He took a drink of his soda. She followed suit, then coughed and sputtered. He grabbed a hand towel off the counter. A consummate actress. He gave her the towel.

"It's strong." She coughed, wiping at her face, then tilted the bottle again.

After lowering it, she belched loud and long. Damn. Any man would've been proud to claim a belch that noisy.

Her eyes grew wide. "Oh. That was an odd feeling."

"Carbonation."

"Strangely refreshing. I think I like this." She smiled.

For a moment, his mind went blank as his gaze drank in the sight of the exquisite creature before him, from her rosy-tipped breasts to the thatch of curls at the juncture between her legs. Damn, she had him wanting her again. Hell, had he ever stopped?

He grabbed a shirt off the back of the sofa and handed it to her. "Do you mind?"

She frowned. "You really have a problem with my nudity, don't you?"

"Yeah, when all I can think about is having sex, then yes, I have a problem with you walking around without any clothes on."

"And you don't want to have sex again?"

"Yes . . . no." He ran a hand through his hair. "I need to get a few things worked out before . . . before . . ." What had he been about to say?

Damn, she was making him crazy with lust. Before they had sex again, he wanted to know exactly who he was having sex with. Period.

"I've been working all day. Kind of tired," he mumbled. Let her think what she would.

He moved to the hide-a-bed sofa and opened it. After he grabbed sheets and a blanket, he made it up. The whole time she watched without saying a word. Good, he liked it that way. If he didn't have to talk, he didn't have to think.

But that left looking, which he was trying very hard not to do. Man, hot did not even begin to describe how damn sweet she looked wearing his shirt. A shirt she hadn't bothered to button. It hung open all the way down the middle.

The contour of her breasts tempted him to spread apart the material, take one of her nipples in his mouth, and see how long it took it to get hard, see how long it would take her to start moaning.

His gaze dropped lower to the dark curls covering her sex. She was going to be the death of him. Sam set him up. No doubt in his mind.

"Okay," he said, ready to escape to the sanctuary of his room and think. He straightened. "You can sleep here tonight and we'll figure out what to do in the morning." He pulled the cover back.

"Thank you."

She said thank you as if she wasn't used to saying it very often. "The bathroom facilities are down the hall.

We passed it . . . uh . . . on the way to my bedroom. If you want to shower or something there're towels in the cabinet. I'll be in my . . . uh . . . room." He quickly left.

Man, if Sam was pulling a fast one, he'd kill him. And if he wasn't . . . maybe it hadn't been such a good idea to bring Kia here. Sam always told him that his knight-in-shining-armor mentality was going to get him killed one day.

He paused after shutting the door to his room, then he firmly turned the lock. Just for good measure, he took his gun out of the drawer and put it under his pillow. Tomorrow he would take her wherever she needed to go.

A vision of her gone from his life flitted across his mind.

He briefly wondered why the thought of never seeing her again didn't really hold any appeal. That, of course, was ridiculous. Yeah, they'd had great sex. Burying himself deep inside her had been like plugging himself into an electrical outlet. He came away charged and ready for more. For a minute he'd even thought there'd been flashing lights.

He was losing it, plain and simple. All the more reason to keep adding to his nest egg. As soon as he had enough money, he was heading down to the Bahamas. Sand, surf, and women. Lots of women but no commitments. Love them and leave them, that was his motto.

He'd open a little oceanside bar and grill, then get someone to run the place. A fishing pole in one hand, a beer in the other. That would be the life. Someday his dream would be a reality. He only had to stay focused on the future. He could do that.

A sound from the other room drew his attention.

He was going to kill Sam. An alien—yeah, right. He didn't buy it. Damn, he had a strange feeling his life would get worse before it got better.

The floor lamp was back.

It popped in a second ago.

Kia frowned. Minus the clothes that had draped across it. Odd. She shrugged. Maybe they would appear eventually. She had another problem. Nick didn't believe her.

She sat on the side of the sofa that he'd made into a bed, then shifted, but it still had lumps. She finally stood and wandered into the next room. Her short nap on the way to Dallas had revived her.

There was another popping noise. She opened her hand and caught the bottle Nick had held and that she'd zapped.

She looked at it, then toward his room. He wouldn't be wanting it since he'd retired for the night.

She took a drink, then spat the liquid across the room. Had he really been going to drink that awful stuff? She shuddered. Not good at all.

Kia set it on the counter and continued to explore the room. She waved her arm in front of the white box. Nothing happened. She sighed before jerking on the metal handle. A very primitive race.

The inside was cold and almost empty. Green fuzz grew on something in a container. Not at all appealing. Nor were the stacks of dirty dishes on the counter.

Did earthmen not clean?

If Adam-4 were this slovenly, she would have pulled his hard drive. She was thoughtful a moment. She rather liked Nick's hard drive.

She shut the door to the white box.

Nick had pleased her in other ways. Maybe he was worth staying with for a short time. She would be able to take back many tales of Earth. Her sisters would love to hear stories of a distant planet. But just until she found Mala.

She wandered toward the bathing room he'd mentioned. Nerakians had the same bodily functions as people from Earth and it had been a long trip.

She waved her hand in front of the door. Nothing happened. Did nothing on Earth work properly? She turned the knob and it opened.

The room was deplorable. She eased inside, weaving her way past the piles of clothes. She stopped at a sunken basin on the counter and waved her hand beneath it. No beams of light. How did one remove the bacteria from their body?

Maybe the knobs on either side had something to do with the beams of light appearing. She rotated one. Water emerged. She jumped back, then bent, staring at this marvel. Water was in scarce supply on Nerak. Not that they really needed any. She reached forward and touched it.

Nice.

She put both hands under the stream of water, then splashed it on her face. Laughter bubbled out of her. She quickly stifled it but couldn't stop the smile from forming. This was very nice. Maybe there were some things on Earth worth exploring. What other wonders were waiting around the corner?

She used the facility, found the towels Nick had mentioned and dried her face, then pulled back a curtain. Interesting. It had shiny knobs like the basin on the counter. She turned and pushed knobs until water flowed from the spout at the top.

Laughing, she stepped under the spray of water,

leaving the curtain open. She raised her face, letting the water cascade over her. Had Mala found this pleasure? Probably.

Trepidation filled her. It might not be quite so easy talking her cousin into returning to Nerak. If Mala had found someone like Nick who could please her body, *and* flowing water, then her task could prove difficult.

And maybe it might not be so easy when it was her time to return. But she would have to leave. She'd made a promise to Lara on the stones. A promise on the stones was sacred. Only the lowest of the low would break their word.

She bit her bottom lip when she remembered how Nick had caressed her body in ways she'd never thought it could be touched. Almost with a mind of their own, her hands retraced the path Nick's had taken over her body.

Her body trembled as her nipples pebbled. Her hands slid lower, slipping between her legs as she touched the spot he'd awakened earlier tonight.

She opened her eyes and caught her reflection in the mirror: hands caressing, trying to bring a response when she knew an orgasm without Nick would be a poor substitute. Frustration filled her as she stepped from beneath the water's spray.

This wasn't good. Finding Mala would be her top priority from now on.

She turned the shiny knobs and stopped the water before reaching for another drying cloth.

There wasn't much she could do right now. When the sun brightened the sky would be soon enough to look for her cousin. But right now she would enjoy the flowing water, the drink Nick had called a soda, and she would remember everything so she could tell her sisters about these marvelous wonders. Especially the sex she'd experienced with Nick. Not that she'd soon forget.

Earth was certainly different from what she'd expected. It wasn't so cold after all.

Chapter 5

"Okay, you can end the prank," Nick whispered into the phone, glancing over his shoulder toward the wall that separated his room from the bathroom.

Only moments ago Kia had been laughing and shouting as if she'd never taken a shower. You'd think she wanted him to join her . . . A vision formed. Oh, man, was that what she'd wanted and he'd passed on an opportunity to have sex in the shower, soaping her body . . .

Focus!

He took a deep breath and cleared his mind. Right now, it was eerily quiet on the other side of the wall. He wasn't sure he liked the silence any better. This had to end.

She'd had him going, and maybe for a second he might've believed she was from another planet, but only for a very brief second.

"You can end the prank," he repeated but with a little more confidence this time.

"What the hell are you talking about?" Sam grumbled, sleep thickening his words.

Nick could hear him moving objects around on his nightstand.

"Crap, it's three in the morning. What the hell are you doing calling this early?"

Nick glanced at the clock. So it was.

If Sam was pulling a stupid practical joke, then it was his own fault. Sam should've known he'd call and wake his ass up. He'd carried the gag a little too far.

How the hell was Nick supposed to resist Kia when she liked taking off her clothes? Man, and she did it very well. He was only human.

And so was she.

"And your reason for calling and waking me up?" Sam prodded.

"You didn't get me." Let him chew on that.

"Get you what? Don't tell me it's your birthday."

"Funny. Real damn funny. You know exactly what I mean. Kia."

"Kia?"

"Yeah, the girl from the bar."

"Can we please stop playing twenty questions? What's your point in calling me at this godawful hour? I really need to get some sleep before we have to face the captain tomorrow. By the way, he wants to see us at nine sharp, so don't be late. He didn't sound happy. We'll be lucky if we're not in the unemployment line by noon."

Great. The last thing he wanted to do was explain why he'd screwed up the drug bust.

"The girl?"

Nick frowned. Sam was trying to throw him off with talk about the captain. It wouldn't work. "You set me up, buddy. Couldn't you have come up with something better than her telling me she was an alien?"

Sam laughed.

Nick moved the phone away from his ear. He didn't see a damn thing funny about the situation. He quickly brought the phone back to his ear when Sam started talking.

"Is that what she told you? That she's an alien?" He snickered.

"Like you didn't already know."

"Sorry to burst your bubble, but I didn't set you up. I told you that you'd better watch out taking strays home. One finally bit you on the ass. Now maybe you'll learn to be a little more cautious."

Nick glanced toward his locked bedroom door. Damn, if Sam hadn't set him up, then who the hell was she?

"Are you sure you didn't—"

"Positive, but I wish I had thought of it. So what did she do? I mean, did she just blurt out she was from another planet?"

"She disintegrated my floor lamp and a beer," he mumbled.

"Huh?"

"Nothing. Hey, forget I said anything. I'll see you in the morning."

"Just don't be late. Nine sharp. Damn, the captain is going to ream our asses for screwing up the bust. He wanted info on the Russian mafia and we pretty well blew it tonight." The tone of Sam's voice changed as he went from taunting to serious. "Hey, you going to be okay? I mean with the girl and all?"

"Yeah, sure, you know me. I'll be fine. See you at nine." He hung up the phone before Sam could say anything more. Damn, his life had just gotten a lot more complicated.

Something Sam had said triggered a thought. What if she was connected with the Russian mafia? Sent to the bar to screw up the bust? That would explain her high-tech equipment. Hell, the Russians were always coming up with something.

There was a noise from the other room.

Now what was she doing? He eased over to the bedroom door and knelt in front of the keyhole. Oh, yeah, this was great surveillance. He felt like a frigging peeping Tom.

He caught flashes of her moving around in the living room. She wasn't getting dressed. He swallowed past the lump in his throat. She wasn't even wearing the shirt he'd loaned her.

Sweat broke out on his forehead.

There was just the slightest bounce to her breasts when she walked past. He held his breath when she ambled over and stood in front of his door as if she wanted to ask him something. Ah, damn, he was looking right at her mound. Up close and personal. He could count the dark curls, see the fleshy skin.

Would his tongue fit through the keyhole?

This wasn't right, man. He'd never denied himself a hot woman, especially if she wanted his bod.

Okay, get your head screwed on straight! Observation was his best tactic right now. He'd watch her, see if he could discover what she was after.

She left his range of vision.

Not good. He needed to keep a close eye on her. He slowly turned the lock on the door and eased it open. She was digging through her satchel. Damn! Why hadn't he thought to get her black box? She could do some serious damage with that thing.

But no, she brought out some pills, not the black box. Drugs. His hunch that she was connected to last night's bust was starting to look like the correct assumption.

He opened the door a little wider as she went to the kitchen. She was frowning as she glanced around at the dirty dishes on his counter.

So he wasn't the best housekeeper in the world.

He had other things to do than clean his apartment. Like catching bad guys and fending off a woman who thought she was an alien, but might be a plant for the Russian mafia.

He squinted his eyes. Now what was she doing?

She turned the water on, leaned down, and watched it flow for a few seconds. Laughter bubbled out of her. You'd think she'd never seen water before.

Next, she waved her hand in front of the cabinet, then frowned. Finally, she opened the door.

Odd behavior.

Taking a glass out, she filled it with water, then took the capsules.

He forced himself to ease the door shut as she came back into the living room. Damn, she had a killer body. But he didn't plan on being her next victim. Hell, who was he kidding? He'd already fallen prey to her charms. It was a wonder he was still alive.

He knelt in front of the door again. He had a perfect view of the sofa bed as she lay down. He swallowed past the lump in his throat when she raised her arms above her head and stretched.

Cover up! Pull the cover above your luscious, rosy-tipped breasts and put me out of my misery!

He closed his eyes and drew in a deep breath, leaning his head against the door.

Don't think with your dick. Think with your brain.

When he opened his eyes she'd pulled the sheet up, but then she began waving her arm. What the hell was she doing now? Her forehead puckered as she glared at the—overhead light? Finally, she pulled the sheet over her head and flopped to her side.

Why the hell didn't she just get up and cut the light off?

He continued his vigil, making himself more comfortable in front of the door. Nothing was happening. He even thought he heard light snores coming from beneath the sheet.

Damn, it'd been a long-ass day. Hell, it'd been a long-ass week as they staked out the bar. It became more difficult to keep his eyes open. They were getting heavier and heavier . . .

His head hit the doorknob. He came awake with a jerk, rubbing his injury. What the hell had happened?

Blinking rapidly, he peered through the keyhole. She'd turned over again. He watched the easy rise and fall of the sheet. She was sound asleep while he was starting to feel like a frigging zombie. He had to get some rest or he wouldn't be worth crap in the morning.

He slowly turned the lock on the door, then tested the knob. That should keep him safe long enough to get an hour or so of sleep. He'd deal with Kia in the morning.

He crawled beneath the sheets, could smell Kia's scent. It enveloped him in sensuous memories, reminding him what they'd shared. He got a hard-on just thinking of the way her legs wrapped around his waist, drawing him farther inside the heat of her body.

Ah, crap, it was going to be a long night. He glanced at his bedside clock. No, morning. It was already the next day. And he still had to think about what he was going to tell the captain.

Great. Just great. The captain was going to chew his ass out royally, and he had the sexiest woman in the next room, naked as the day she was born, and he was afraid she was the reason the bust went wrong. A member of the Russian mafia was probably in the next room. Under his covers—undercover.

Like Deep Throat.

Ah, damn, why'd his brain have to go there? He

wasn't even thinking about her ferreting his deep dark secrets. Not that he knew any. Hell, even on a good day he couldn't remember his driver's license number.

At least he was safe for now. He was a light sleeper. If she tried anything, he would be instantly alert.

Kia snuggled against Nick's back. Much better than the lumpy pillow and the equally lumpy bed in the other room and the glaring overhead light that refused to go out. She liked his lumps much better.

Light had started to filter into his room some time ago, but it was softer than the light above where she'd slept.

She pushed the covers down, needing to feel him against her naked skin. He wiggled closer to her warmth. Her sensitive nipples pressed against his back as her hand moved downward, sliding over his hip, her nails brushing through his pubic hair, grazing his sex, which began to grow firm. She sighed, laying her cheek against his back.

They were going to have sex again.

This was good. It had been all she could think about while in the other room. So much that she hadn't been able to stay by herself any longer. His body heat had beckoned her to draw nearer. How could she resist?

His breathing pattern changed. He inhaled, then slowly exhaled. Nick was awake.

"Uh . . . how did you get in here?" he asked.

She trailed her lips across his back. "I made your door go away."

"How . . ."

"Phazer." She rubbed against him, moaning softly. He groaned and rolled over, raising up on an elbow and looking to where his door used to be. "My door's gone."

"An observant earthman."

He arched an eyebrow and glared down at her. "Not funny. I want to know where you got that black box and who you're working for."

"Phazer. It's a phazer and I'm not working for anyone." She sighed, snuggling her front to his. This was nice—now if he would just quit talking so they could enjoy sex.

"Stop that." He scooted away from her.

"Why?"

"Because." When she raised an eyebrow, he continued, "I don't even know who you are or where you come from."

"Earthmen are very forgetful. Remember, I'm Kia, from Nerak."

"I'm still not buying you're from another planet. I need more proof than a little black box." His gaze moved to her breasts, then jerked back up.

Nick really had a problem with her nudity. "How do I prove to you I'm from Nerak?"

He snorted. "You're supposed to be the alien. You tell me. Do you have antennae that come out of the top of your head?"

"No." Now he was getting absurd. Her species hadn't needed antennae for a very long time.

He looked intently into her eyes. She stared back. "Ever heard of the Russian mafia?"

"No, but you can explain about this mafia while we have sex."

He slid from the bed. "Until I know exactly who you are, there won't be any . . . any . . ."

She rolled to her back, parting her legs just slightly. "Any what? Sex? Don't you want to bury yourself deep inside my body? Feel the heat as it closes around you?" She lazily stretched her arms above her head.

Nick couldn't stop his gaze from sweeping over her one more time. God, she was magnificent with her luscious breasts crying out for him to caress . . . to . . .

"Ah . . . ba . . . ba . . ." Now she had him stuttering and talking as if he was feebleminded. Hell, for all he knew, maybe he was. He cleared his throat. "I'll be in the bathroom taking a cold shower." He grabbed a pair of jeans off his dresser and a black T-shirt he was almost certain hadn't been worn more than once.

He stopped in the doorway. How the hell had she removed his door without him hearing anything? Oh, yeah, the little black box. Her phazer.

Did the United States have anything that even came close to this kind of technology?

With a shake of his head, he continued on toward the bathroom. The next thing he knew she'd be making him disappear. He stumbled, then made a quick U-turn and hurried back into his bedroom.

He came to an abrupt stop. She had his gun. He swallowed past the lump in his throat. "Put the gun down."

"Is that what it's called? What will it do?" She turned the barrel toward him.

His life flashed before his eyes.

"You're very pale. Are you ill?" she asked.

"Just put the gun down."

She laid the gun on his pillow. He rushed over and scooped it up, then had to sit on the side of the bed before he collapsed.

"Is something the matter?"

"Guns kill," he barked before he could rein in his anger. Her games weren't fun anymore.

"Kill?" She sucked in a breath. "It's an instrument of destruction. In the forbidden archives they tell of these weapons. That's what killed the men on my planet."

"You don't have men on your planet?" He rolled his eyes. Damn it, he could almost believe her. Almost.

"Men died in the wars they created. The Elders manipulated the DNA so only girl children would be born in the laboratories. Eventually, there were only females populating Nerak."

"Yet you're not a virgin." Ha! Explain that. The truth would win every time. Now she would have to admit who she really was.

"We have companion units to see to our needs."

"Companion units?" He raised a skeptical eyebrow.

"They are mechanical men. It was the perfect solution. The companion units don't argue or talk back, unlike what I've heard about the male of the species."

He snorted. "*Us* not argue or talk back? Your Elders have it all wrong." Great, he was encouraging her again. He bet she was pretty good at interrogation.

"But haven't you argued that I'm not from another planet?"

"That's different."

He took the gun to the living room and stashed it away in a locked drawer. When he turned around, he noticed the floor lamp was back, minus his clothes.

So maybe he couldn't explain that, but he knew someone who could. He'd have Weldon look at her so-called phazer. Weldon worked for the police, and the man was a genius when it came to high-tech gadgets. He'd be able to tell Nick quick enough who'd made it.

As he walked toward the bathroom, he wondered if she might have been in an accident—hit her head or something. It was possible. Maybe she wasn't with the Russian mafia. She could have been a scientist and someone was trying to steal her invention and she'd been running away from them when she hurt herself. Hell, he'd grasp at any straw, but that one was really weak.

But what if that was the correct explanation? If she had some form of amnesia, then she might even be married. Not good. The last time he'd been with a married woman, he'd almost gotten the crap beat out of him. She'd told him she was divorced. The ideal situation. He wasn't looking for a long-term relationship and she only wanted a good time. When Hubby showed up, she'd smiled and said she'd meant "almost."

Women. He should wash his hands of the whole lot of them. He snorted. Find a planet with no women. He could have his own companion unit . . .

He stumbled to a stop in the doorway of his bathroom.

Jesus! What the hell had she done? There were puddles of water everywhere, along with foamy clouds of shaving cream. The lid was off his toothpaste and a runner of minty green stretched from one end of the counter to the other. Did she have some kind of masochistic streak? Was she getting back at him for not believing she was an alien?

At least she'd left him a towel. He laid his clothes on the back of the toilet and jumped in the shower. He didn't want to leave her alone too long. No telling what she'd do.

When he was once again dressed, he went into the living room. He found Kia looking at his small collection of books. Thankfully, she was dressed in her black pants and top again. He didn't know how much temptation he could handle. He was only human.

She looked up when he came into the room. "What is this, *Where The Red Fern Grows?*"

He could feel the heat rise up his face. Okay, so he liked dogs. No big deal. A lot of people liked them. "Just a book I read in school. I liked it."

She nodded.

"I have to be at the station by nine. If you want to go, you can wait in the car. I shouldn't be long." He only had so much butt left the captain hadn't already chewed. Besides, he had a feeling keeping an eye on her was a good idea and he couldn't do it if she was alone in his apartment. "I don't have anything to eat. We can stop at a Micky D's for breakfast."

From the confused look on her face, he didn't think she even knew what a McDonald's was. His amnesia theory was starting to make a lot more sense. "I just have to get my wallet."

Nick hurried to the bedroom but there was a pop as he reached the place where his door used to be. His head smacked into a hard surface.

His door was back.

Great timing.

He rubbed his forehead.

"She is not an alien. She is not an alien," he mumbled as he opened the door and grabbed his wallet off the dresser.

On the way to the fast-food joint, he covertly observed her every move and noticed how she watched him before repeating what he did. He still hadn't ruled out that she could be from another country.

He parked in front of the fast-food place and they went inside.

"What do you want?" he asked, looking up at the menu.

"I've never had food before."

He glanced around. Good thing everyone was busy and no one had come over to wait on them yet. "You don't eat . . . where you're from?" he asked, keeping his voice down.

"Food capsules. It provides plenty of nourishment and we don't have to bother with using space to grow anything."

She turned those dark blue eyes on him and his insides began to melt.

"But I'd like to try your food. The soda was quite refreshing."

Hell, he'd give her anything she wanted if she kept looking at him like that. Food, sex . . . state secrets.

He cleared his throat and ordered two pancake breakfasts and two milks, then carried them to a booth in the far corner. Keep a low profile, that was the name of the game.

He covertly watched her as she slid across from him. Man, if she was playing him for a fool and Sam was in on this, he'd kill them both.

She just stared at the white Styrofoam, then pinched off a corner of the lid and put it in her mouth. Before he had a chance to react, she spit it out. "Ugh, your food isn't good."

He quickly glanced around to make sure she hadn't been seen, breathing a sigh of relief. No one was paying them the least bit of attention.

"That's the box," he told her, then opened it and poured syrup over the stack. "Like this." He cut into one, then forked it into his mouth. She followed suit.

Her eyes closed, she moaned. The overhead lights began to flash. A bulb popped.

"Mmm . . . this is good. Oh, yes . . . yes!"

Nick's gaze scanned the room. A busload of geriatrics had just come inside. Their expressions ranged from amusement to reprimanding looks to fear as some noticed the wild light display above their heads.

"This is so wonderful, Nick." She rolled her shoulders, her back arched, her tight nipples clearly outlined through the material of her top. "I've never had anything this good before."

He realized he was holding his breath when the room began to spin. He exhaled, but continued to stare. She was giving him a major hard-on as her tongue came out to slowly lick the syrup off her lips.

She opened her eyes and forked another bite into her mouth. "I think I love your food, Nick." Her words were raspy, like a woman ready to smear syrup all over his body and lick off every drop.

He grabbed a paper napkin and wiped the sweat from his forehead. That's when his attention was drawn to the lights. They were still flickering, but that wasn't all. A wave of bright blues, yellows, and pinks swirled like the aurora borealis.

Damn, the same thing had happened last night when they'd had sex, but he'd dismissed it as a figment of his imagination. She'd been really hot in the sack and it'd been a while for him so he hadn't really thought much about them. Only that his eyes had to be playing tricks. It had been a really fantastic orgasm.

Kia squirmed in her seat as she shoved another bite in her already stuffed mouth. Syrup drizzled down her chin. She swallowed.

"More. I want more . . . thank you."

She looked like a woman in the throes of passion.

Holy shit, he had a feeling she was telling the truth about being an alien. And people were really gawking at them now. He scooped up the food and grabbed her arm.

"Man, there must be some kind of wild electrical storm blowing in," he said in a loud voice, then cleared his throat as he tried to keep the cartons in front of him to hide his obvious condition. "Better be careful when you go back outside."

None of the patrons looked convinced as he dumped the food in the trash bin.

"I heard about this on the news last night," he added.

They kept staring. Not saying a blasted word. Just looking at them like they were crazy—or from another planet.

Crap, this wasn't good.

As he opened the door, the elderly people began speaking all at once.

"Pancakes! Give us all your pancakes!"

Chapter 6

Kia gazed longingly over her shoulder as Nick hurried her out of the place he'd called "fast food." Why couldn't she have more? She really liked the pancakes.

But when he opened the door of his car, she slid across the seat without complaining. He was a great warrior, so there must be a reason for his behavior. Yes, she was almost certain there was a legitimate explanation for taking her away from the pancakes and that wonderful topping.

She couldn't stop the sigh of regret that escaped past her lips, though.

After he was seated on his side of the conveyance, he twisted around in his seat until they were looking at each other. "Okay, tell me again where you're from."

Earthmen were so forgetful. She wondered if the affliction carried from one male to the next. She would try to explain in words he might understand.

"I'm . . . from . . . the . . . planet . . . Nerak." She spoke very slowly so that it might be easier for him to remember. "I've already told you this. Don't you have the capacity to retain information?"

He gripped the navigational wheel until his knuckles turned white. Had she said something wrong?

"I know what you said, but I want to hear it again."
He slapped his hand down on the wheel. "There are
no such things as aliens."

"You still do not believe me?"

"What happened to the lights in there?"

"What lights?"

"The psychedelic ones flashing and . . . and everything." He waved his arm around. "For that matter,
the lights I thought I saw when we were having sex
last night?"

She shrugged. "I suppose my . . . enthusiasm might
have created some kind of electrical energy. I'm not
sure. On Nerak we're rarely exposed to such extreme
emotions. Our planet is perfect—calm."

"Sounds boring if you ask me," he mumbled.

She bristled. "It's not boring. We have everything
we need. Can you say the same for Earth?" How dare
he judge her world when his still had wars. It was as
she suspected, men thought everything they did was
superior.

Nick closed his eyes and it looked as if he was
counting to himself. She could clearly see that earthmen had many problems. She wondered how long
he'd suffered from this affliction where he would apparently lose his train of thought.

He opened his eyes and stared at her long and
hard. "Okay, okay, let's just say I might—*I might*—believe your story. Now, I'm not saying I do or anything.
I'm just going to consider the possibility."

"Would it help if I showed you my third eye?"

His face lost some of its color. "You have a third
eye?" He swallowed hard.

Men could be very gullible. "No, but if I grow one
you'll be the first to know."

His jaw began to twitch, just as Sam's had when
they left the bar.

"Can you at least keep a low profile until we find your cousin?"

She bowed her head slightly. "Of course. I had already planned to do so. I don't wish to cause a problem. I came to Earth only to find my cousin, then I shall depart your planet. You will not even know I was here."

He mumbled something beneath his breath. She didn't think his attitude was conducive to forming an amicable relationship. Sex was probably out of the question too, even though she noticed his pants were rather snug. He was denying himself again—and her.

Maybe she should've brought Adam-4. He would have given her some measure of relief. And he vibrated. But he hadn't made her tremble. No, he'd never made her do that.

As Nick started his conveyance, she leaned against the back of the seat, but she couldn't stop one last look at the place that served food. She would've liked to have more. Food was a good thing. This she would miss.

And probably the sex, even though Nick had only indulged that craving once—once was enough to hook her. Their joining had been very good.

She watched him from the corners of her eyes. He was a very handsome earthman. Too handsome. Her nipples were already straining against her top and a familiar warmth began to build deep inside her. Looking at him only made it worse.

The sooner she found Mala the better, but how hard would it be to convince Mala she needed to leave? Sex and food. They would be difficult for her cousin to give up. Life was getting very complicated.

Nick pulled in front of a tall building and came to a stop.

"Wait here," he told her as he started to get out,

but turned back at the last second. "Don't leave the car."

"I'm not lacking in brains, Nick. I do know what you're asking of me."

"Okay." He nodded but he didn't look too sure of himself. "The black box."

She raised her eyebrows. "My phazer?"

"I want to show it to someone. Do you mind?"

She paused. Her phazer in the hands of an earth person could get her into a lot of trouble with the Elders.

"He's trustworthy. I promise you that Weldon will be very discreet."

She finally reached inside her satchel and brought out the device. "Be careful."

"I'll be back as soon as I can."

She brightened. "And we can have more food?"

"We'll stop by the grocery store."

She supposed that meant yes. She leaned back in the seat when Nick got out of the car, closing his door behind him. The thought of more food made her insides quiver. And perhaps after they ate, she could convince him more sex would be a good thing as well.

Shortly after Nick disappeared inside the building, Sam appeared. He stopped at the car and opened the door on Nick's side, squatting so they were on eye level.

"Hi. Kia, right?"

"Yes. Can you read minds?" She had a sister who read minds.

Sam chuckled and shook his head. "I spoke with Nick last night. He tells me you're from another planet." His smile grew wider and she found she rather liked it.

"And you believed him?"

"No."

She frowned. "Then why do you seem happy about it?" His green eyes twinkled with merriment.

He chuckled. "Because I think Nick may just learn his lesson this time."

"But I *am* from another planet."

He studied her for a few seconds, his expression turning serious. "No matter where you come from, Nick will help you get home again. He's like that, you know."

Her gaze moved to the building. "Yes, I do know. He immediately went into protector mode when that man in the bar was bothering me. Your friend is a very good person."

"Sometimes too good." He stood. "If you get cold, come inside, but Nick shouldn't be too long."

She nodded, but he was already closing the door. She pulled her cape closer to her body. It was warmer today. Odd that the temperature could change so quickly from what it had been yesterday. On Nerak, the climate was controlled. Her home was perfect.

Conveyances of different sizes moved up and down the street and people walked on the walkway. They were different sizes, too. Some rotund, some short, some tall.

She looked at the building where Nick had gone. Her gaze strayed back to a glass-fronted building with clothes and bright shiny things displayed in the window, tempting her to take a closer look.

A warrior should explore her surroundings, know the territory in case trouble should break out. Especially as fond as these earthmen were of having wars. One could erupt any second. How could she defend herself properly if she didn't know the terrain?

Decision made, she waved her arm in front of the

door. Nothing happened. She reached into her satchel, then remembered Nick had her phazer.

It didn't matter. She had observed Nick opening his door. This was only an inconvenience. She was quite pleased when she pushed down on the handle and heard a click. A primitive place but she could learn to adapt. How hard could it be to survive on an inferior planet?

She shoved against the door, then jumped back when a vehicle crashed into it and the thing went flying. Conveyances skidded to a stop, barely missing each other. There were loud blasts of noises and angry voices.

If they would make conveyances that could fly, they wouldn't have these problems. She stepped out of Nick's vehicle and marched down the walkway to the store that had caught her attention.

Her sister would want details about Kia's time on Earth. If she could tell Lara it was a very dull planet, then maybe she would lose her fixation with this barbaric place.

"Hey, lady, what are ya goin' to do about my car? You're parked on the wrong side of the street!" a male voice called out, but she refused to turn around.

She ignored the stranger who had hit Nick's door with his conveyance. Better not to be confrontational and thus bring attention to herself. She would let the stranger explain to Nick why he'd ripped off the door. She had a feeling Nick wouldn't be happy with the man.

The captain looked up from the papers he was shuffling through. His brown hair was liberally streaked with gray, as were his bushy eyebrows, which were lowered in a menacing scowl.

It was an expression Nick had seen many times over the ten-year span of his career. His gut clenched. The look didn't bode well for him or Sam. He only hoped Sam didn't go down, too.

Beside him, Sam squared his shoulders. Finally, the captain dropped the papers on his desk and leaned back in his chair.

"Nick, you're on suspension pending an Internal Affairs investigation. I couldn't stop it this time."

"This is crazy and you know it, Cap'n! Suspension, maybe, but what the hell is IA doing butting their noses into it?"

Damn it! He couldn't say he hadn't seen some kind of reprimand coming. IA, though? What was he supposed to do when that biker started pawing Kia?

"We need an informant. The Russian mafia is trying to horn in on the drugs coming into the country. They want a piece of the action. When all hell broke loose at the bar, IA found you were the cause—over a woman. What the hell were you thinking, Nick?" He shook his head. "Never mind. I don't even want to know."

"It wasn't his fault," Sam jumped in.

The captain turned his attention to Sam. "The only reason you're not on suspension is because I talked Candace out of it."

"Candy? What the hell is she doing on the case?" Damn it, Nick had known her since she was wet behind the ears. She'd gotten lucky a few times and moved up the ranks. Once she'd made a pass and he'd brushed her off.

Ah, hell, he was in deep shit.

"You've had a pretty clean record—up until now." The captain continued speaking to Sam as if Nick hadn't said a word. "Despite Nick flagrantly throwing away the rule book."

"We're partners," Sam spoke up. "If Nick goes down, then so do I."

"It wasn't your fault." Nick intervened. Damn, he didn't want his friend on suspension with him. "I screwed up. Me. Not you."

"I hope she was worth it." The captain eyed Nick.

"She was in trouble. What was I supposed to do? I thought we were supposed to protect people."

"Around you, someone's always in trouble." He sighed long and deep. "You're a damn good cop, Nick, but you've got to learn to follow the rules. This informant was important to the operation. I'd suggest until the investigation is over you keep a low profile."

"Yes, sir."

"Sam, give us a minute."

Sam hesitated.

"Don't worry," the captain said. "I haven't shot anyone in all my years on the force."

Sam nodded toward Nick. A silent look that said no matter what, Sam had his back. But he'd always known Sam would. As soon as the door shut, Nick turned to the captain.

"At least I've never shot anyone that didn't need shooting," the captain finished. His expression said the jury was still out whether Nick was on his hit list or not.

"You've got what it takes to be the best cop on the force, Nick. Your gut instinct is better than anyone I've ever seen. Being a maverick is all well and good until you start messing with your job. You've pushed it to the limit this time. Let's just hope it wasn't too damn far. I'll do what I can. Now get out of here."

Nick clenched his fist. There wasn't a damn thing he could do. Not until IA finished their investigation. He turned to leave.

"And don't forget to keep a low profile. It just might save your hide."

Nick drew in a deep breath as he left the captain's office. He couldn't afford to lose his job. Two more years and he could buy his bar. All he had to do was keep Kia under wraps until he could locate her cousin. He'd lay low. Not draw any attention to himself. At least long enough to find this cousin of hers.

He ran a hand through his hair. An alien. He had an alien living in his apartment. His gut rumbled. Candy would be all over his ass if she found out about Kia. What was left of his career would be sucked right down the toilet.

But what else could he do? Throw Kia out on the streets? Send her to a homeless shelter? Bring her to the station?

He could see it now. "Hey, Cap'n, I don't have a Russian mafia informant, but will an alien do?"

None of those solutions sat well with him.

Nick couldn't believe this was happening. Damn, he'd expected a slap on the wrist, not suspension.

Not that he was that worried. They wouldn't find anything because there wasn't anything to find. He wasn't on the take and had never been on the take. Hell, they could check his bank accounts and see he didn't have that much money, and he damn sure didn't have any hidden in his mattress.

It seemed Kia was now his responsibility, though. Sure, she handled herself pretty well at the bar, but there was something vulnerable about her.

Duh. Like maybe this was her first visit to Earth?

Yep, he was in deep shit.

Chapter 7

A tall, thin woman went inside the dress store as Kia approached the door. Kia watched carefully as the lady pulled on the handle, then repeated what she had done. Most everything on this planet was manual, it seemed. How disgustingly archaic.

The sights and smells assaulted her senses as soon as she stepped inside. The shop was a fantasy world of colors, sights, and sounds that she'd never experienced on Nerak. For a brief moment, she regretted the stark whiteness of her home.

Maybe she wouldn't describe this place to Lara.

"May I help you?" A young girl with pale blond hair approached her. The tag on her shirt identified her as Sherry. A worker in the establishment?

Her hair wasn't as long as Lara's, but the girl reminded her of her little sister. Maybe it was the smile on her face, but Kia felt an instant liking toward Sherry.

"I wanted to see inside your building," Kia told her.

The young woman's smile grew wider. "Is there anything in particular you wanted to look at?"

Kia glanced at all the clothes hanging on circular chrome pipes. "Clothes. I need more clothes."

The girl nodded. "You just flew in, right? The airlines lost my luggage when I went to Cancun." She rolled her eyes and shook her head. "What a pain."

"You were hurt?"

The girl laughed. "I'm sorry. You must be from another country. What I meant is that I had to buy enough clothes to last me while I was there. It was . . . bothersome."

"Bothersome. I know this." She would like to go home but it looked like she would be stuck here for a little while at least.

"I bet we can take care of all your needs. Will you be here long?"

"I'm not sure."

The girl took a step back and studied her for a moment. "Nice outfit. Kind of Goth. I don't think I've ever seen material that exquisite. It shimmers in the light." Her mouth twisted to the side of her face. "You look like you're a size six. We can start there."

"Do you have food?"

The girl had started toward one of the racks but turned back around. Before she could answer, a woman a little older than Sherry joined her. The name on her tag said Manager Aims. Her name wasn't nearly as nice. Kia had a feeling their names suited their personalities.

"Will you be paying by credit card or check?" Manager asked.

Kia didn't know what "credit card" or "check" meant. Maybe she should've stayed in the car. "I don't know these things you talk about."

Manager gave Sherry a knowing look before turning back to Kia. "Do you have any way you could pay your bill? You know, coins?"

Kia shook her head. She didn't like the way the woman snickered. It sounded very rude. Females on her planet didn't treat other females as if they were lesser Nerakians. Every woman was equal except for the Elders and their direct descendents, and of course, healers. Lara was a healer, therefore, highly respected. She didn't think Manager ranked very high.

"Maybe you have precious gems?" The older woman laughed outright. "You know, diamonds? Rocks? Stones?"

Kia straightened to her full height of five foot eight inches. "I have promise stones." She pulled her pouch from her pocket and opened it. Raising her palm, she dumped the contents into her hand.

Deep purple, brilliant blue and green stones as big as her thumb flashed under the bright lights. Ten sparkling gems. She had more at home, but these were her favorites. Out of these, she liked best the clear ones with yellow and blue colors hidden deep within.

Manager choked. "Are those real?"

"Yes." Her promise stones were quite dazzling. She'd collected them over the years. They were easy to find on her planet, but you did have to know exactly where to look.

Sherry turned toward Manager. "That princess from another country is visiting. I saw it on the news last night. I didn't get a good look but she was tall and had dark hair. I bet it's her," she whispered.

Kia wondered if a sudden illness had stricken Sherry that she could no longer speak in a normal tone.

"So where are her bodyguards?" Manager asked, her eyes narrowing as she glanced around the store.

"Didn't you see that show where the princess escaped . . ."

Manager's eyes grew round. ". . . and fell in love with the reporter."

They talked as if she weren't there, and now they

stared at her as if she were an alien. Oh, right, she was an alien. A frown furrowed her forehead. But they didn't know she was from another planet.

"Uh," Sherry began. "Where exactly are you from?"

Kia doubted they would have heard of her planet. She didn't see the harm in mentioning the name of her home. "I'm from Nerak."

The younger woman jumped up and down. "It sounds foreign! I knew you were from another country!"

The older woman still looked skeptical. "There's a jewelry store next door. Do you mind if I take one of your . . . stones in for a quick appraisal? Just so we'll know how to adjust your bill."

Kia didn't like her attitude, but the younger woman was bobbing her head up and down until Kia thought it might come unhinged. She held out her hand and the woman took one of her clear stones. As soon as she went out the door, Sherry turned back to her.

"You might want to put them away for safekeeping."

Sherry eyed another customer, the woman who came in right before Kia. She seemed interested in their conversation. The woman quickly turned away when she was caught eavesdropping.

Kia returned her stones to the pouch and tucked them away in her pocket.

"Why don't we look at some clothes? I'm sure there won't be a problem with payment. I'm sorry, I didn't get your name . . ."

"Kia."

Sherry covertly looked around the interior. "No last name," she whispered. "I understand."

Last name. Of course, the woman called Manager had more than one name. On Nerak they only had one name and it worked fine since they were basically related in some way to each other.

When one strayed, as Mala had, then they were erased from memory to ease one's pain, every trace of them forgotten, but maybe because the family units were critical to everyone's well-being, Kia hadn't been able to let go of Mala. Family was important and nothing to take lightly. If she couldn't convince Mala to go home, then and only then would Kia permit her memory to be obliterated.

"What about this?" Sherry held up a bright yellow top and a pair of white slacks with yellow pinstripes. "You can try it on in the dressing room."

The color was pretty. So different from her monochromatic black wardrobe.

"It would look really good with your dark coloring," Sherry prodded. "And you can try this silver number, too." She held up a dress that glittered. "Is it sexy or what? No man will be able to resist you."

Maybe that was her problem. Right now, Nick *was* able to resist her. If she wore the silver dress he would want to have sex with her again.

For just a second she closed her eyes and remembered his hands on her body. The way he'd lightly pinched her nipples, rubbing them between thumb and forefinger. Ripples of pleasure ran through her.

Her eyes flew open. "Yes, I will try everything on and you will tell me if I'm irresistible."

Sherry smiled knowingly. "Ah, so there *is* a man involved. I thought so. Your secret is safe with me," she whispered.

Sherry hung the clothes up in a small room, then stepped out so Kia could go inside, shutting the door behind her.

Kia almost had the silver dress on when she heard a bell jingle. The same one that jingled when she'd entered the store.

"It's real!" Manager whispered, but her words traveled into the changing room.

"I told you so!" Sherry said.

"No, there's more. It's the finest cut diamond the jeweler has ever seen. She can buy almost everything in the store and still have change coming. And that was the smallest of the stones. I think you're right about her being this princess who's visiting."

"And there's a man involved. I knew there would be. Maybe they're planning on running off and getting married. Isn't it romantic?"

"Where is she?"

Kia listened, but apparently they had lowered their voices or walked farther away from the changing room. Odd how the mention of money had put Manager into such a state of excitement.

Nick had asked if she had money last night. Money so she could get a motel room. Then again, he'd handed the woman paper and round metal disks for their food this morning. Apparently this money was held in high esteem on Earth.

Her stones were much prettier.

She stepped out of the changing room. Sherry smiled warmly. Manager's smile was much more calculating. Apparently, the thought of owning one of her stones was very important. Not that it really mattered as long as she had the right clothes—clothes that would entice Nick to have sex again. And maybe she could use Manager's greed to her own satisfaction.

"Sherry, you didn't say if you have food."

"We'll order anything you want. Do you have a preference?"

"Pancakes."

Manager and Sherry looked confused. Didn't they

know what pancakes were? A shame they were missing out on such a delicious food. But Manager said she had plenty of money now.

"You will order pancakes for everyone . . . thank you."

Today was going to be very good. She had money. She had clothes to seduce Nick. And soon, she would also have pancakes.

"And lots of the topping, too!" Maybe she would order extra for when she seduced Nick. She could drizzle it all over him, then lick it off.

He was going to be so pleased with her!

Sam caught up with Nick as he rounded a corner. "Hey, it's only for a few weeks. They won't let an officer with your reputation for catching the bad guys stay on ice very long. Besides, we're short handed. They need you on the streets."

Nick slowed his steps. "Yeah, I know. I guess I'm just pissed I screwed up."

"Hey, you got the girl. The good guy always gets the girl."

"Yeah, and she's in the car waiting for me."

"I saw her. We spoke briefly before I came inside. Damn, she's a looker. I don't know how you always manage to get the sexiest women on the planet. So what are you going to do about her?"

Nick started walking again. "I think she may actually be telling the truth," he mumbled.

Sam grabbed his arm. "What?"

Nick looked around the hallway, waiting for a curious clerk to pass out of hearing range.

He shrugged, feeling like a complete idiot. "I think she might be telling the truth." He'd known Sam would look at him as if he was crazy. Hell, he sounded crazy.

"You're serious?"

Nick frowned. "She has a little black box that makes things disappear. I've never seen anything like it. She calls it a phazer. I dropped it off with Weldon. He's checking it out, seeing if he can discover who made it. I've never seen Weldon as excited as when I handed it to him."

Sam raised an eyebrow. "Weldon? The computer geek?"

"Yeah. He said he'd never seen anything like it."

"That still doesn't prove anything."

"Then when she eats there are all these flashing lights . . ."

Sam looked at him as if he'd lost his mind. A blast of heat flooded Nick's face.

"It's possible. Who's to say we're the only ones?" Why did he feel like the hole he'd started digging was only getting deeper?

Sam raised an eyebrow. "*The only ones?* Do you hear what you're saying?"

Nick turned on his heel and marched toward the front door. Why did he even think Sam would believe him? Straight-and-narrow by-the-book Sam. Yeah, of course his best friend would believe in aliens—not! "Yes, I know what I'm saying, but everything she says points in that direction. My list of logical explanations gets shorter by the second."

"She could just be crazy."

Nick glanced at Sam.

"Okay, I admit, she doesn't look or sound crazy, but it doesn't mean she didn't escape from the state hospital. Look at some of the criminals who are locked up in the loony bin right now. They look perfectly normal. It doesn't mean they are, though."

"I know. But she insists she's from another planet."

Sam's eyes narrowed. "Do you think she might be a spy? Undercover operative?"

"I thought about that. It still doesn't explain the bizarre lights."

"Have you slept with her?"

Nick stumbled.

"Ah, geez, why'd you want to do that?" Sam ran a hand through his hair. "This complicates everything."

"You think I don't know that?" He blew out a breath. "Kia didn't mention she was from another planet until *after* we'd had sex. But no matter what, it was the most incredible sex. She was so . . ." He swallowed hard. "I've never had . . ."

"Oh, shut up! You don't have to rub it in."

Nick grinned. "Yeah, I do—it was that damn good."

They walked out the front door and started down the steps. Nick looked toward his car and came to a grinding halt. Kia was gone—and so was his passenger-side door.

"What the hell . . ." It looked like it had been ripped right off.

"Is this your car, Nick?" a young officer asked. He stood beside Nick's vehicle, jotting down information. A big bruiser of a man stood beside him. He didn't look happy. Nick glanced up the street a short distance. A car with a damaged right fender was pulled to the side.

But no Kia.

His gaze swept the area, but she wasn't in sight.

A hazy blue light hovered over one of the stores. He blinked. It disappeared. He had a feeling he knew where she was, though.

Nick strode down the last steps. "There was a girl in the car . . ."

The irate man planted his fists on his hips. "That would be the woman who got out of the car, after she opened the door and I slammed into it, then left without a by-your-leave or anything. What I want to know is who's going to fix my car? You're parked illegally."

He'd parked on the wrong side of the street. A bad habit of his. That wasn't his top priority right now. What if Kia was hurt? "First, I'd like to hear exactly what happened," Nick said.

The stranger looked at the officer, his eyes narrowed. "I know how you cops stick together. If you don't think I won't get a lawyer, then you'd better think again."

Crap. Who the hell had he pissed off upstairs . . .

"Nick," Kia called out.

Everyone turned toward her. How could they not when his name came out of her mouth like a hot caress on a cold day? She wore a silver dress that was totally inappropriate for the daytime, but she had a body that could pull it off. Boy, did she pull it off. He'd like to pull it off!

She looked like a million dollars in a white fur coat that was open enough to show off the deep vee neckline of the sparkling dress. The hem reached midthigh, brushing across incredibly long, silk-stocking-clad legs. His gaze continued downward until it ended at her silver stiletto heels.

She was the epitome of every man's wet dream.

And every man within sight of her stopped to unabashedly stare. She didn't even seem to notice. Her gaze had fixed on him.

Male pride washed over him. How the hell could

he stop it? A hot chick said his name like he was Super-man or something and every man within hearing dis-tance looked at him like he was the luckiest son of a bitch around.

She didn't stop until she stood in front of him. "Can we have sex now?"

Chapter 8

Can they have sex now?

Nick quickly glanced around.

Sam was choking because he was trying hard not to laugh. *When the hell did he get a sense of humor?*

The young cop was sputtering and turning red-faced while the irate driver's mouth had dropped to his jaw.

Kia really had a way with words.

"Uh . . . where were you?" he finally managed to ask, ignoring her question.

"I have new clothes."

When she smiled, he could feel his legs tremble. What was she doing to him? He closed his eyes for a second and regrouped. When he opened them, she was still smiling, still looking incredibly hot.

He took a deep breath and tried to think. There was something important that didn't quite compute inside his head. He let his gaze travel over her and when he did, it came to him. "I thought you didn't have any money?"

"I don't. I didn't. Manager said I could buy things with a promise stone." She looked behind her. "See?"

A small troop of men marched briskly down the sidewalk carrying bags in each arm. Good Lord, had she bought out the store?

"Manager helped me."

"Manager?"

She nodded. "She wore a name tag on her clothes: Manager Aims."

"If you can go shopping, then you can pay for my fender," the man growled.

"With money?" She turned her gaze on the man, and his anger immediately evaporated.

"Uh, well, yeah, but I don't think it'll cost too much. If you have insurance, then . . ."

"I have money. Manager gave me back money." She reached inside her pocket and pulled out a wad of bills, shoving them toward Nick. "Will this be enough?" she asked in an innocent way that only someone who didn't know the meaning of cold hard cash would ask.

He looked at the money—at least a couple of thousand dollars—and grabbed it. What the hell was she doing flashing that kind of cash around? The officer looked at her with more than a touch of suspicion.

Nick quickly peeled off some bills and handed them to the guy. More than enough since he drove an older-model Olds and it didn't look like one more dent would hurt it. "Will this take care of the damage?"

The guy grabbed the money and shoved it in his pocket. "That'll take care of everything." He hurried to his car and climbed inside.

"Hey," the officer called out. "Don't you want to file a claim?"

"No claim to file," the man tossed out and peeled away from the curb.

"I guess you got lucky." The officer eyed Kia as he closed his ticket book, and he didn't look as if he was admiring her new clothes. "What exactly are those stones you mentioned?"

"I'm sure you have more important things to do, Officer." Sam spoke up, patting him on the back. He leaned over and whispered something close to the kid's ear.

"Oh, uh, yeah, sorry to interfere. I mean, uh, have a good day." He adjusted his hat before hurrying up the steps and into the building.

After the young cop left, Nick looked at Sam. "What did you say?"

"I just mentioned we were undercover cops." Sam grinned. "Can I help it if he read more into the situation than was there?"

"For someone who doesn't break the rules, you sure don't mind bending a few when it suits you."

"If we're not going to have sex, then can we have food?" Kia asked, looking hopeful.

At least sex ranked above food. That had to say something for his performance scale.

Sam grinned.

Nick had a feeling his friend was enjoying all this. In fact, he'd wager his next paycheck that Sam was having the time of his life. "Aren't you the least bit concerned for my safety?" he asked.

"No." Sam walked over to where Nick's car door lay and hefted one side.

Nick grabbed the other end and they carried it to the back of his car. After popping the trunk, they put it inside. Damn, he'd just washed his car, too.

As they straightened, Sam tossed his keys to Nick. "Take mine. I'll get the boys in the shop to put your door back on. It shouldn't take them too long. I'll drop it by your place when it's fixed."

"And you're doing this because . . ."

"I'm a nice guy. Besides, you can fill me in on

everything." He eyed Kia. "It should be better than what they've been showing on TV."

"Funny."

Nick looked at the guys who quietly stood on the sidewalk, holding Kia's packages. "This way."

They trooped behind them. He felt like the friggin' Pied Piper. The sidewalk was fairly busy with pedestrians who turned to stare. The nosy rubberneckers acted as if he and Kia were from outer space or something . . .

He gritted his teeth.

What the hell was he supposed to do with her? Beam her back to Nerak?

When they got to Sam's car, he pushed the button that popped open the trunk. One by one, her entourage placed the packages inside, then moved back to the sidewalk and stood as stiff as soldiers at attention.

"What are they waiting for?" Kia whispered. "Did I also purchase the men?"

He didn't like the speculative gleam in her eyes. She didn't have a very high regard for the male population if she thought she could just buy one. "They're waiting for a tip. You know. Money." He rubbed his fingers together.

"I have more!" She reached into her other pocket and pulled out another wad of cash and hurried forward. She gave each man a bill.

He choked. "Do you realize you just tipped them twenty dollars each?"

"Should I give them more?"

As one, the men leaned forward until Nick glared at them. "No, I don't think you need to give them more."

Seeing they weren't getting anything else, the men left. Marching right back down the sidewalk like little troopers. And why shouldn't they, after getting a good tip?

He opened the passenger-side door of the car and motioned for her to get in, then walked around and climbed in on his side.

"Your jaw is twitching and you look grim. Are you angry?" she asked.

"Angry? Why should I be angry? I'm on suspension pending an investigation, you're flashing money around that could get me into even hotter water than I already am, you weren't waiting for me when I got back, the door on my car was ripped off, there was an angry man ready to tear me limb from limb . . . Why would you even think I was angry?"

"I guess I was wrong. Can we get food now?"

He closed his eyes and counted to ten.

"You do that a lot," she said.

He opened his eyes. "What?"

"Lose your train of thought and start counting. Have you suffered this condition for a long time?"

"Only since I met you."

She frowned. "I don't think you meant that in a nice way."

Damn it, none of this was her fault. Not really. She just didn't know any better. "I'm sorry."

"Can we get food now?"

"First, you're going to tell me about those stones."

"My promise stones?"

"Show them to me."

She reached into her coat pocket and brought out a small bag. After opening it, she poured them onto the palm of her hand. The sun shone inside the car, causing them to sparkle and glow with a life all their own.

He stared. They couldn't be real. But how else was

she able to buy all the clothes if they weren't? Ah, crap, he had a feeling if IA got wind of this, they'd lock him up and throw away the key. They'd think he was on the take, and he wouldn't blame them.

"Are they genuine?"

"Do you think I've created an illusion?"

He didn't answer. Instead, Nick picked up one and held it toward the light. The brilliant ruby had an inner fire that warmed his hand. "Where did you get these?"

"They're not hard to find. You only have to know where to look. My sisters and my cousin Mala have always called them our promise stones. Whenever we make a promise that we swear we'll keep, we make them on the stones."

He took each stone and replaced it in the bag before giving everything back to her.

Why the hell did she pick him to torment?

"What are you thinking?" she asked.

That his day had just gotten a whole lot worse. He started Sam's car and pulled into traffic.

"Nothing."

Kia thought Nick looked like he was thinking *something*. Not a very good something, either. If only Lara were here to give him a massage.

She watched him closely. The twitch in his jaw was more pronounced.

"You *are* angry?"

"No, I passed anger a long time ago. I'd say I'm more pissed off now."

"And I made you *pissed off?*"

"It's not your fault." His frown deepened. "Well, it really kind of is, but shh . . . stuff happens."

He was angry because she'd left the car. This wasn't good. She didn't like his anger. Not when it was because of something she did. "I only went inside the building with apparel in the window because I needed clothes."

"A typical female. She says she comes from another planet, traveling long distances, and the first thing she does is go shopping."

She had to strain to hear his words. It was almost as if he were talking to himself, but he didn't seem quite as angry as a moment ago. His shoulders had relaxed and the twitching had all but ceased.

"I'm sorry I didn't wait in your vehicle as you asked."

He glanced her way, then quickly returned his gaze to the road. "When I saw you weren't in the car, I was worried," he said brusquely.

She could see her leaving had deeply affected him. He really had been concerned for her safety. On Nerak, no one worried about anyone. She would be gone for months sometimes and only be missed, but never worried about. What could possibly happen to her on such a peaceful planet?

But Nick had been worried. An odd feeling swept through her. His concern pleased her. She had a sudden urge to throw her arms around him and stick her tongue in his mouth.

Not good.

Their relationship was getting complicated. She was starting to have odd feelings for this earthman. She would explore these emotions later, when she was alone.

She turned her gaze toward the window and watched the scenery as they drove down the road. Some of the people on the sidewalk looked menacing. Others seemed to be uncaring of the people who walked near them. They all carried bags or satchels, clutching the items close to their bodies as if someone might try to steal their things.

Nerak suddenly seemed very far away.

No wonder Nick had worried about her. She would be more cautious in the future. He must think she made a poor excuse for a warrior.

Feeling bad wasn't an emotion she normally experienced. Food would make her happy again. She really wanted more pancakes. The ones Manager had ordered had been very small.

Nick turned a corner and pulled in front of a store where other vehicles were parked.

"Is this the food place?"

"It's called a grocery store."

"But you can get food?"

"If you have money."

She could see how money would be very important on Earth. It seemed a person needed it to have food and clothes. There was no such requirement on Nerak. The Elders provided everything.

When Nick stopped the car, they got out. Sam's door had to be manually opened, too. An inconvenience, but eating was a good trade-off.

"Just try to keep a low profile—okay?"

"Well, of course." That's exactly what she'd been trying to do.

They walked inside the store. The doors automatically opened. At least these worked. As soon as she stepped into the interior, her nose was assaulted with wondrous aromas. She closed her eyes and inhaled, letting her senses be aroused.

Food! Oh, yes!

The overhead lights flickered for a brief instant.

"This is . . . very good."

An older woman passed them, smiling. An elder. Kia bowed to her.

Nick cleared his throat. "Maybe we should get a cart."

"You don't revere the elders on your planet?"

His brow knit. "Well . . . yeah . . . sort of . . ." He sighed. "Not nearly as much as we should, I guess."

"A shame. Elders have great wisdom."

Nick got a cart on wheels and she followed him as he pushed it toward a sign that marked this as the produce section. What an array of colors! Yellows and reds. Deep purples and bright greens. They reminded Kia of her promise stones.

She picked up an orange ball. Though the texture felt odd, the aroma was mouth-wateringly pleasant. "What's this?"

"An orange."

She frowned. Whoever had named it hadn't been very creative.

"It's fruit. You eat it."

Oh good! This is what she'd been wanting. Food! She took a huge bite and chewed, then immediately spit it out. "Ugh, this is awful."

Why would anyone want to eat something that tasted so vile? Nick had lied to her. She glared at him, wishing for a moment she had her phazer.

He looked around before kicking the orange chunk under one of the tables, then grabbed the fruit from her.

"You have to peel it first. And you can't eat the food until you pay for it."

The money issue again. Nick could've mentioned that fact a little sooner, and that she would need to peel the fruit. She didn't dwell on it long as more food caught her eye.

"What's that?" She pointed toward a red shiny object.

"An apple. Don't you have food on your plan . . . on Nerak?"

She shook her head. "Just capsules. I told you."

"You weren't lying?"

"Lie? I don't lie. Why would I do that?" People didn't lie on Nerak. There was no need. She picked up the apple and brought it close to her face, inhaling the fragrance of this fruit. This one had a lot of promise, too. But would it taste as bad as the orange?

"Like I said, Nerak has to be a pretty boring place. No men, no food . . ."

Her head whipped around. "You truly believe me? That I'm from another planet?"

His frown deepened. "Yeah," he mumbled, casting his gaze toward two women who were approaching with carts on wheels.

The women hadn't heard their conversation, but *she* had and it greatly pleased her. She threw her arms around his neck. "I'm happy you finally believe me and not just maybe believe."

"Uh, we're in a grocery store . . . low profile," he mumbled and stepped away, but then smiled to ease the harshness of his actions, a smile that made her body tingle. "But I'm glad you're pleased."

"Can we have sex after we get back to your apartment?"

The two women, who were closer now, jerked their heads around to stare.

Nick coughed.

People seemed to do a lot of choking when she mentioned sex, then they looked around at other people. Odd behavior. Maybe she should explain.

"You said we could have sex when you discovered who I am. Now that you have accepted the truth, we can have sex."

"We don't discuss sex in grocery stores," he whispered.

The women chuckled. She could see they were friendly.

"Then where do you discuss it?" she asked, turning her attention back to Nick.

"In private."

She thought about it for a second. "If you insist, but you do realize I'm not wearing any undergarments beneath this dress. The material rubbing against my nipples is causing numerous sensations inside me. I don't know how long I can go without fulfilling my desires. I want to have sex with you very much."

When her gaze lowered, she saw the familiar tightening in his pants. She liked that she hadn't even pushed a button to make him expand.

As she returned her gaze to his face, she noticed a bright yellow fruit. Momentarily distracted, she picked it up, lightly running her fingernails over the length.

"What's this?" It reminded her of the male anatomy. Interesting.

"A banana." He grabbed it from her hands and dropped it into the cart along with some other things as he hurried her up and down the aisles at a brisk pace. He seemed to be in a hurry. Maybe he did want to have sex with her after all.

She snuggled inside the fur coat, pulling the collar up. The soft pelt felt wonderful against her skin. Sherry had been right when she told Kia that no man would be able to resist her when she wore this dress. And she had more clothes in which to seduce Nick. Before she left Earth, she would have many sexual experiences with him.

Sex first, then they would begin the search for Mala.

And food. She couldn't forget about eating.

She sighed. Earth might not be as bad as she'd first thought.

Nick slowed, leaning over a bin with fogged glass. She joined him. The temperature had dropped considerably in this area and strange things were happening. She laughed.

"What's so funny?"

She opened her coat. "Look, the cold air has made my nipples hard. You can see them through my dress."

"Ah, shit."

People were staring again. When she smiled, though, they smiled back.

But Nick didn't seem to want to stay and interact with them. He hurried down another aisle with boxes and boxes of food. When he stopped, so did she. Good, she wanted to see what other treats were in store for her. She read some of the containers.

Chocolate.

She scanned the labels. Chocolate cupcakes, bags of chocolate candy, chocolate cookies.

It must be a favorite Earth diet staple since they had so much of it. Would it taste as good as pancakes?

She cast a covert look in Nick's direction as he reached the end of the aisle and disappeared around the corner. She had money. They shouldn't mind if she tried their product if she was able to pay for it.

The aromas in this area were so very tantalizing and she was so hungry. The food capsules she'd taken last night no longer made her feel full and Nick hadn't given her a chance to finish her pancakes and the ones Manager had ordered hadn't filled her nearly enough.

She squared her shoulders. Wasn't she a warrior? Afraid of nothing? Besides, she was a superior being. It was her right to try this food called chocolate.

Having made her decision, she opened the bag of chocolate candy bars.

Chapter 9

"They went into Albertsons," Darla said into her cell phone.

"And you say she has a pouch full of jewels?" Slava sounded skeptical.

"Well, yeah, I saw them when she was shopping for clothes. I heard the clerk say she was some kind of princess or something."

Slava didn't believe her. He could be such an ass, just because his Uncle Yuri was a hot shot with the Russian Mafia. Yeah, well, he was only living in the shadow of his uncle. Now *he* was one to worry about. Even Darla didn't screw with the mafia—Russian or Italian.

But Slava was a different matter. He didn't even sound or act Russian, and he thought he knew everything just because he'd been in the joint. Some big-time con he was. He'd stolen some checks, signed his own damn name, then written his driver's license number at the top. What a moron.

Darla snorted with laughter but quickly turned it into a cough.

She'd make him eat crow. This so-called princess had a bag full of jewels. She'd seen the precious gems flashing when the overhead lights hit them. Enough that it made her mouth water. The princess didn't have a clue she would soon be parting company with her stones. An innocent just waiting to be ripped off.

The job would've been simple, one Darla could've handled herself. Hell, it wouldn't have been the first job she'd done alone. But almost as soon as the chick left the store, she'd joined the man.

Good-looking SOB, and he was stuck to the princess like a bee on honey. Nope, he knew he had a good thing and he wasn't about to let her out of his sight.

She still might have attempted to rob them, but it didn't take her long to figure out he was a cop. Crap, just her damned luck.

There'd been some kind of wreck in front of the police station and the good-looking cuss seemed to know the uniform handling the accident. Probably undercover, since he wore his hair longer than the average street cop.

But Darla wanted those jewels.

That's where Slava came in. He might not have much for a brain, but he damn sure had muscle. He could distract the guy long enough for her to get the jewels. If Slava got caught in the middle—oh, well. She'd be out of the country and she wouldn't have to divvy up the jewels.

She could see it now. An Italian villa complete with a pool boy. She might even have a pool installed.

"So what am I supposed to do?" Slava asked, interrupting her delicious fantasy.

"Just hang close to the phone until I give the word."

"Gotcha." There was a pause. "I was going to the store later. Outta beer."

She pinched her nose between her thumb and forefinger. "Take your cell phone."

"Oh, yeah." He chuckled. "I forgot about that."

"I'll call you when I need you. Make sure you keep gas in your car just in case." It was bad enough his brain ran on empty.

"Gotcha."

She snapped her phone shut and dropped it back inside her purse. She really had to choose her partners better. And with the princess's jewels, she could have just about any partner she wanted.

The lights above the grocery store began to flicker. Darla frowned. What the hell was going on? Power outage? Bad weather blowing in?

Not a cloud in the blue sky. In fact, it was pretty clear.

She scrunched down in her seat. If there was an impending storm, she sure didn't want to be in the path of a lightning bolt. It'd be just her luck she'd get struck.

No, she was going to be really careful until she had those jewels in her hot little hands.

Chapter 10

Nick grabbed a loaf of bread and tossed it in the cart. The sooner he got out of the store, the better. The next thing he knew . . .

The lights flickered.

His feet came to a grinding halt. He jerked his head around, almost giving himself whiplash.

No Kia.

The lights flickered again.

He looked up as a hazy blue and yellow cloud formed, floating above the next aisle over.

Ah, crap!

He whirled the cart around and ran to the end of the aisle, taking the corner on two wheels, then came to a dead stop.

Kia sat on the floor, surrounded by open boxes and bags of chocolate cookies, snack cakes, and candy bars. She looked up, smiling. Her teeth were evidence enough of what she'd been doing.

"Chocolate, Nick. It's wonderful."

A man came around the corner, took one look, and hastily left.

She came to her feet, sauntering toward Nick. He couldn't breathe. Even covered in chocolate, she had all the right moves.

"Chocolate is good. The only thing better is sex." Her heated gaze caressed him. "I want you," she breathed in a sultry voice that drizzled over him like hot fudge. "Do you want me, too?" She stopped in front of him, leaning against his chest, then ran her hands through his hair, pulling his mouth down to hers.

He couldn't breathe. And he damn sure couldn't move away from her. Not when she looked at him like this. Her deep blue eyes hypnotized him.

She ran her tongue lightly over his lips. She smelled like chocolate.

He captured her mouth, tugging on her bottom lip with his teeth before he pulled her closer and deepened the kiss.

She tasted like chocolate.

Everything faded. It was just the two of them and a kaleidoscope of swirling clouds.

Heat swelled inside him. More, he had to have more. He fondled her breast, squeezing the nipple. She moaned, then coughed.

Coughed?

She coughed again, louder this time. Except the sound was deep and kind of hoarse, and he didn't think Kia had made the noise.

A damn good way to kill a mood. Someone was going to catch hell for interrupting him.

He pulled away from Kia, blinking his eyes. Ah, crap, they were still in the grocery store.

"Are we not going to have sex, Nick?" Kia's face showed her disappointment.

A clerk stood behind her. Short, squat, and looking more irate than the driver who'd ripped off Nick's door. Oh, yeah, this was really keeping a low profile.

The clerk straightened to his full height of five four, and tugged on his deep blue apron. "This is a family store," he huffed. "We can't allow this kind of behavior."

"I'm sorry." Nick set Kia away from him.

The clerk waved his hand. "Who's going to clean up this mess?" He glared at Nick. "And who's going to pay for all this?"

Kia turned toward the clerk. "Pay? I have money."

The clerk's jaw dropped open as he caught the full effect of her.

"The chocolate smelled so tempting that I couldn't resist."

The clerk snapped his mouth shut. "Uh, oh, that's okay. We just need to pick up a bit, but we can do that."

"Come on," Nick said under his breath, grabbing Kia's arm. "But chocolate, Nick."

He grabbed some boxes and bags, tossing them into the cart. "Okay, let's go." He didn't add "before he changes his mind and calls the cops."

Damn, he'd been thrown out of a few bars before, and once a bedroom shop—it was a bedroom shop, for Pete's sake. What the hell had they expected? But a grocery store? This was a first. Or at least it would be if they didn't get a move on.

He hurried to the checkout, dodging other carts and keeping one hand firmly on Kia's arm. He wasn't taking a chance that she might wander over to the ice cream section. No telling what the cold creamy fudge bars would do to her libido.

He piled the groceries on the revolving counter, then looked at the kid behind the cash register. Was he even out of high school? The boy wasn't moving. No frigging wonder. Kia was licking the chocolate off each finger—slowly, one finger at a time. Hell, he couldn't blame the teen. Kia made a simple, innocent act look so damned hot.

"Do you mind?" he asked.

The boy didn't take his gaze off Kia. "Huh-uh. I don't mind a bit."

"The groceries!"

The boy's head jerked around to Nick. "Oh, yeah, sorry." He grabbed the food and quickly ran each item past the scanner.

Nick dug some cash out of his pocket and handed it to the clerk, who took the bills without even counting them. No, he was too busy mooning over Kia.

"Can I carry the bags?" he asked hopefully.

"We've got them," Nick said before Kia could say a word.

He hurried her out to the car, dumped the bags into the trunk, and got in on the driver's side.

"Are you angry?" she asked.

"No." He started the car and pulled out of the parking lot and into traffic.

"Your jaw is twitching."

He glanced in the mirror. She was right. It was twitching. He took a deep breath, slowly exhaling.

"Are you going to start counting?"

He opened his mouth, then snapped it closed.

"I'm sorry about the chocolate."

He glanced at her. She didn't look sorry. "You agreed to keep a low profile."

"You're right."

She crossed her legs. Her dress barely skimmed her upper thighs. His grip tightened on the steering wheel.

Don't look at her legs. Don't remember how they wrapped around your waist and pulled you in deeper . . . and deeper . . .

Damn, the way she made him sweat he'd have to watch that he didn't get dehydrated. And what was she doing while he was being tormented by images of her naked body pressed close to his? She'd turned slightly and was looking out the window. All innocent. Yeah, right, he knew better—innocent she wasn't.

Man, he had to get control of his emotions and quit thinking with his dick. What did he really know about Kia? She was from another planet—that was it.

He'd seen all the Star Wars and Star Trek movies. Who could really say for sure there weren't other planets in the universe? He'd always secretly wondered if Earth was where other planets had sent their rejects and humans had evolved over time into their own species.

So he could buy that she was from another planet. Stranger things had happened. But was this her true form? What if underneath that sexy bod was something green and slimy? Hell, maybe she did have a third eye or another head.

Cold chills swept over him.

This wasn't right. Not at all. And having sex . . . well, that was out of the question. From here on out, he had complete control and he wouldn't let her seduce him.

Who was to say his dick *wouldn't* fall off if he kept having sex with her?

He cast a covert look in her direction. Her face was in profile. Sinfully long lashes outlined those incredible eyes. And those lips. Damn, they were sweet.

He squared his shoulders. It didn't matter what she looked like. Wherever the hell Kia came from, she was his responsibility for the time being, but that was as far as it would go. He wouldn't fall to temptation. It wasn't going to happen.

What the hell had happened to his vow not to have any commitments? No long-term relationships? Hadn't his father walking out when Nick was sixteen taught him anything? Dear old Dad had just gotten tired of being a husband and father.

And now look at him. Not only was he stuck with Kia, but she was an alien. Could his life get any worse?

He hit his right blinker before turning into the parking garage and pulling into an open space.

He'd get the stuff unloaded and into his apartment, feed her, then they would start looking for this cousin of hers.

And there would be no sex—at least until he knew what he was dealing with. With IA on his ass he'd have to keep his nose clean. Ah, man, if Candy questioned Kia he'd be in deep shit.

Low profile. He could do it.

He wouldn't even think about his ripped-off car door . . . or Albertsons. He would start with a clean slate.

He put the car in park and killed the engine before going around to the passenger side, but Kia had already opened her door. He couldn't move. Hell, he could barely breathe as she swung her legs around.

What was it about a long-legged woman who wore a short dress and stiletto heels that could make his brain stop working? Sexy didn't even come close to describing how she looked.

"Is something wrong?" she asked as she stood.

"You look nice. Really nice. Did I mention that?"

Her smile came slow but it reached all the way to her eyes and made them sparkle.

"No, you didn't." She raised her wrist to his nose. "Sherry showed me scents. Isn't it nice?"

He took her hand in his. He couldn't resist touching her. Her skin was soft . . . smooth and warm. It didn't take much imagination to envision her hands sliding over his body, caressing every inch of him.

"Smell." She nudged her wrist closer.

He inhaled. This was what he'd been smelling. A

light scent that blended with the chocolate. It had wrapped around his senses, warming his blood.

"It's nice, isn't it?"

"Yeah, it's real nice." He let go of her hand, mentally shaking his mind clear of all the sexual thoughts he was having. He kept repeating "no sex" until he felt in control of his sexual urges, then pushed the button that would pop the trunk.

Kia sauntered past him as she went to the back of the car. He'd let her get a few packages, then he'd grab a couple and whisk her toward the elevator. He wouldn't think about sex or the way her perfume had enclosed him in a cocoon of sensual images and made him think thoughts he had no business thinking.

Like scooping her up and carrying her up to the apartment, then slowly stripping off her clothes and having hot and wild sex for the rest of the day.

And if she liked chocolate? Oh, baby, he could think up a lot of different ways to use chocolate that would please her and him.

"Oh," she began as she reached into a bag. "I have this, too. Sherry said you would enjoy it."

He really liked her voice. It was sultry yet held a touch of innocence, too. As if she was unsullied by the world at large.

"What's that?" he asked.

"Body oil that heats as you massage it into the skin. They had a . . ." She pursed her lips, then smiled when she thought of the word she wanted. "They have a whole line of sensual products." She grabbed some packages as she straightened.

His gut clenched and his dick went full salute. Ah, man, this wasn't good. How the hell was he going to resist? He was only human.

He grabbed an armful of packages and shut the trunk. "Let's get this stuff upstairs." Maybe trekking back and forth to the car would cool his ardor. Cool? Had it ever dropped to below hot and horny since he encountered Kia? He didn't think so.

"Are we going to have food again?"

Food and sex. Did she think of nothing else? He frowned. Yesterday, if someone would've told him that he was going to have a sexy woman staying in his apartment who only thought about food and sex and he would try to keep her at arm's length, Nick would've laughed and said they were crazy.

Too bad that's exactly what had happened. Maybe he should just give the lady what she wanted. Worry about the consequences later. But that's exactly what he'd been doing all his life. Sam was right. He lived on the edge. This time he wouldn't succumb to temptation.

He followed Kia toward the door. She stopped in front of it and waved her arm, then turned toward him. "It's broken."

"You have to push it open." He shoved the door open and let her go past him. She stopped halfway through the threshold and looked at him as if she'd just thought of something.

"Thank you," she said.

Her words drifted over him, touching parts of his body he didn't even want to think about. He swallowed past the sudden lump in his throat. "You're welcome," he croaked.

She stopped in front of the elevator, then pushed on the door. She looked back at him as if to tell him this door was broken, too. He walked over and pushed the button and the door swished open.

"So much to remember," she mumbled as she went inside.

He went in behind her and pushed the button to the fourth floor, casting sideways glances at her as they ascended.

How the hell was he going to resist her? Was he retarded? She was sexy, vibrant . . . and horny. How often did he get a horny woman in his bed? Sure, he'd had his share of hot women, but Kia was different.

Earthy, that's what she was. Not exactly Earthy. Nerakian would probably be correct since she wasn't from Earth.

Nothing seemed to embarrass her. Oh, man, she looked so friggin' hot without a stitch of clothes. Her high, pointed breasts begged him to suck on them.

The elevator stopped, but it took a few more seconds for his mind to clear. Kia was killing him.

As soon as they went inside his apartment, he carried the bags to the bar and set them down.

"We can have food now?" Kia set her bags beside his, then slipped off her coat. When she turned around to place it across the sofa, something close to a gurgle escaped from him.

There was no damn back to the dress. At least, there might as well not have been, as low cut as it was. It formed to a vee so low that he found himself raising on his toes for a better look.

He really had to get hold of himself, but how the hell could he, when the silvery material clung to every damn curve?

"Nick?" She turned back around and glided toward him.

"Huh?"

"Can we eat now?"

He cleared his throat. "Uh, sure." He reached into the bag and grabbed the first thing he came to—a banana. "Here, this should hold you until lunch."

When she started to put it in her mouth, he

grabbed it back. "No, you have to peel it first." He peeled the banana, leaving only part of the bottom skin so she could hold it.

She took it, paused, then said, "Thank you."

Tentatively, she placed the tip in her mouth. "Mmm . . ." She closed her eyes, swirling her tongue around the banana, licking up the side. "Wonderful."

He couldn't move if he'd wanted to. Her mouth on the banana took on a whole other meaning as she licked and sucked. Damn, he was going to bust out of his jeans watching her eat a friggin' piece of fruit.

Until she bit the end off and began to chew.

Ouch!

His world-class boner shriveled right up. She might as well have tossed a bucket of ice water on his lower regions.

He drew in a deep breath. "I'll get the rest of the packages."

She nodded, still going to town on the banana. This was good, he told himself. She was occupied and he'd have time to get his mind in order.

No sex, no sex, no sex.

Why exactly was it such a bad idea to have sex, anyway? It wasn't like he ever followed rules—even his own. There was a good reason, though. He just couldn't quite think what the hell it was right now.

Chapter 11

Kia finished the banana and tossed the outer hull back on the counter. She was still hungry. She pulled out a pretty package.

Chocolate!

This would fill her stomach. She carried the bag back to the lounging sofa and got comfortable. Chocolate was good. Better than sex—almost.

What about chocolate and sex at the same time?

Her nipples tightened and began to ache as a burst of heat inflamed her body. Just as quickly, passion's fire extinguished. An emotion she was only vaguely familiar with ran through her.

Guilt? She didn't like guilt.

Succumbing to temptation made her feel guilty because she knew how hard it would be to give all this up.

Had Mala tasted chocolate?

Her brow puckered. If Mala had discovered men, sex, water that cascaded over one's body, and chocolate, it might be impossible to get her to leave Earth.

She unwrapped another bar and chewed slowly, savoring the taste.

What other things had Mala discovered that Kia hadn't? She could feel the blood drain from her face as a wave of dizziness washed over her. Would she dis-

cover more pleasure while on Earth? How hard would
it be for her to leave when it was time to go home?

She worried her bottom lip, realized there was
chocolate on it, and licked it off. Chocolate was so
good. She closed her eyes for a moment and savored
the taste of it on her tongue, then sighed when it was
gone.

Already she could feel the tug to stay longer—discover everything she could about this marvelous
planet. But what about her promise to her sister? Lara
would be so hurt if she broke her word. And if she
stayed longer, maybe *she* wouldn't want to go home
at all.

Lara wasn't the only one who would be affected.
All her sisters would have to erase her from their
memories. She sniffed. Not fair. She didn't want to
be forgotten forever and ever. Never to have existed.

She jumped to her feet. No, she was a warrior, and
warriors were not weak! They didn't fall prey to temptation. Warriors had more control than the average
Nerakian. When it was time to leave, she would go without looking back.

The door opened and Nick strolled inside, dropping his packages onto the lounging sofa, his gaze
never leaving hers.

Sweet temptation!

"You have chocolate on your cheek," he croaked,
then quickly cleared his throat.

As long as she was on Earth, why not indulge in
the pleasures of the senses? She was a Nerakian warrior, even if it was in name only. She was highly trained,
and she would be able to walk away.

This was only research—sort of.

She sauntered toward Nick, her gaze moving over
him, liking what she saw. There was something about

him that drew her like a powerful magnet. The pull surprised her. His black T-shirt was a little wrinkled, but it fit snug to his muscled chest. And his pants rode low on his hips, begging her to strip them off.

No, he wasn't at all perfect. He was better than that.

When she stopped in front of him, she wiped the chocolate off her cheek with one finger, then touched it to his mouth.

"Chocolate is good," she whispered.

His pupils dilated. Then with excruciating slowness, he licked his lips, brushing across her finger before sucking it inside his mouth. She gasped with delight. Heat swirled inside her.

Nick released her finger, and she stroked her hand down the side of his face, relishing how it felt to touch him. His skin was tanned and still smooth from this morning when he'd scraped away his facial hair. She enjoyed the smoothness.

"I wasn't going to do this," he rasped.

"What?" Her eyes widened.

"Have sex with you again."

"But I want you. I'm not good at denying myself." She slid her hand down the front of his slacks until she came to the object of her desire. She squeezed his erection. There was pleasure on his face.

"Ah, fuck," he groaned.

"I know this word. Our language is very similar. It means to have sexual intercourse. Yes, that's what I want, too," she breathed.

He slid his hand behind her head and jerked her closer. The heat of his hands moved over her bare back. She moaned, her arms going around his waist, moving nearer.

Her sensitive nipples pressed against his chest,

while his erection pushed against her lower half. Automatically, she rubbed against him, feeling his heat even through the material of her dress.

A shudder swept over her.

Nick shoved her dress down. It puddled at her feet. He ended the kiss and stepped back, his gaze slowly moving over her, his eyes telling her that he liked what he saw.

"You look good in thigh-high stockings and stiletto heels . . . and nothing else. Damn good."

His words sent a rush of excitement over her. "Then you do want to have sex."

"God help me, but yeah, I want to have sex with you."

She smiled and raised his shirt, then pushed it off his shoulders. "I think you look damn good, too." His body was harder than hers—more firm. She ran her hands over the sinewy muscles, the hard ridges.

Leaning forward, she brushed her nipples against his chest. He sucked in a deep breath; her body tingled. She reached for the waistband of his pants, their gazes locked as she tugged the button from the hole, then slid the metal tab down. Her hands shook as she pushed his pants down, then his briefs, freeing him from the restraints of his clothing.

His erection was hard like the strongest metal on Nerak, strong like the warrior he was. She brushed her fingertips over it and watched it quiver. Nick was the stronger warrior, she knew this. Experience would always tell. But she felt very powerful as she slid her hand downward and cupped his testicles, gently squeezing, feeling his body tremble beneath her touch.

He cupped her butt, drawing her closer, rubbing his erection against her mound. She moved her hands to his shoulders, biting her bottom lip as tremors of excitement washed over her.

Rubbing against him created a friction. Her breathing grew ragged as she quickened the pace. He pulled her closer, letting her have her way. But before she had a chance to climax, he pulled back ever so slightly.

"Nick!"

"It's okay, baby. We've got plenty of time."

She drew in a deep, ragged breath, knowing he was right. He would bring her close to the edge many more times before she found the ultimate release, and that would make it all the sweeter.

When the room stopped spinning, she began to touch him again. She flicked a finger over his nipple, watched it tighten before she leaned forward and licked across the hard nub. "You taste salty."

"You think so?" His words were laced with passion and humor. He was letting her explore his body. She glanced at him and saw the restraint it took for him not to touch her any more than he already had.

Nick had tried to resist, but she'd tempted him. A smidgen of guilt rushed through her. "You were probably right not to want to have sex again."

He frowned. "Why?"

"Because it will be harder for me to leave. Like the chocolate."

One eyebrow shot up. "You're comparing me to chocolate?" He casually brushed his fingers over her nipples, then tugged on each one, rolling the hard nubs between his thumb and forefinger. Liquid heat pooled between her legs.

"Chocolate is very good," she hissed as he lowered his mouth and drew one tight nipple inside. His restraint hadn't lasted long but she didn't care. This was good. He sucked on one breast before moving to the other and giving it just as much attention.

"You don't have chocolate on Nerak, and sex is just something to relieve stress. Right?"

She nodded.

He moved his hands lower, tracing her hips, lightly trailing them over her abdomen. For a moment, Nick stole her thoughts. It took a conscious effort for her to remember what he'd said. He brushed his fingers through her curls. She nudged her sex against his hand, seeking satisfaction.

"On Nerak sex is the same as taking a food capsule. Each companion unit is programmed by its owner to perform in a certain manner. When climax is reached, the duty is finished."

"You mean there's none of this?" He tugged on the fleshy part of her sex.

She gasped, grabbing his shoulders as heat swirled inside her. "No . . . no. I'm a warrior. Warriors do not indulge in personal gratification. Having sex is only a way to release pent-up emotions."

"You mean you don't touch each other?"

"I'm a warrior, and therefore above such things."

Incredible sensations washed over her. How could she think when he was caressing her like this? Even her thoughts were no longer coherent.

"Then you've never had anyone kiss you right here?" He cupped her sex.

Her eyes flew open. "No . . . I mean . . ." Confusion filled her. Confusion . . . heat, excitement . . . and lots and lots of heat! "You have done this before?"

He grinned and her heart did a little flip-flop.

Rather than answer, he moved to his knees and she grabbed his shoulders, not even realizing how much she'd been leaning on him. Before she could do much more than catch her balance, he was blowing warm air over her sex. She gritted her teeth. If his breath felt this wonderful, then what would his tongue . . . his tongue . . .

He ran his tongue over her sex, then sucked her inside his mouth.

"Oh . . . oh . . . Nick . . ."

"Let it happen, baby."

He scraped his teeth over her most sensitive area before sucking her inside his mouth again. His tongue was hot as it swirled around her.

It took a supreme effort on her part to stay on her feet, but she didn't want him to stop . . . ever.

He slid a finger inside her and began to move it in and out. Lights swirled around her. The air filled with electricity. Something close to a whimper escaped past her lips.

Her orgasm hit her in waves, rolling down her body, pulsating against her sex. She cried out. Her legs refused to hold her a second longer but she didn't have to worry because Nick scooped her into his arms and carried her to bed, then gently laid her down. She felt like a puddle, without substance.

Adam-4 had never done this for her. About the best he could do was vibrate, and while that was awesome, it didn't even come close to this. She doubted if she would be able to move for at least . . .

After sheathing himself, he nudged her legs open and slowly slid into her depth, but he didn't move. His heat filled her. Still, he didn't move. Suddenly she wanted more. She arched toward him and he raised his hips, then lowered into her again.

She sighed.

He kept a slow rhythm. The heat began to build. Her gaze met his and she saw the knowing look in his eyes. Ahh, he knew what he was doing, building her up for another orgasm. As soon as the thought formed, the fire burst into a roaring flame.

She wrapped her legs around his waist and clenched

her inner muscles. He sucked in a breath, picking up the pace. Her breathing grew more rapid, matching his. Fire spread through her body and exploded all at once. He cried out and collapsed on top of her.

Her eyes barely noted the fading haze of colors above them. She'd never thought it could be like this. Never this incredible.

He rolled to his side, taking her with him.

"I think you're more than just a great warrior. I think you're also a great lover."

The temptation of Nick was so very bad, and while she was on Earth, Kia planned to discover just how bad he could be.

Chapter 12

Nick mumbled an excuse and hurried to the bathroom. *What the hell was he doing?* He was having sex with an alien, for Christ's sake.

Fear swept over him.

His gaze snapped to his dick. It looked okay—was still attached to the rest of his body and it wasn't green or anything. He breathed a sigh of relief. For a second there he'd thought . . .

Kia was making him crazy, that's what it was.

He turned the shower on and stepped beneath the spray, letting it wash away his problems. At least for a few seconds. The muscles in his back relaxed as the hot water cascaded over him.

Kia was incredible, though. Sex with her had been even better this time. He couldn't imagine what it would be like next time.

No! There wouldn't be a next time.

He'd been weak. He'd succumbed to temptation. It was over.

Damn, so much for wishing his troubles down the drain. No escaping. He sighed, reviewing his options. The IA investigation would take a few days, at the very least. Two weeks tops if Candy wanted to make a personal vendetta out of it. He wouldn't put it past her. She really liked this new job, and she didn't like him. But that should give him enough time to find Kia's cousin.

Crap, how many aliens were living amongst them? He could feel the blood drain from his face.

Now that he thought about it, one of the dispatchers acted kind of odd. She was always giving him funny looks. Not the come-hither kind. More like she wondered what he would taste like—as in for her next meal. Kia did seem to have this weird obsession with food.

The shower curtain was flung back.

He jumped, ramming his shoulder against the wall. "You scared the hell out of me!"

Kia's bottom lip trembled.

Ah, man, what was he supposed to do when she looked at him like that? "Hey, I'm sorry. I was . . . deep in thought." He didn't have to tell her *what* he was thinking.

She nodded, but still looked dejected.

"Want to join me?"

She immediately brightened. "I love the water! I didn't know you were going to stand beneath it. We can stand under it together." She stepped inside the shower with him.

He swallowed past the lump in his throat.

Do you want to join me?

Oh, yeah, nice shootin', Tex.

What the hell had he been thinking? Him . . . Kia . . . naked in the shower. So much for that vow about not touching her again.

"Yeah, sure," he told her. "We'll stand under the shower together. Want to invite the neighbors?"

"Do you think they'd like to join us?"

He shook his head. "Never mind." He closed the curtain.

She scooted in front of him and stood beneath the showerhead.

That's all she did. Just stood beneath it.

"This is fun, and cozy with the curtain closed," she said, brushing her hair out of her face.

"It also keeps the bathroom floor dry."

"Oh, that's what it's for."

He laughed. How could he not? The tension drained from him.

"Don't they have showers on Nerak?"

She shook her head, slinging water in his eyes. He blinked several times until his vision cleared. Another bright idea. He should've left it blurry so he wouldn't have to see her glistening, naked body.

Damn, she looked sexy with water running down the curve of her back, then sliding down the gently rounded cheeks of her ass. If he stepped a little closer, his dick would be nestled quite nicely against her backside.

"No, we have beams of light that remove the bacteria from our body and clothes," she said. "Water is not in plentiful supply on Nerak."

"Then you don't have soap?"

"What's that?"

"I'll show you." Hell, he was already as hard as a friggin' rock. It was more of a have-to-touch-her than anything else. If he didn't, he could quite possibly go insane.

He reached for the shampoo. "This is to wash your hair. It's called shampoo." He poured a dollop in his hand, then set the bottle back down before he began to massage her head.

"I like shampoo." She leaned her back against him, her body rubbing against his.

Ah, screw it. If his dick rotted off because he had

sex with an alien, then it rotted off, but how many people could say they'd had sex as incredible as what he'd had so far with Kia? He'd bet his bottom dollar there weren't many.

But he still couldn't resist looking closely at her scalp as he lathered her head. No third eye, and he didn't see a miniature head hidden away. No seams that he could tell, either. Maybe this *was* the skin she was born with. Yeah, he was losing it all right.

"Keep your eyes closed tight," he told her. "If the soap gets in them, it'll burn. Ready?"

She nodded.

He rinsed her hair, then turned her to face him before reaching for the soap. "This is body soap." He wet the bar before running the smooth surface over her shoulders, leaving a trail of tiny bubbles in its wake.

"You're so beautiful," he said. And she was. Her golden tan was all over—no lines that he could see.

"So are you," she said.

He grinned. Okay, so her words made him feel good. Big deal.

His smile quickly faded.

As if she could make any big comparisons, since there were no men on her planet. So far, all she'd really had to measure him against was the trucker who got her this far, the biker at the bar, and Sam. Okay, he was better than Sam. Now he felt mollified.

She took the soap from him and began to run it over his chest. "It feels soft and . . . and . . ."

"Soapy?"

She laughed. "Yes. Soapy."

He liked her laugh. Throaty, sexy. She learned quickly how to work up lather in her hands. When she had enough, she set the soap down. There was a mischie-

vous twinkle in her eyes when she faced him again.
He raised an eyebrow.

Her hands closed over his erection. He sucked
wind, closing his eyes as she moved her hands up
and down him.

"You like this?"

He couldn't speak, only nodded.

"I want to take you inside my mouth like you took
me inside yours. Do earthmen like this act?"

Do they like . . . He cleared his throat. "Yeah, we . . .
I like that." His brain quit functioning as she moved
to the side and rinsed the soap from him. She met
his eyes and smiled. A slow, seductive lifting of the
sides of her mouth.

"Good, because I want to taste you, feel you inside
my mouth."

She moved to her knees in front of him. He couldn't
breathe. With the water lightly pelting them, she ran
her tongue down his length, then back up before she
took the end of his penis in her mouth. He gasped as
incredible pleasure drenched him in waves.

Without even thinking, he moved one hand to the
back of her head and began to caress her, and with the
other, he braced against the bathroom wall. Ah damn,
her mouth sucking his dick felt so fucking sweet.
There might not be any men on her planet, but she
damn sure knew what she was doing as she ran her
tongue over the tip.

He clenched his ass when she sucked him inside
her mouth. His thought processes immediately stopped
working. All he wanted to do was feel. He leaned
against the shower tiles. The water from the showerhead was like a gentle waterfall against him as her
mouth worked magic. The pressure inside began to
build higher and higher.

As much as he enjoyed what she was doing, he knew he had to make her stop. Reaching beneath her arms, he pulled her up. Damn, the look of disappointment on her face was another turn-on.

"I was enjoying myself, Nick."

He snaked his hand downward and rubbed lightly between her legs. "I want to be inside you when I come. I want to give you just as much pleasure."

She rubbed against him and he forgot what he'd been about to do.

"Then come inside me," she moaned. Her eyes were glazed with passion.

Ah, damn, she was definitely killing him. "Hold that thought. Protection," he mumbled.

"Hurry."

He stepped from the shower, slipping and sliding on the wet tiles. He finally managed to grab the counter and regain his balance.

She chuckled.

He glanced over his shoulder. The curtain was open. She stood gloriously naked in front of him. Her nipples puckered, inviting him to cover each one with his mouth.

His gaze lowered, skimming past her gently rounded hips and lower, to the thatch of damp curls at the juncture of her legs.

"Nick?"

What the hell was he doing? Yeah, right, condom. He opened the medicine cabinet and grabbed a package, ripping it open with his teeth.

"Hurry. I want you." She ran her hands over her breasts, her mouth opening, her tongue running across her lips.

He sucked in a deep breath, inhaling the part of the foil packet he'd just torn off. He coughed and choked before he got it spit out. Sweat beaded his forehead and he trembled with anticipation.

Hands don't fail me now!

He nearly had the condom on when she stepped from the shower and sauntered toward him. As he slid it the rest of the way down, she wrapped her arms around his neck and pulled his mouth to hers. Her tongue sparred with his until she captured it, sucking gently. His dick quivered in response.

The lady learned fast. Real fast.

She pushed him toward the toilet. He sat on the lid, wondering exactly what she was up to but not minding a bit that she'd taken control.

She straddled him, moving against his erection and kissing his neck. He cupped her ass, drawing her nearer. She arched her back, giving him full access to those incredibly sexy breasts. He was never one to waste an opportunity.

He drew one ripe nipple into his mouth and began to suck. She moaned. He massaged her other breast. She raised her hips and positioned him so she could slide onto him.

Heat enveloped and surrounded his dick. Incredibly moist heat. Slowly, she raised her hips and lowered them. He slipped his hands around her waist, holding her in place, and raised his hips, sinking even deeper into her hot body.

Through his passion-glazed eyes, he saw the swirls of color surrounding them, caressing their bodies. Bolder and stronger than before. Deep purples and wild reds infused him with the most fantastic energy.

She increased her movement. He thrust in perfect timing with her. Their ragged breathing filled the room.

Her inner muscles clenched as she called out his

name. He saw the look of ecstasy on her face. There was something incredibly beautiful about watching a woman come, especially this one. Pure passion shone on her face as she bit her bottom lip, straining toward complete fulfillment.

He gripped her waist as an explosion of color burst around him. He came hard. His body quivered from head to toe. He gasped for air, finally was able to draw in enough so he didn't pass out.

He knew without a doubt sex would never be this good with anyone but Kia.

She laid her head on his shoulder, close to his heart. The clean rain-forest scent of the shampoo wafted to his nose. He breathed it in, nuzzling her hair.

Sweet.

It wasn't going to be easy letting her go. How much longer did they have together? Damn, he'd been afraid of this. He'd let her get under his skin.

That wasn't good for a man who had never had a relationship that lasted longer than a week. But then, the week wasn't up yet.

Chapter 13

Kia had on a green jogging suit that should've been unsexy as hell but for some reason looked hot on her.

"Did you hear me, Nick?"

He hadn't. "What?"

"I have to find Mala. You'll help me?"

He propped his feet on the coffee table. Of course he would. What kind of guy did she take him for?

Not that she had much to compare him with, but yeah, he'd help her get home. He ignored the little ache that went with the thought of her leaving. The sooner she was out of his life, the sooner his could get back to normal. Some of the things she was making him feel just didn't suit the life he'd mapped out for himself.

Okay, he'd help her find this cousin of hers. "Where did you land?"

"Against a tree."

He raised an eyebrow.

She shrugged. "There were lots of trees. I walked until I came to a fence. I climbed over it and a very large conveyance stopped and brought me to the bar. He said it was an eighteen-wheeler." Her forehead wrinkled. "But he lied about it flying. It didn't. I fell asleep and when I awoke, the sun had disappeared and it was dark."

"Okay, that could be anywhere. Do you remember any symbols? Anything that would tell me the name of his trucking company?"

She brightened. "Yes!"

"Good, now we're getting someplace. What was it?" He took a drink of his soda.

"'I'm a Mother Trucker and Proud of It!'"

He coughed and choked on his drink. It took him a few seconds to get his breath. He set his can on the coffee table and wiped the tears from his eyes. Oh, God, he had to remember not to take a drink after he asked her a question. Her answers could be the death of him.

He groaned. *I'm a Mother Trucker and Proud of It!* This might take longer than he'd first thought. "On the shirt he wore, right?"

She nodded, then took a big drink, belching like a sailor as she plunked the can down on the end table. "Oh, that was a damn good one!"

Great. She was belching and cursing now. "Where did you hear that word?"

Her eyes innocently widened. "What word?"

"Damn."

"You say it a lot. I think to emphasize something. You also say 'frigging,' 'fuck,' and 'ah, hell.'"

He'd created a monster.

His gaze swept over her. A damned sexy one, though.

"Maybe you should stick with the basic language. I shouldn't say words like that."

"Why?"

"They're not nice words."

She leaned against the sofa pillows. Her top gaped open, exposing the curves of her breasts.

"Okay," she said.

Okay what? Okay sex? It hadn't been that long, but he thought he could manage . . .

"Are you going to count again?"

His brow furrowed. "Count what?"

"When you get silent like this you usually start counting." She tucked her arm under her head.

Sex? Counting? Hell, he couldn't remember what they'd been doing.

"Are we going to find Mala?"

"Mala!" He let his breath out. That's what they'd been doing. Man, when he was around Kia he forgot everything.

"Yes, we're going to try to find your cousin. The sooner the better."

"Good." She smiled.

Focus. That's all he had to remember. Just focus on what he was doing. "Tell me everything you remember." He grabbed a pencil and paper, then leaned back again. This time she might even tell him something he could use.

"His name was Hank."

"Okay, that's a start." He jotted down the name. "Did he have a last name?"

"He didn't say."

First name only. Not good. His job just got a lot harder. Why should this be any different? Kia made everything hard. He attempted to clear his mind of just what she could do to make him hard. It didn't work.

"Is there anything else you can tell me about him?"

"He has a brother who should be a singer, but I didn't agree and it seemed to upset him but it was only the truth." She met Nick's gaze. "I never lie."

"Never?" He found that hard to believe, and he didn't care what planet she came from.

She shook her head. "Never."

Alrighty. "Do you remember anything else about the truck?"

"There was writing on the side." She was thoughtful for a moment. "Bountiful Earth, I think. Does that help?"

"Bountiful Earth. They have a fleet of trucks all over the country. It'll be like trying to find a needle in a haystack."

"And is it hard finding a needle in a haystack?" She drew her legs under her.

The movement was simple . . . and sexy as hel— heck.

"Why don't you tell me more about Hank?" If he had a description, he might be able to narrow it down.

"He had hair only on the sides." She made a half circle from one side of her head to the other, then patted the top. "But nothing up here. And a lot of his teeth were missing." She sucked her lips in. "Like this. I think the truck had jarred them loose and they fell out."

Oh, Lord, it was worse than he'd thought. That could describe any number of truckers, any number of people, in fact. This was going to take forever.

"And his stomach stuck way out here." She moved her hands in front of her. "He smelled very bad, too, and he talked funny."

"Talked funny?" Talking funny was good. Now maybe they would get somewhere. If this Hank had an accent, he might be easier to find. "How did he talk?"

"Name's Hank." She spoke from deep in her throat, bringing her chin to her chest. "You gotta name?" She smiled. "That's how he talked."

Nick started laughing.

She frowned. "Why are you laughing?"

Ah, Lord, she was going to be the death of him. He shook his head. "Don't worry, we'll find your cousin. It might take some time, but we'll find her."

"What'll we do next?"

She looked so damned tempting. "Narrow down the Hanks who work for the trucking company. There can't be more than ten or fifteen."

"I trust you."

He wanted to tell her not to. That he wasn't that honorable. Not when he had a beautiful sexy woman staying in his apartment. Just like Sam had told him a million times, he was in over his head.

He cleared his thoughts and got back to the subject at hand. "How did you expect to find your cousin when you arrived?" Maybe if she had coordinates of some sort, he could work from them.

"My locator, but it broke."

"Locator?"

She reached into her satchel and dug around. "Here it is, but the screen wouldn't come on."

The locator was about the size of a cell phone. Kia handed it to him. "What do you do with it?"

"I put a drop of DNA on a small strip and insert it into the locator. In a few seconds it gives me the directions where to find the person."

Wouldn't law enforcement love this? A people GPS system. Any criminal, at any time, could be apprehended. Parole violators, jailbreaks . . .

"Maybe it's just a loose wire or something." He turned it over.

"There are no wires, only chips."

There was a knock on the door. A nervous tap-tap. Nick handed the locator back to Kia and stood.

Sam? He looked at his watch. Too early for him to return his car. IA investigator? Oh, crap, he hoped not.
He looked through the peephole.

What the hell was Weldon doing here? Nick had
told him that he would check in with him in a day or
so. He opened the door a few inches.

"Is there something wrong?"

Weldon shoved his thick glasses higher on his nose
before nervously glancing around. "I need to talk to
you."

His voice squeaked. Nick had never seen Weldon
this antsy. Something must really be wrong. "Come
in."

Weldon didn't hesitate to scurry inside the apartment, but skidded to a halt when he spotted Kia on
the couch.

"Oh, I thought you'd be alone." His face turned
bright red. "There are things I need to talk to you
about that might be better said without anyone else
around." His eyebrows rose almost to his hairline as
he tried to get his secondary meaning across.

"It's okay. You can say anything in front of Kia,"
Nick assured him.

"Are you sure?"

"Positive."

Weldon still didn't look convinced. "The object
you . . . uh . . . had me check out . . . It . . . uh . . ."

"Just spit it out, Weldon."

"It's not . . . uh . . . from around here." He cast his
gaze in Kia's direction, then stared pointedly at Nick.

"Texas?" Nick asked.

"Earth," he whispered. "At least, not anything I've
ever seen."

"No high-tech company involved?" Okay, so he'd
already known that. There was just something about
having his fears confirmed.

Weldon furiously shook his head. "No one is this advanced." He slipped the phazer out of his pocket, attempting unsuccessfully to shield it from Kia's view.

"Oh, you have my phazer," Kia said, coming to her feet.

"Your phazer," he croaked. He looked from Kia to Nick. "Did you know you have an alien in your apartment?" he frantically whispered, shielding his mouth with his hand.

"Yeah, she's mentioned it a few times."

"Oh . . . uh . . ."

"You don't look so good, Weldon." The little man's face had gone pasty. Nick caught his arm and led him to the couch, pushing him down onto the cushions.

"She's not going to disintegrate me, is she?" he whimpered.

"I don't think so. You have her phazer."

"Oh, I forgot." He pulled a white handkerchief out of his pants pocket and mopped at his forehead.

"Is he all right?" Kia asked.

"I would imagine you're the first alien he's ever met."

"Yes." Weldon looked up. "Correct assumption. It's a little . . . uh . . . unnerving."

"You want some water or something?" Nick hadn't known Weldon could be this excitable. He'd never even seen the man crack a smile. Weldon was always hunkered over a computer staring at whatever wires he was trying to connect. Not a life Nick would be happy living. To each his own.

"Do you have a beer?" Weldon stuffed his handkerchief back in his pocket.

Nick raised an eyebrow. "A beer?"

Weldon puffed out his chest. "Yes, a beer, if you have one."

Nick nodded. "Yeah, I've got one. I just never took you for a beer drinker."

"I know perfectly well what your opinion and everyone at the station's opinion is of me. You think because I enjoy pursuing a career in computers rather than taking a more hands-on approach, that I'm a nerd." He pursed his lips. "Just remember, Bill Gates is considered a nerd and look where it's gotten him."

"You're right. The worst thing a person can do is have preconceived notions of who someone is just because of what they do for a living." Nick went into the kitchen.

Keeping an eye on Weldon so he didn't scare Kia, Nick opened the refrigerator and got a beer from the six-pack he'd bought. When he straightened, he saw Weldon was staring at her as if she were . . . okay, she was from another planet.

"You don't have a problem believing I'm from another planet?" Kia asked.

Weldon straightened. "Of course not. Scientifically, it's quite possible. There are many planets that we on Earth know nothing about but that are inhabited by different species."

"You're a very intelligent man."

Weldon beamed. Nick frowned. So what the hell did that make him? He'd eventually come around.

"I like to think I'm more open minded than most." Weldon took the beer Nick handed him, then looked at Kia. "I'd really like to ask you some questions."

Nick sat in one of the chairs, crossing his legs at the ankle. Kia looked at him, he nodded.

"What would you like to know?"

Weldon laughed. "Everything. What's it like on your planet? What kind of ecosystem do you have? Are there animals?"

She snuggled a pillow close to her. "We don't have

plants in abundance as I've seen on Earth. Nor do we have animals, but then I haven't seen any on Earth yet."

"But how do you live? What do you eat?"

"We have food capsules that provide adequate nourishment." She frowned. "But they're not as good as chocolate."

"Amazing." Weldon's attention turned to Nick. "Do you realize what you have here? Another species that's different from humankind." He set his beer on the end table and opened his hands. "The significance of this is beyond anything I could ever have imagined."

Nick sat up. "You can't tell anyone. You do understand that, don't you?"

Weldon seemed to snap out of his self-induced trance. "Of course, that's beyond saying. The government would destroy this . . . this . . ." He sighed. "You are quite beautiful, you know. Like a delicate flower that has just started to bloom."

What the fuck?

"Thank you," Kia said.

"You're welcome." Weldon blushed.

"She has something else for you to look at," Nick said, interrupting them. When Weldon dragged his gaze from Kia, Nick frowned at him.

Weldon cleared his throat. "Of course." He shoved his glasses a little higher up the bridge of his nose as he reverted to his nerd side. "What do you have?"

"Give me your locator, Kia."

When she handed it to him, Nick gave it to Weldon. "You put a drop of DNA on the pad and push a button. It's supposed to locate the person for you."

"So much more advanced than we are," he mumbled as he turned it over in his hand and examined the other side.

"It's broken," Kia said. "Can you fix it? I need to locate my cousin."

"There are more aliens? I mean, here on Earth?" Weldon's eyes widened.

"I'm not sure how many. But yes, there are Nerakians who live on Earth as humans."

"Nerakians?"

"I'm from the planet Nerak."

"Someday I would love to visit your planet."

Kia's eyes turned sad. Something inside Nick clenched, twisting like a knife. When she left, he'd never see her again. He didn't like that—not one damn bit. It wouldn't be so bad if he knew she was in another state or something. Not that he wanted anything permanent, but it would be nice to call her up occasionally and . . . talk.

"It wouldn't be possible for you to visit," she told Weldon. "There are no men on Nerak. The Elders will not permit them."

"I understand," he said.

Weldon glanced from the heartache apparent in Kia's eyes, then back to him. Nick had a feeling Weldon knew what was going on between them. He shifted in his seat when Weldon gave him a reprimanding look.

"What?" he finally asked.

"She's a visitor from another planet. I would think you'd be able to control . . . uh . . . certain urges."

"Yeah, right, like you wouldn't if you'd had the opportunity."

"What are these *urges*? Hell, you're talking as if I'm not here, and I don't think I like it."

Weldon raised his eyebrows. "And the language, too?"

Nick felt the heat rising up his face. "How the hell . . ."

Weldon's eyes widened.

"I didn't know she would pick it up so fast." He cleared his throat and pointed toward the locator. "Can you fix it or not?"

Weldon shrugged. "I'll see what I can do."

"Good."

Weldon sat on the sofa without moving, just staring at Kia like a lovesick puppy.

"Today, maybe?"

"Oh, yes, of course." He stood. "It might take me longer than a day, if I can fix it at all."

"You'll try?" Kia asked.

Weldon seemed to melt into a puddle at her feet. "For you, I would move heaven and earth to do your bidding, lovely lady."

"Give me a break," Nick mumbled.

Chapter 14

Kia and Nick walked inside the front door of the Bountiful Earth offices. It was nearly five o'clock and the place looked deserted. No one sat at the front desk.

Their footsteps sounded loud in the eerie quiet of the building. Kia rubbed her arms as chill bumps popped up. "They'll give us the information on Hank?"

"Maybe."

That didn't sound promising. "But you have a plan?"

He glanced her way. "No."

For a moment, she lost herself in his deep brown eyes. She shouldn't have made Adam-4 quite so perfect. Nick's hair looked as if he'd been out in the wind. It wasn't short, with every hair in place, like Adam-4's.

Nick's words sank in, effectively bringing her out of her comparative analysis of his body and that of Adam-4. "What do you mean, you don't have a plan?"

He shrugged. "Exactly what I said. I don't have a plan. I thought we'd just wing it."

Wing it? That must be another saying. If the eighteen-wheeler couldn't fly, she was almost certain humans couldn't. Even Nerakians weren't that advanced.

The only species she knew that could fly were the Nagems.

She sighed. She'd seen a hologram of a Nagem once. They were very delicate creatures with gossamer wings. The little creature's hair had been white with streaks of lavender.

She brought herself back to the present. No, she really didn't think Nick would sprout wings and swoop through the building demanding to know which Hank had brought her to the bar. Nick might be a great fighter, but she wasn't too sure about his tactical maneuvers.

Heat flooded her body. He was an expert at sexual maneuvers, though. Maybe tactical was his weakness. She would make up for his deficiency with her skills. Together, they would be perfect.

She narrowed her eyes as her gaze swept the large open room. "No one is here," she said.

Nick glanced around. "Someone has to be. The front door wasn't locked. We just have to find them." He nodded toward a long corridor. "Maybe in the back. Just remember to do what I do. I still think you should've waited at the apartment."

She squared her shoulders. "I'm a warrior and have no intention of being left behind."

He didn't look happy.

"Just hang back. Remember, low profile."

"Of course."

The office doors on either side were closed and no light showed from underneath, except for the one at the end. It was partially open and a weak glow seeped around the edges. As they approached the door, Kia read the writing on the opaque glass: Operations Manager. The title sounded important.

Nick tapped on the glass, three sharp raps with his

knuckles. Weldon had also made noise on the door. It must be some sort of ritual. She repeated his action.

He frowned.

Maybe only one person should do the tapping? What did he expect when she didn't know Earth's customs? He should inform her next time. Besides, he had said to do what he did.

The woman behind the desk glanced up as they entered. She wasn't quite an elder, but she was approaching the age of wisdom. Her dark hair was liberally streaked with gray.

"Can I help you?" she asked in a superior tone, looking directly at Kia.

Kia didn't care for the woman's manner. She was in need of an attitude-adjusting smoothie.

"I hope so." Nick leaned against the counter and smiled at her, the kind of smile that made Kia's knees weak.

The almost-elder was not immune to his charms. She batted her lashes and simpered like a much younger female.

Now Kia knew she didn't care for this woman. Some strange emotion inside her simmered to the surface. For a brief second, or two, she wanted to hit this female over the head with her satchel. She frowned instead, remembering Nick's warning about keeping a low profile. But if all the pre-elders acted like her, then no wonder they didn't garner the respect of others.

"What did you need? A job application?" she asked hopefully, fluttering her hands close to her face. "I have a little . . . uh . . . stroke with the boss. I'm his assistant. I can almost guarantee you employment."

Kia was so tempted to zap the woman with her phazer, pre-elder or not!

"Well, darlin'," Nick began. "We just need to find someone who works here. A man named Hank."

The elder's eyes narrowed to mere slits. "I see. You want information and you think you can sweet-talk it out of me."

"Now, don't be that way . . ."

"You're cute, but I wasn't born yesterday."

"That is certainly true," Kia agreed.

The pre-elder glared at her. "I bet you think you're just really smart." Her gaze swung to Nick. "Both of you."

"Actually," Kia began. "I am quite intelligent. A much superior being to you." She thought it would be obvious.

The pre-elder puffed up, expanding her already wide girth. Was she about to explode? The Adnams grew very big when they sucked in their breath, then they would explode poison juices all over their victims.

"I'm calling security to have you both thrown out." She picked up a black object and placed it near her ear.

Kia couldn't let that happen, either. She pulled out her phazer and zapped her. One second the woman was there, and the next, she was gone.

Nick's mouth dropped open, then snapped closed. "Where . . . what . . ."

"She was very rude," she explained.

"So you killed her?"

She frowned as she walked behind the desk. "Of course not. I told you we are not aggressive on Nerak."

"But you're not *on* Nerak."

She raised one eyebrow. "We are not an aggressive race," she clarified. "We don't kill." He really did have a problem retaining information. Maybe it was a good thing he was such a skilled warrior.

"Okay, you don't kill. You just go around making people disappear."

"We're wasting time. From my calculations, we have about twenty minutes before she reappears. Do you want to discuss this or see if we can find information about locating Hank?" It would be so much easier if Earth were more technically advanced.

He glanced at his watch. "All right, but don't zap anyone else. It gives me the creeps."

Men. No wonder the elders had let them die out.

Nick came around the desk and sat in the chair. He swiveled it around to face the computer, then tapped on the buttons. Very antiquated machinery, if you asked her. It took forever for the screen to appear.

He opened and closed out of different programs, scrolling through each one until he came to an employee list.

"There're a lot of people who work for the company, but it looks like they're all listed." He glanced at his watch. "If your calculations are right, then we haven't got much time. We'd better print out all the names and go through them back at the apartment."

Nick pushed some more buttons and one of the machines began spitting out papers, with the list of names.

"The time to leave is nearing," she reminded him.

"That's the last of them." He clicked out of the screen, scooped up the papers, and grabbed Kia by the arm. "Let's go."

There was a popping noise as they hurried out of the office door and down the corridor, then a heavy thud.

Eghhhhhhhhh!

"She's back. Just as I told you."

"In one piece?" He cast a worried look over his shoulder and started back toward the office.

"Pretty much. She might be missing her clothes."

He skidded to a halt, his gaze swiveling to hers. "No clothes? I'm not even going there. I don't want to know and I definitely don't want to see."

Anger swarmed around Darla like killer bees. Why wasn't Slava answering his cell phone? This was the third time she'd called his number. *Imbecile!* She slapped it shut and dropped the phone in her pocket, not bothering to leave a message this time.

The princess and her boyfriend had gone into the offices at Bountiful Earth twenty-five minutes ago. What was their business with the trucking company? Was that how the so-called princess was getting her jewels? Could this be a front for a smuggling ring?

Money signs danced before her eyes.

What if there were more than jewels involved? They could be bringing in treasures from all over the world. If she could just get a portion of it, she would cash in and be set for life. Her Italian villa was sounding better and better. Or maybe a little place on a beach somewhere. Hell, she'd buy the whole frigging island. A resort for the rich and famous with her at the helm.

She slid down in her seat as the man and woman came running out carrying a shitload of papers. Not that they could see her. She'd parked behind some bushes and trees. She wasn't stupid. No, her daddy hadn't raised any fools.

She covertly watched as the two hurried to a car and climbed inside. Now what were they up to? Must be something big going on for them to be in such a hurry.

They took off. There was no need to follow them. She knew his apartment building. No, she was more interested in who they'd met inside the Bountiful Earth building.

She shook her head in amazement. There was a lot more going on here than met the eye. The pieces of the puzzle were all starting to fit.

Trucking company plus transportation equaled big-time smuggling operation.

And she wanted a part of the pie. Correction, she was going to get a part of the pie . . . period!

After the two had driven off, Darla slipped from the car and into the building.

Most everyone had left for the day, but if anyone approached, she'd make up some excuse for being there.

She took off her shoes and crept over to a hall that ran off to the side. At the end, one office door stood slightly ajar and she could hear a female talking.

What was going on?

The closer she got to the office, the better she could make out what was being said. The woman was apparently speaking to someone on the phone, because it was a one-sided conversation.

She eased nearer and listened, ready to bolt if anyone spotted her.

"Get them here as fast as you can!"

Darla's ears perked up. She knew it! Something was going down. She'd hit the big time.

"If I have to leave here without anything to cover me, you'll regret every breath you take from now until the day you die."

Trepidation filled Darla. Cover? A bodyguard? She swallowed past her fear. A hit man? This bitch sounded serious.

Maybe she'd gotten in over her head?

"Yeah, okay, just bring me whatever the hell you grab and make it fast."

A phone being slammed down echoed through the hallway. Man, this woman was really desperate for her shipment. Darla hugged the wall and continued to listen.

"Damned incompetent asshole. What right does he have to question me? He should know by now I'm the boss and whatever I say goes."

Darla knew it! This was Ms. Big.

She slipped back down the hallway and out the front door. There was no reason to take any chances and get caught. She didn't even want to tangle with this lady or the cover that could arrive at any time.

But she didn't leave, either. No, she wanted to see where this woman lived. She went back to her car, slipped inside, and eased the door closed. Better not to take any chances when there were others around who might hear the door slam.

And she waited.

She jumped when her cell phone rang just as a car pulled up and a man in his mid-sixties got out. She pulled her cell out of her pocket as he covertly looked around. He tucked the bag he carried a little tighter under his arm.

"What!" she whispered in the phone.

"Did you call me?" Slava asked. "I went to the store."

"Shh!"

She waited until the man went inside the building before she turned her attention back to Slava. "You're supposed to take your phone with you." She didn't add, *you moron!*

"I forgot."

Why did she even bother with him? If it weren't

for his uncle, Slava would have a bullet in his head, be wearing a pair of concrete shoes, and be feeding the fish at the bottom of some river.

"What did you want?" he asked.

"They were alone and we missed our chance to take them."

"Who?"

Maybe she'd face the Russian mafia's wrath and be the one who put a bullet in his head.

She took a couple of deep breaths to calm herself. "The girl with the jewels and her boyfriend. We could've nabbed them."

"Want me to get them now?"

"They've already gone."

"You mad, Darla?"

"Not anymore. I think we have bigger fish to fry."

"Good. I'm hungry."

She closed her eyes, pinching her nose between her thumb and forefinger. "Not that kind of fish. I meant there might be more going down than just a bag full of jewels."

"Are we going to be rich?"

One of them was. She almost laughed, but held back. Slava was stupid, but she didn't want to rile him. He was also the meanest son of a bitch when he was mad. Which was why she liked using his brawn. About a year ago, some guy had shot him in the leg and Slava still beat the crap out of him.

She watched as a few minutes later the man and a woman came hurrying out of the building. The woman wore a beige trench coat cinched tight at the waist and a hat pulled low on her forehead. When he said something to her and reached for her hand, she slapped his away.

The guy downed his head, then ran to the passenger side of the car to open the door so she could get in. Definitely her flunky.

Something was up. She'd bet her bottom dollar there was some smuggling going on somewhere.

"Yeah," she told Slava. "We're going to be rich. Next time, don't forget your phone." She closed hers as the man started up the car and they drove away.

Easy street, here I come!

She kept her distance as she followed them. No use alerting them that they were being tailed.

Her smile was calculating. She'd find out where they lived. It wouldn't take her long to figure out just what was going down.

She frowned.

There was one thing that bothered her. Why wasn't the woman wearing any shoes?

Chapter 15

"There are one hundred twenty-six Hanks who work for that trucking company," Nick said.

Kia's heart thumped hard inside her chest. Earth didn't have the advanced technical capabilities of Nerak. One hundred and twenty-six sounded like an incredible number of Hanks. It could take a very long time to find the one who had dropped her off across from the bar.

"Don't worry. We'll find Mala." Nick patted her hand, then went back to perusing the list.

She frowned, not at all sure she liked his calm attitude about her leaving. Was he sorry he'd brought her to his apartment? Was he in a hurry to be rid of her? Did he want to locate Mala so she would go? She did not like this feeling. It created an uncomfortable ache.

"You want me to leave?" she asked.

He didn't seem upset that she would depart from Earth, never to see him again. Pain rippled through her, stopping in the center of her chest. Not good! She didn't like this emotion. It hurt and made her feel empty inside.

Nick's eyebrows drew together. "Of course I don't want you to go." He shuffled through the papers, his face taking on a rosy hue. "Not right now."

"Then you enjoy being with me."

His shoulders relaxed and he smiled. Her pulse rate increased.

"Yeah, you're growing on me."

She shook her head. "Oh, no, I don't have that capability."

His hands stilled. "You mean there's a race who can do that?"

"The Adnams." A shudder swept over her. "They're blue and slimy. They attach themselves to you and suck out your personality. They haven't dared create havoc in years. We have an agreement with our neighboring planets. The Adnams would have to attack all of us if they made war, and they're not strong enough."

Nick chuckled. "You're pulling my leg, right?"

"No, my hands are in my lap." She raised them. "See, they're right here. I promise I didn't pull your leg."

His smile grew wider. She really liked when his mouth turned upward. It made her warm and tingly all over. She liked even more that he wasn't trying to get rid of her so that his life would return to the way it was before she arrived.

"That was a figure of speech," he said. "I was asking if you'd made that up."

She shook her head. "I told you that I don't lie." Maybe someday she would make him a smoothie that would help him to retain information.

"It's not exactly lying. Just stretching the truth," he explained.

"I don't do that, either."

He opened his mouth, then closed it. After a few seconds, he said, "What were we talking about?"

He definitely needed that memory smoothie. If only she'd brought some with her.

Her gaze swept over him. His recall might not be

very good, but he did have other qualities that she liked. He was cute and sex with him was very nice—more than nice. Just thinking about it started an ache deep inside her. Maybe it didn't matter that his intellect and cognitive skills were inferior to hers.

"We were talking about Hank," she reminded him. "Then you asked about the Adnams, and we also discussed the fact that I never lie."

"Yeah, right. Then I guess we can say we've established the fact that I would like to get to know you better, there are different races out there that boggle the mind, and you don't lie."

She nodded.

"But you *do* want to find your cousin?"

She nodded again, but wore a thoughtful expression. "I think you are growing on me, too." She glanced down at her hands, but quickly looked up. "In a good way, like you said. I think I'll miss you when I return to Nerak."

He cleared his throat and glanced down at the papers again. "Okay, let's see what we can discover about this Hank guy." He shuffled through the papers. "At least their phone numbers are listed. We can start calling to find out if any were in Dallas around the time you were dropped off."

"Phone?"

"A way of communication." He raised a black object. "Phone."

The black object was the phone, a device for communication. She understood that, but her attention was drawn to his arms, namely his bulging biceps.

She licked her lips as the heat inside her began to build. He had nice muscles. She liked the way they felt beneath her hands: every texture, every ridge. His whole body was hard, sinewy strength made for passionate sex that lasted for long periods of time.

If she closed her eyes, it wouldn't be difficult to imagine him naked, his body pressed against hers, his hands caressing her breasts.

Flames licked at her body, flicking over her most sensitive places. Her breasts ached to feel his mouth sucking, his teeth scraping across her tight nipples while his hand slid between her legs and caressed, bringing her to climax.

She drew in a ragged breath. "Can we have sex?" she blurted.

He jumped, dropping the phone. "Can we have . . ."

"Sex. S-e-x," she repeated very slowly.

His forehead furrowed again. "Yeah, I know what it is."

Garbled noise came from the communicating device. "Your phone is corresponding."

He mumbled one of the words he'd said was bad and scooped it off the floor, placing it next to his ear. He was silent for a moment.

"No, ma'am, this isn't an obscene phone call. I have the . . . television on."

He paused.

"Yes, that's probably what you heard. I'm terribly sorry."

He paused again, his brow furrowing into deep grooves.

"No, ma'am, I'm not lonely and I don't need a date." He pushed a button on his communicator and laid it back on the table in front of the lounging sofa.

She sighed. "I guess you don't want to have sex."

"It's not that. I just think we should take it a little slower. I don't want you to get hurt or anything."

Hurt? Why would he think she would be hurt? Before she could ask, there was a knock on his door. Was that relief she saw on his face? Did he not enjoy having sex with her? She had certainly enjoyed having sex with him. Earth was becoming more complicated the longer she was here. No wonder there were so many wars.

"The door." He pointed toward the wooden structure. "Someone's at it."

"I assumed as much." She wondered if it was possible for a man's brain to grow.

Nick stood and hurried over to the door, looked through the little hole, then opened it.

"Sam, come on in." Nick opened the door wide.

"Your car keys." Sam dropped them into Nick's open hand.

"Thanks, man."

"Kia." He nodded toward her, then glanced at the papers on the small table in front of the lounging sofa. "What are you two doing?"

Kia sighed. "We were going to have sex, maybe, but you tapped on the door and Nick let you in. I guess we won't be having sex now. Nick didn't want to invite the neighbors, so I guess you're probably out of the equation, too." Hmm . . . Now that she thought about it, she didn't think she wanted to share Nick. Another strange emotion.

Sam chuckled and turned toward Nick. "You having fun yet? I warned you about being a good Samaritan."

"Funny." Nick closed the door.

"Since I interrupted your almost sex, what are you doing?" Sam nodded toward the papers again.

"Looking for Hank," Kia supplied.

Sam raised his eyebrows. "Hank?"

Apparently, Sam had the same affliction as Nick about retaining information. It must affect the entire male population.

"Hank . . . is . . . the . . . man . . . who . . . brought . . . me . . . here."

"Why is she talking so slow?" Sam frowned.

"Because you can't retain information," Nick supplied.

She brightened. "You remembered!" It was as she suspected, Nick needed to be around a female so he could learn.

Sam's forehead puckered. "I can't what?"

"Don't worry about it, buddy." He went in the kitchen and grabbed one of the awful-tasting sodas out of the refrigerator and brought it back to Sam. "Beer?"

"Sure." He twisted off the cap, then took a long drink.

She reached for her can. Why they would want to have that rather than a strawberry soda was beyond her. After taking a drink, she set the can down and looked at Sam. "Are you going to help us find Hank? My sister will start to worry if I stay on Earth too long."

Sam gave Nick a funny look.

It didn't take a genius to figure out what he thought. "You still don't believe I'm from Nerak."

Sam grimaced. "I'm sorry. I think you're a lovely woman who is a little confused."

"Would you like to meet my sister?" Maybe that would convince him.

Nick straightened. "You can bring her here? From your planet?"

"Not physically." She was good, but she wasn't that good.

"Why are you encouraging her?" Sam asked. "It'll only make it harder for her when she has to face the truth."

Kia ignored Sam and reached for her satchel.

"What's she getting, Nick?" Sam edged toward the door.

Men. They acted strange. No wonder the Elders had manipulated the DNA.

Still, they hadn't looked at what they'd be giving up. Mala had known there was something missing. Kia couldn't really blame her now that she'd tasted a bit of what Earth had to offer.

She pulled out a small white box and stood. "This might help you to believe." She walked to the center of the room and set the box down. Before she straightened, she opened the top, then stepped back.

The room went dark and a bright yellow light began to swirl in the center. This was her little sister's color. A bright healing yellow, like the person she was inside.

"Nick?"

"Kia?" Nick sounded just as worried as Sam.

"Don't worry, it can't hurt you."

Lara formed from the mist. She sat on a flat plane with her legs tucked beneath her, head bowed, hands together. As the mists swirled around her, then settled, she looked up.

She wore a shimmering green dress that sparkled with every movement of her body. Her pale blond hair reached past her waist as was in keeping with her profession of a healer. She was educated in all the ways that could heal the body, whereas Mala was in tune to a person's mind. Kia was more adept at the physical side of the body, along with mental strategies.

Lara smiled.

Kia's heart swelled with pride and a deep longing. This was her baby sister.

"Hello, Kia."

"Hello, Lara."

"You can communicate with her?" Nick whispered. Kia shook her head. "It's a hologram. We create them as a way of connecting when we'll be separated for any length of time. It helps with the loneliness."

"Sure beats the heck out of writing a letter." Nick sat on the arm of the sofa.

She didn't know this letter he spoke about, but when she turned to question him, she saw Sam's face. He seemed mesmerized by Lara. Not that she could blame him. Lara was a strikingly beautiful woman.

"I hope your journey was safe." Lara came to her feet and walked over to a closed window panel. "You're missed but I have kept busy so the pain is bearable. I know you'll return soon and have much to tell.

"The air is quite pleasant today. The Elders have misted it with a new scent. It's very nice."

"These Elders spray the air?" Sam asked, then frowned when he apparently realized he'd even asked such a question.

"They create different scents that are put through a filtering system that goes into the population. It's quite pleasant."

Sam turned to Nick. "And you're still buying into her fantasy?"

"I believe her, what can I say?"

"That it's a crock of bull? That instead of looking for a trucker named Hank, you should be checking the state hospitals? I can think of a number of things you could be doing." He waved his arm. "This is a terrific show. I'm sure there's a device around here somewhere that's creating the 3-D effect. What were you before you took one giant leap over the edge of reason? A photography student?"

Before anyone could answer, Sam turned back to her with a sarcastic smile plastered on his face.

"So tell me about this planet of yours."

"You won't trip her up if that's what you're planning. Don't you think I've already tried?"

Sam ignored him. "What about plants? What kind do you have on this so-called planet?"

"We don't have plant life on Nerak."

"Yet you know about it," he quickly countered.

"Our planets are similar. Early travelers, my grandmother for one, came to Earth and brought back documentation of your planet. That is why my cousin Mala traveled here even though it's forbidden. She found the documentary tape."

Nick raised his eyebrows. "Documentary?"

She nodded. "The one titled *Debbie Does the Sheriff*. She came in search of Sheriff."

Sam sputtered and coughed. "*Debbie Does* . . ."

"Watch and you will see where I come from." She nodded toward her sister. "This is not a trick, I promise."

Lara waved her hand, and the window panel silently opened. Nerak was there in front of them. It sparkled beneath the bright sunlight. Aero units whizzed past.

Sam jumped back, then took a tentative step forward. "This isn't real." Sam looked between them. "I mean, it can't be. Aliens don't really exist." His laugh held no humor.

"My planet is as genuine as your planet."

He shook his head. "Nope, I'm not joining in on your fantasy. I'd like to meet the actress who plays your sister, though. Now, she's a beauty. And you did a damn good job with the special effects. Those craft were pretty cool looking."

Kia had hoped the hologram might convince Sam. She didn't want him thinking his friend was crazy . . . or her. She walked to the box and closed the lid, saying a silent good-bye to her sister before replacing the box in her satchel.

"She *is* from another planet," Nick said.

Kia's heart swelled with pride that he would take

her side. But then, she had given him more proof. Maybe that's what she had to do. Give Sam more proof that she was from another world. She pulled her phazer out and pointed it at Sam. The red beam landed in the center of his chest.

She pushed the button.

Chapter 16

Nick stopped mid-sentence. One second he'd been talking to his partner and the next . . . poof! No more Sam. His gaze swung to every corner of the room. Still no Sam.

Nah, she didn't just . . . just . . . Nick opened his mouth, then snapped it closed. His stomach knotted. This wasn't good. Not good at all. He turned and stared at Kia.

Oh, Lord, she had her phazer in her hand, looking calm as could be as if she hadn't just eliminated his best friend. He swallowed past the lump in his throat. Ah, man, he was going to be sick. No, he couldn't be sick. He had to find Sam.

Then he could puke his guts out.

"Where's . . . uh . . . Sam?"

Her eyebrows drew together. "I don't know the exact location."

She didn't know? He drew in a deep, shuddering breath. This was great. What if Sam got stuck . . . wherever the hell he was?

"Don't worry, he'll return."

"Are you sure?"

"Pretty sure."

"But not positive."

"Who can really say for certain what will happen from one minute to the next?"

And if he didn't return—then what? How would he explain Sam's disappearance? "Hey, Captain, you might want to find me another partner. It seems this girl I picked up the other night in a biker bar—yeah, that would be the same one who screwed up the bust. See, it's like this, she's really an alien from the planet Nerak, and she zapped Sam with her phazer and now he's pffft."

Nick didn't even want to think about how he'd explain everything to Sam's mom and dad or his older brother . . .

Ah, crap, Sam's older brother was going to beat the living hell out of him. The guy was six-five and all muscle. He'd thumped a guy once and sent him staggering across the room. One little thump, that's all it took.

Yeah, he was dead meat.

"Nick, are you feeling okay? You're sweating." Kia's forehead was puckered with worry.

"Am I feeling okay? No, I'm not. You zapped my best friend. His brother is going to pulverize me, and my parents are going to be out the expense of my funeral because I didn't plan ahead."

Her face lost some of its color.

Damn, he didn't mean to scare her or anything, but he wanted to get the point across that she couldn't go around zapping people—especially people he liked. Now what the hell was he supposed to do?

He scraped his fingers through his hair and tried to stay calm. He didn't like seeing Kia this upset. It wasn't as if she knew any better. Maybe he'd laid into her a little hard. Not good.

He moved from the sofa and went to her, taking her into his arms. "Hey, it'll be okay."

She shook her head, not saying a word. He hadn't thought he could feel any worse. Wrong!

"Let's sit down." He led her to the sofa, nudging her down onto the cushions. "I'm sure Sam's brother won't beat me up too badly . . ."

She looked up at him with unshed tears shimmering in her eyes. "You know your parents?"

He frowned. That's what had her looking as if she was about to cry? The fact that he knew his parents? She wasn't worried he'd be pounded to a pulp by Sam's brother?

His ego rapidly deflated.

So maybe if she saw him being beat to a pulp, then she would be worried. She probably didn't understand what he'd meant.

"You weren't created in a laboratory?" she asked.

He forgot about what Sam's brother was going to do to him when he realized she was serious. Had Kia really thought he'd been born in a laboratory?

The thought of kids being born in a lab was a little weird. A whole race? More than a little weird. "You're joking, right?"

She shook her head.

It made sense—sort of. Why would he even think babies would be born naturally, since these Elders had gotten rid of men so they could create the perfect world? Of course they'd get rid of childbirth pain, too. Not that he could blame them.

"On Earth, women have babies naturally."

"Naturally?" She blinked her tears away, confusion mixed with a little skepticism now furrowed her brow. "They're not delivered to the home?"

"Are you sure Sam will return?"

She nodded.

What choice did he have but to hope for the best?

"I think I have a health book around here some-where." He looked in a couple of cabinets and one drawer before he found the book with a pile of other books that had been stacked against one wall. "This should explain everything about reproduction." He scanned the index, then flipped through the pages until he came to the section on the stages of preg-nancy, and handed her the book.

She glanced through the pages. Her face went from a healthy color to a very unhealthy pallor.

She looked up, a sickly expression on her face. "The woman's stomach will get this big without bursting?"

"Well, yeah, the skin stretches."

She swallowed hard and turned the page, then dropped the book and took a step back. "The child emerges from between the female's legs!"

Damn, he'd never thought about the process of birth before now. To someone who hadn't taken health classes, had never known a child could be born another way, he guessed it would seem pretty bizarre. Kind of like cruel and unusual punishment.

"Women have babies every day." Now that sounded like the biggest copout he'd ever uttered.

"They aren't torn apart?"

"They stretch there, too."

Her eyes narrowed. "It sounds like a lot of stretch-ing."

Kia didn't look one bit convinced, and he didn't really blame her. He didn't even like talking about it. His sister had told him he was a big wuss when it came to a pregnant woman. Okay, he was, so what.

She retrieved the book and turned a few more pages, becoming transfixed with the pictures of babies, skimming her fingers over the infants.

Now he knew he didn't like the look on her face.

He wasn't daddy material, and he didn't want any child of his raised on a planet that didn't care a whole hell of a lot for men.

"Would you like some dinner?" Anything to get her mind off pregnancy and babies.

She closed the book. "Food? How can you think about food at a time like this?"

Uh-oh. "A time like what?" he hedged.

"Babies. The fact that you actually know your parents."

"You have sisters."

Her bottom lip trembled. Ah, no, not the trembling bottom lip. He was a sucker for the trembling lip.

"It's not the same thing." She sniffed.

He pulled her across his lap and tucked her head beneath his chin. Funny how she fit so damn perfectly. Some tough warrior she was now.

"I'm sorry you didn't have parents." He frowned. "Didn't you have a mother? I know you mentioned a grandmother."

Her head moved in the direction he thought might be a yes.

"Some DNAs are linked stronger than others. Within those ties are created a form of bonding, but I don't think it's as strong as when a woman carries a child inside her."

"I bet you love Lara just as much as I love my sister." He brushed her hair behind her ear in a gentle caress.

She was silent for a few seconds. "You're right, of course."

"How about that food?"

She sucked in a ragged breath. "Food is good."

He breathed a silent sigh of relief as she scooted off his lap and stood.

"I showed weakness." She squared her shoulders. "I apologize. I'm feeling strange new emotions that I find hard to control."

"You don't have to be strong all the time. Besides, it's probably just hormones. You're only like millions of other females."

She cocked an eyebrow. "I'm not like millions of other women. I am a warrior, and we have better control."

And the Kia he'd first met returned. He wanted to tell her it was okay to cry, but he had a feeling she wouldn't appreciate his suggestion.

As they started toward the kitchen, there was a popping sound. Nick stopped in his tracks, immediately recognizing the noise.

Sam appeared looking none the worse for wear, except he was naked. He looked around the room as if he'd just awakened from a long sleep.

"What happened?"

Nick didn't think Sam was going to like his explanation. "She zapped you with her phazer."

He slowly shook his head. "I don't buy it. I blanked out for a second. That's all."

Kia's gaze moved downward. "They're not all the same. Amazing."

Nick wasn't sure he liked the idea of Kia comparing him to Sam. Not that he thought he wouldn't measure up.

"There must be something different in the components of your clothing and that of Nerak's," Kia said. "I can't understand why the clothes don't return."

Sam looked down. "What the fu . . ." He grabbed a pillow off the sofa and placed it in front of him. "Where the hell are my clothes?"

"Who knows," Nick told him. "Somewhere in the wide-open universe?"

There was another pop and Sam's wallet and cell phone dropped out of the blue and landed at his feet.

"You don't look so good, buddy," Nick said. "Maybe you should sit for a minute. Get your equilibrium back."

"Is there a reason he holds the pillow in front of him? Is this a custom?"

"He's naked," Nick explained.

"And this is a bad thing? He has no reason to be ashamed. He's built very well. Any woman would be proud to have him between her legs."

Now he knew he didn't like the turn this conversation was taking. Sam wasn't hung that well. Not that Nick had really looked. Guys just didn't do things like that.

"Maybe you could search in the cabinets for something you'd like to eat. Just read the back of the boxes and it'll tell you what's inside." Anything to keep her busy until he could find Sam something to wear.

She nodded and went into the kitchen. That should keep her occupied for a while.

"Is she always like this?" Sam whispered, still looking as if he was trying to digest everything that had happened.

"Yeah, pretty much."

"Where are my clothes?"

"I haven't the slightest idea." There was something he wanted to know. "Where the hell were you?"

Sam shook his head. "I don't know. I feel different, though."

"What do you mean?"

He shrugged. "I don't know. Sort of like I was

asleep, but awake. Suspended animation or something. I know, it sounds crazy . . ."

Nick raised an eyebrow.

"Or maybe it doesn't." He drew in a deep breath. "She's an alien."

"I know."

"I found chocolate," Kia called out.

"That's not healthy."

"What's healthy?"

"Protein . . . vegetables."

"They don't sound as good as chocolate."

Sam cleared his throat. "You think I could borrow some clothes? It's damned chilly in here."

"Sorry."

Kia was distracting him again.

"Just keep looking," he called over his shoulder.

Sam did a sideways shuffle as he followed Nick across the room and down the hall into his bedroom. If the situation weren't so serious, he might laugh.

That and the fact Sam would probably get really pissed. He might seem laid-back, but make him mad and you'd better hope you could outrun him.

Nick grabbed a pair of jeans and a T-shirt that he didn't think he'd worn and tossed them toward Sam, then a pair of briefs. He looked at Sam's feet.

"Your feet are bigger but I think I have a pair of flip-flops that'll work."

He dug around the bottom of his closet and found one. The other was hiding under his bed, along with a favorite shirt. He'd wondered where it had disappeared. When he straightened, Sam was already dressed.

"She really is an alien?"

Disbelief showed on Sam's face. The poor guy still had a problem accepting the truth.

"Yeah, she is. It took me a while to believe her, but then I've always been more open-minded than you when it comes to this kind of stuff."

"It changes everything I've ever believed in. That's hard to swallow all at once. It might take some getting used to."

"Kind of feel like you're in a sci-fi movie, don't you?"

"Yeah, and I'm the only one without a script." He cleared his throat, his gaze darting around the room. "She doesn't have, like, a third eye or anything, does she? Maybe a tiny head hidden by her hair?"

"Don't be ridiculous." Nick wasn't about to tell Sam that he'd already checked.

Sam's face turned beet red. "Yeah, I guess that's a little crazy."

"Just accept her and the rest will come with time." He started toward the door but stopped at the last minute. "You heard anything from the IA investigation?"

"Nothing. But if they release you to go back to work, what are you going to do with Kia?"

His stomach rumbled, and it wasn't because he was hungry. He quickly dismissed the feeling before he could wonder about it too much. "We'll find her cousin and they'll go back to Nerak."

Sam stared long and hard until Nick became damned uncomfortable.

"What?" he finally asked.

"You still sleeping with her?"

He tensed. "What if I am?"

"Alien sex? That's not good and you know it. She's from another planet, for Pete's sake. Don't get stupid about her."

"Me? Not on your life. I like her—that's it."

Sam raised an eyebrow. "You know long-distance

relationships never work. This one's about as distant as it gets."

"Okay, I like her a lot," Nick conceded. "But look at her. She's damned sexy. It's just a bad case of lust. When she leaves, I'll move on. You know me. I don't do long-lasting relationships."

"Just make sure the one time you do decide to jump in for the long haul it's with someone from our planet."

Sam didn't look convinced but dropped the subject. Nick knew it wouldn't work between him and Kia. He'd seen her look of longing when Lara appeared, and that's when he'd realized he couldn't compete. Hell, he felt the same way toward his sister and brother.

But him and a lasting relationship? No, his dad had showed him those don't work when he'd walked away from a twenty-two-year marriage. As far as he'd known, they'd never even had a real fight.

"Nick, I found pizza," Kia called out, drawing his attention back to the present. "Is that healthy?"

Some of his tension disappeared. How could he help but like someone who was experiencing life on Earth for the very first time? And what living, breathing man wouldn't get horny being around a woman who looked like her?

But he would let her go when the time came. Hell, he probably wouldn't have any say in the matter. As soon as she found her cousin, Kia would be out of his life without a backward glance.

A sharp pain stabbed him in the chest.

"You okay?" Sam asked.

"Gas pain." And that's all it was.

"Nick, is pizza good?" Kia called out again.

"Pizza is good," he called back.

"What's an oven? It says I have to put it in the oven."

"I'd better get back out there before she burns the apartment down."

Before Sam said another word, Nick continued.

"I'll be careful, but hell, I might as well enjoy the time we have together."

He left his bedroom and hurried back to the kitchen. If they only had a short time, then he was damn well going to make the most of it.

He stopped at the doorway. Kia faced away from him. She'd removed the pizza from the box and set it to the side. She'd found the strip that opened the clear plastic cover and taken that off. He silently watched as she tentatively took a bite of frozen pepperoni, then made a face and spit it out in the sink. When she turned back around, she noticed him.

"I don't think I like your pizza."

"You will when it's done." He turned the oven on and dug out the pizza pan. "It has to cook first, then I'll guarantee you'll love it."

When she smiled, his heart squeezed tight. What was it about her that struck such a deep chord inside him? Damn, it would be hard letting her go.

But he *would* let her go.

Pizza was good.

Nick had named off all the toppings for her and he was right about the little round pepperoni tasting better after it cooked.

Not that she was that fond of it. She much rather liked the bigger ones he'd called Canadian bacon. But she liked the cheese the very best of all. She could stretch it out really far and then eat it all the way back to the crust.

"Why are there lights swirling above us?" Sam asked, his gaze riveted above them.

Poor Sam. He still looked a little disoriented. "We've come to the conclusion that deep physical responses create the lights," she explained, talking around a mouthful of pizza. "You should see them when we have sex."

"Uh . . . I think I'll pass on that one."

Nick's face was red again. Men really had a problem with nudity and talking about sex.

Chapter 17

Sam still looked a little dazed when he'd left the apartment but apparently he recovered pretty fast because the next afternoon, he was back at the apartment.

"What's your plan?" Sam asked.

"I thought I'd start calling everyone on the list until we find the Hank who brought Kia to Dallas," Nick said, changing the subject.

"Need some help?" Sam asked. "I have the rest of the day off and I brought my cell phone. I'm taking a wild guess here that it still functions properly."

His face lost some of its color as his gaze dropped down to his lap.

"Nothing was damaged while I was . . . uh . . . gone?"

Men also worried a lot about their penises.

"I don't think so," Kia assured him.

"But you're not sure."

"Not positively."

"You can't win," Nick interrupted. "Believe me, I've already had this conversation."

Just as they sat on the sofa, the door chimed. She liked the bells better than the rat-a-tat-tat.

"What is this, Grand Central Station?" Nick muttered as he stood and went to the door. He looked through the peephole and groaned.

"What?" Sam asked.

"It's Becca. What am I going to do?"

"Nick, open the door. My back is killing me and Mom sent food."

"Food?" Kia sat straighter.

Nick frowned at her. "How can you still be hungry? We just ate lunch."

He was being rather judgmental. An attitude-adjusting smoothie would fix him, except she didn't have one handy. She jutted her chin out instead. "I like food."

"Nick, I can hear you." The person pounded on the door.

No pretty chimes this time. She wanted in, and Kia had a feeling she would get her way. There was something in the way she said Nick's name. Curiosity filled Kia. Who was this woman Nick called Becca?

"Damn." Nick opened the door.

The woman strode into the room, holding a package in front of her. Her red hair reminded Kia of her burgundy stones—a deep, bold color. The female had cute little dots across her nose, too.

"You'd think with my condition you could at least open the door a little faster. Hi, Sam." She shoved the bag into Nick's arms and stared at Kia. "I'm Becca, Nick's sister, and who are you?" she asked, shrugging out of her heavy coat.

Kia's gaze traveled to the woman's protruding abdomen. "Your stomach is so large."

"Yeah, well, that usually happens when you have a baby growing inside you for nearly nine months."

Kia stood, walking toward Nick's sister. "You have a baby inside you?" she asked with awe. "Does it hurt?" She stared at the woman's rotund figure.

"Let me tell you," Becca said as she made her way to the sofa and eased down onto the cushions with a groan. "Nick, get me something to drink." She looked at Kia. "I didn't catch your name."

"Kia."

"Well, for the first three months I puked my guts out."

"But how did you survive without them?" A Nerakian couldn't live without her internal organs.

"It's a figure of speech," Nick quickly supplied as he hurried to the kitchen. When he came back, he handed them each a can of soda. "Kia isn't from America."

"Oh." Becca nodded. "I was so sick it felt as if I were puking my guts up," she amended. "Then when I finally got over the morning sickness, along came the emotional ups and downs, the swollen feet, and having to run to the bathroom every five minutes."

"Do we have to discuss this now?" Sam asked. "I mean, I feel for you and everything, but . . ."

Men had no sympathy. Kia patted Becca's hand. "It sounds terrible. I don't think I would want to have a baby."

Becca took Kia's hand and placed it on her stomach. Nothing happened at first, then something thumped against her palm. She jumped back. It was alive!

"Did you feel that?"

Kia nodded.

"That's the baby kicking inside me." Becca's face softened and glowed.

"And this makes you happy?"

Becca smiled and gently rubbed her stomach. "Very."

Kia tentatively reached out and laid her hand upon Becca's stomach once more. When the baby kicked again, Kia laughed. She liked being able to feel the little one's strength.

"This child is a part of me and my husband. There's

nothing I want more than to love the baby we created."

"And this is done by having sex?"

Nick choked and Sam coughed, but Becca only
chuckled. "That's the best way I know to create life."

Kia looked at Nick. "Are we going to have a child
because we had sex?"

"Uh . . . Kia . . ." Nick gave her what she now
thought of as his warning look.

She rolled her eyes and turned back to Nick's sister. "Why are men so afraid to mention the word
sex?"

"I like her, Nick," Becca said. "Where in the world
did you meet?"

Kia opened her mouth, but Nick began to speak
before she could get a word out.

"It doesn't matter."

She shook her head. Of course it mattered, but she
wouldn't say anything. She remembered a low profile
was better than telling anyone else she was an alien.
She wasn't the one who couldn't retain information.

Her forehead wrinkled in thought. *Speaking of
which* . . . She turned back to Becca. "Have you noticed how men have a terrible time remembering
things?"

"You don't have to tell me something I know. My
Jack can't remember from one day to the next what
he's supposed to do."

"It's exactly as I thought."

"We can hear you," Nick pointed out.

"Good, then run down to my car and get the other
stuff Mom sent over. I don't know why she thinks you
can't survive on your own. TV dinners never killed anyone." She eyed Kia. "But then, if you married, Mom
wouldn't feel the need to baby you."

"Sis . . ."

She waved him away. "The stuff in my car? Both of you—go!"

As soon as the door closed, the women's gazes met, each one measuring the other.

"I'm sure if he's around a woman's influence, his memory will improve," Kia said, breaking the silence.

Becca chuckled. "I knew I liked you."

Something warm began to grow inside Kia. It tingled like fingers reaching to every part of her body. This was a good feeling. But one she couldn't afford.

"I like you, too."

"Okay, give me the scoop on you and Nick." Becca leaned closer.

"The scoop? I don't know what you mean."

"Sorry, I forgot. Where are you from anyway?"

She hesitated. "Nerak." Nick said not to tell anyone she was an alien. He was right. If too many people knew, it could cause problems, and although she enjoyed being with his sister, she would keep some things to herself. "Nerak is very far away."

Becca nodded. "I saw the way Nick looked at you. He may be a cop, but he isn't the greatest person at hiding what he's feeling. Do you like my brother a lot?"

Kia wasn't sure what Becca meant about the way Nick looked at her, but she didn't have to think long about her question. "Yes, I'm positive I do."

"Interesting."

"Why?" She didn't understand Becca's line of questioning. There seemed to be a hidden meaning that she couldn't grasp.

"And you're living together?" Becca asked without answering Kia's question.

"Yes."

"You're not married, are you? He dated a woman

who he thought was divorced, and the lady's husband beat the crap out of him. I'd hate for that to happen again."

"What does *married* mean?"

Becca was thoughtful. "Sleeping with another man. You know, having sex with someone other than Nick."

Adam-4 didn't really count since they didn't sleep in the same bed. They hadn't had sex for months, either. "No."

"And what do you do for a living?"

Becca asked a lot of questions but she could answer this one as well. "I'm a code enforcer—like Nick."

"Same kind of job." She nodded. "That's good."

"Why are you asking the questions?"

"Better safe than sorry."

This Kia understood. "Yes, that's what Nick has told me." Right before they had sex, in fact.

"Do you love him?"

Her question took Kia by surprise. Like was one thing—love quite another. She knew love. She loved Lara and her other sisters. She loved Mala and in another way, she loved the Elders. But what she felt for Nick was different.

"I'm not sure."

"Then let's do a test. Close your eyes."

Kia did as Becca asked and closed her eyes.

"What do you enjoy most about him?"

That was easy. "The way he smiles and the way he holds me close. The way he smells." She sighed. "The way I feel when we have sex."

"If you never saw him again, how would you feel?"

Pain ripped through her. She opened her eyes. "This isn't a good test. I don't like the thought of never seeing Nick again."

"That's what I thought." A knowing smile curved Becca's lips.

"What?"

"You're falling in love with my brother. I thought I saw the signs. It's about time. The family had almost given up on him."

"But I can't stay. I'll have to leave." No, this wasn't good. With love came pain, and she didn't like how it made her feel.

"Don't worry," Becca told her. "Love always finds a way. And if my brother is falling in love, then he'll move heaven and Earth to keep you here with him."

Could Nick somehow move Earth closer to Nerak? No, Kia didn't think so. This must be another figure of speech.

She would leave when she found Mala. She couldn't stay. Not just because of Lara, but the Elders weren't ones to be crossed.

The Elders were amicable most of the time, but they could become fierce when annoyed—or so she'd heard. She hadn't actually seen them angry. Nor the princesses, who were the direct descendents of the Elders. They would take over when the Elders' life cycle was no more.

But cross them? No, she didn't think that would be a good plan. Mala must have been terrified to face them. What had caused her to want to stay so much that she would give up everything she'd ever known?

The door opened and Nick and Sam carried in the bags. Maybe Kia did understand to some degree, but she wasn't willing to pay that kind of price—she couldn't.

Nick glanced her way, a question in his eyes. Becca was in conversation with Sam, so she quickly shook her head to let him know she'd continued with her low profile.

He seemed to breathe a sigh of relief. And why wouldn't he? She'd disrupted his life, and he'd want it to go back to normal. The fewer people who knew she was an alien, the better it would be for him.

"Did you get everything?" Becca asked, interrupting her thoughts.

"Doesn't it look like we have everything?" Nick raised the bags he held.

"Well, put them down and help me off the sofa. I want to go by Baby Stork and pick up a cute little outfit that's going on sale today."

"You have more clothes now than the baby will ever wear."

She shrugged, then held out her hand. "I want more, and who's going to deny a pregnant, emotionally fragile female?"

Nick helped her to her feet. "You have a point." He pulled her all the way into his arms and held her. "You doing okay, sis? I mean with the pregnancy and everything."

"Better than okay. We're excited—a little nervous, but women have been having babies for years. I'll be all right."

"Make sure you are." He released her and stepped back. "I'll walk you down."

"I made it up here without a problem. I don't need anyone to hold my hand going to the car." She gave him a look of exasperation. "I guess I could argue until I'm blue in the face and you'd still see me out."

"Yep."

She sighed. "I'd better use the restroom before I leave." She started toward the hall, but turned and hugged Kia at the last minute.

As soon as the bathroom door closed, Kia turned to Nick. "I kept a low profile."

"My sister can be pretty tricky."

She hugged her middle. "She has a baby growing inside her." She rubbed her hand over her stomach and for just a second, imagined what it would feel like to be carrying Nick's baby.

"What are you thinking?" Nick asked with a little hesitation.

"Okay, I think it's time I grabbed another beer." Sam quickly exited to the kitchen.

"Kia?" Nick prodded.

"I'm thinking that it would be a wonderful experience to carry a child. To feel it growing inside. The love would be incredible."

"Nerakians don't have children, right?"

"No, there are a lot of things that I'm discovering we don't have." She moved her hand away from her abdomen and was left with a feeling of emptiness. Maybe Nerak wasn't as perfect as she'd always thought.

But then, a pregnant warrior would look very odd.

Sam came back into the living room a few minutes later, and their conversation about babies ended. What else did they have to say? Nothing. Nick had been right when he said she would never have a child. Nerakians did not experience any of the stretching or the pain that came with carrying a baby, but then, they didn't experience any of the first seconds of life, either. That moment when a tiny heart began to beat on its own.

Her idea of the perfect world had begun to crumble. Returning to Nerak would be hard knowing what she'd learned on Earth.

And she would miss Nick.

She squared her shoulders; she was a warrior. She'd known the time would come. There was much to love about her planet. Nerak was perfect. It was. And her family was there. Lara waited for her return.

And when Kia did go home, she would warn everyone that Earth was a terrible place. She would tell about wars and horrible cruelties, starvation, and pestilence. For the first time in her life, she would tell an outright lie, but she had a good reason.

If she lied well enough, then maybe none of her family would want to explore Earth, they wouldn't want to leave their own planet, and maybe, just maybe, they wouldn't have to feel the pull between two worlds. They wouldn't feel their heart breaking into a thousand little pieces at the thought of leaving someone, at the thought of what their perfect planet was missing.

Becca came out of the bathroom. "Okay, Nick, come on if you're going to walk me to my car. I have a credit card with my name on it and I know how to use it." There was a wicked twinkle in her eyes. "Bye, Sam, bye, Kia."

They both said good-bye at the same time.

Nick opened the door, bowed gallantly, and waved his sister through. As soon as he closed the door, Becca turned to him.

"I like her."

Uh-oh, he could see the matchmaking wheels turning in her head. His sister had been trying to marry him off ever since she fell in love with Jack. She thought the whole world should be as happy as they were.

"She belches like a sailor," he told her.

She lightly slapped his arm as they stopped in front of the elevator. "Oh, she does not. I'm going to tell her you said that."

The doors opened. He waited for her to go inside and stepped in behind her, punching the lower level.

"Kia won't be around long enough for you to tell her anything, sis."

"Why do you always do this?" She sighed very loudly and very dramatically.

He didn't say anything, hoping his lack of response would make her realize he didn't want to rehash ancient history. As soon as she opened her mouth he knew his tactic hadn't worked.

"Don't pretend you didn't hear me, because I know you did. You never stay with a woman longer than a couple of weeks."

He could've told her his relationships only lasted about a week, but that would only be adding fuel to her fire.

"Everyone doesn't have to be in love just because you are."

"I don't think that and you know it."

The elevator opened and they exited. He held the door to the parking garage open for her and there was blessed silence all the way to her car.

"I know how much you were affected when Dad left. Mom was a lot better off for it. Their marriage didn't work out. It happens sometimes. That's the chance you have to take."

His insides twisted. Yeah, he remembered that day all too well. He'd come in from football practice and his father was gone. He didn't hear a word from him for six months.

He and his dad had barely spoken since then. It wasn't because his dad hadn't made the effort. Nick just hadn't had anything to say to him. Too little too late.

He pushed the painful memories away and held Becca's car door open so she could slide in.

"Dad's leaving has nothing to do with my relationships with women."

She got in and looked up at him. "Doesn't it?"

He didn't say anything.

She gave him one of her long-suffering sighs again. "You need to talk to Mom. She's a lot happier without Dad."

He didn't want to talk about it at all. "Don't run the credit card up too high."

Her mouth turned down, showing his sister knew exactly what he was doing. "Yeah, yeah. Clean your apartment. There is such a thing as a closet somewhere—that is, if you can find it."

He grinned and closed her door, waving her off. He loved his sister but he wasn't going to get married just to make everyone happy. He and marriage just didn't go together.

Darla stayed a car length behind the pregnant woman. Was she in on the illegal goings-on? Or innocent?

Darla had been hiding in her car when Nick Scericino walked the pregnant lady to her vehicle. The same vehicle he and Sam Jones had taken packages out of and carried up in the elevator.

Oh yes, she knew all about Sam and Nick. They were partners. Cops—probably on the take. She had a friend on the inside who told her everything she needed to know. Like the fact Internal Affairs was investigating Nick.

There wasn't anything she disliked more than a dirty cop. A cop had inside information a crook didn't have access to. That wasn't at all right.

But she planned to get her fair share.

And now the plot had thickened. Was the woman only pretending to be carrying a kid? Maybe she had loot under her clothes. The perfect carrier. No one would suspect a pregnant lady.

She'd follow the woman, to see where she was going, just like she had Ms. Big. Now that was one crafty person. She even had a home in the suburbs and pretended to be married to the man who'd picked her up.

Darla was good, though. She'd crept close to the house and watched through a window. The woman had been furiously waving her arms, and although Darla couldn't hear the words, her tone was unmistakable. The man had slunk further inside himself, never once raising his voice.

Darla narrowed her eyes. Yes, the woman was the one in charge. That was obvious.

But then someone had come to the door. The buyer? Possibly. Ms. Big had changed and began smiling but Darla knew her game.

Ms. Big had talked with the other woman, then given her a plastic bag. The handoff! She'd known it. How damn big *was* this operation? She could almost smell the cash flow.

She knew where she could find Ms. Big, so she'd followed the other woman. Just a couple of blocks away, she'd pulled into a driveway. Everything looked perfect about the place. Typical middle-class neighborhood.

Darla knew better.

She parked down the street and crept back to the house, peeking into the window. The woman was smiling as she held up a vase. It looked oriental.

Ming?

Damn, she knew this was the big time. Hell, the way everything was coming together, she'd be set for life and then some because she damn sure wasn't going to walk away empty-handed.

When the pregnant woman pulled into traffic, Darla was right behind her. She followed her all the way to the baby store and pulled in close beside her. Darla watched as the woman heaved her body out of the car.

"Need some help?" Darla asked as she hurried over.

The woman laughed. "Unfortunately, I think I'm getting used to the extra weight."

"When is the baby due?"

"Any day."

"Congratulations." Darla smiled and walked away.

Wild goose chase. The woman was definitely pregnant. But the others—she had them dead to rights.

Chapter 18

"This is bigger than the two of us can handle," Darla told Slava.

Damn, she hated to do what she was about to do, but losing part of her gold mine was a hell of a lot better than losing it all. And if it was as big as she thought, she and Slava didn't have the resources to handle the entire operation.

But she knew someone who could. Slava's Uncle Yuri.

A cold chill of foreboding ran down her spine, but she resolutely pushed it away. She had no other choice. Uncle Yuri had everything they would need. But she would insist her cut be at least fifty percent. If he didn't agree, she wouldn't give him the information.

Slava closed his cell phone. "He'll meet us."

A deep frown furrowed his forehead. She didn't like the way he looked.

"You're right about this being a big smuggling operation, aren't you? I thought I had something good the last time when I told him about those drug dealers." His frown deepened. "But they turned out to be grade-school kids trading lunches. He got really mad at me."

"That's because you're an imbecile," she muttered

under her breath, then in a louder voice said, "These aren't grade-school kids. Not even close. I found out who two of them are: Nick Scericino and Sam Jones—cops."

Slava sat down hard on the sofa, bouncing the other end off the floor. "I don't like messing with no cops."

"These aren't just any cops. They're on the take." She laughed. "You think Scericino is a good old American name?" She shook her head. "No, that's Italian. Want to bet he's got a few relatives in the mafia? Yeah, I think your uncle would like to know more about these two and what's going on."

He laughed. "Yeah, I understand you now. Uncle Yuri might even let me have a gun this time."

Please, someone give him a gun, Darla silently prayed. Maybe it would accidentally go off while he was holding it next to his head. She mentally shook off the image. The idiot would probably miss and shoot her instead.

Sam had left an hour ago, and they were no closer to finding the real Hank than when they'd started. At least, it seemed that way to Nick. Half the people they called weren't at home.

Nick was tired and getting irritated because he knew the more they narrowed it down, the closer Kia was to leaving and he'd never see her again. The logical part of his brain said it was inevitable and for the best. But there was another part of him that said his life would be forever changed because of her.

Hell, she was a lot of fun to be around. And Becca was so wrong about his not wanting to commit. He just wasn't ready, and that's all there was to it.

Suddenly, he felt as if the walls were closing in on him. He might as well make the most of the time they had left. "Hey, you want to see another side of Dallas?"

She glanced up from the papers that were laid out on the kitchen table. "What do you mean?"

"Maybe we could take in a show or something. It's still early."

"A show?"

Of course, she wouldn't know what a show was. "You'll like it, trust me."

The look in her eyes warmed his entire body, and he knew without a doubt that she did trust him. It was a heady feeling and did a hell of a lot for his ego.

"Let me change first." He wanted to take her somewhere nice—somewhere that would give her a special memory for the rest of her life. Or maybe he was the one who wanted that memory. Whatever the reason, he didn't want to take her anywhere wearing scruffy jeans and a T-shirt that had seen better days.

"Should I change clothes, too?"

"You look beautiful just the way you are."

She frowned. "I think I'll wear something else anyway."

Laughter erupted from him. She was already adapting to Earth, even if she didn't realize it.

Half an hour later, he glanced at the clock on the wall. Yeah, she'd adapted all right. How long did it take her to change?

The door to the bathroom opened, and she stepped out wearing a slinky deep blue one-piece suit.

"Is this all right?"

"Yeah." His gaze moved slowly over her. The silky material clung to every curve, every hollow. She showed just enough cleavage to be tempting, to keep a man's gaze on her and only her.

Not that he planned to look at another female tonight.

He drew in a deep breath. "Better than all right. You look sexy, tempting."

"Thank you."

He helped her on with her coat and grabbed his.

A show—maybe a romance—some dinner at a nice restaurant, a little wine, then home and . . . and if he didn't stop thinking about what would happen at the end of the evening, he'd never make it out the door, and he really did want to show her some of Dallas.

They stepped inside the elevator and descended to the garage level. As they walked to the car, Nick had the strangest feeling they were being watched. He glanced around but nothing seemed out of the ordinary.

He was losing his touch if he was starting to think there were criminals around every corner. He shrugged off the feeling and opened the door on the passenger side.

Still, as he pulled out of the parking garage, he reached up and adjusted the rearview mirror. His eyes narrowed. A blue car tailed them.

Man, he was really losing it. The IA investigation was making him punchy. But just in case, he pulled into traffic and took the first left. The car was still behind him. He took another left. Still there.

Rule of thumb: three lefts, and if a strange car was still behind you then you'd better start getting a little suspicious.

He made another left. The car went straight. Okay, maybe he was just being paranoid.

Leaning over, he bumped the radio button. Maybe some music would relax him.

Kia smiled. "Nice," she said when he glanced her way.

"You don't have music?"

"Not like this."

It didn't seem as if she had much of anything on her perfect planet. Not good. He was starting to feel sorry for her.

"What's that?" Kia asked after they'd been driving for a while.

He glanced in the direction she pointed. "The mall."

"Mall?"

"Stores and stuff."

"I'd like to go there, please, thank you."

Did women from every race or species have a homing device when it came to malls? But the way Kia looked, he'd give her the world on a silver platter if she asked for it.

He found a parking place and they went inside. "Oh, this is wonderful." She walked around in a circle looking at the Christmas decorations and the twinkling lights.

"It's beautiful." She grabbed his hand and pulled him forward, laughing with joy. "Who is this Santa Claus? He must be a very important person if he is so honored."

"He's a tradition. December twenty-fifth is Christmas, and people exchange lots of gifts." He didn't want to confuse her with the different religions.

"And when is this December twenty-fifth?"

"Not long."

She smiled. "I think I like your traditions. We don't have this on Nerak."

As if she'd just realized that she'd admitted Earth might have some advantages that Nerak didn't, she straightened.

"As a warrior, traditions aren't necessary," she stated. "The giving of many gifts would create a lot of clutter in one's life. All Nerakians are in harmony with who they are. We have few possessions that accumulate in our lifetime. It's better this way."

He glanced up and read the name of the store, a smile lifting the corners of his mouth. "But then, you've never been in a toy store, either."

"I don't know this toy you speak of."

"Nope, didn't think you did." He grabbed her hand and pulled her inside.

"Oh . . ." Her eyes filled with wonder. When she saw he was watching, she masked her face of all emotion. "I'll look at the things in this store, but only for research purposes."

He knew better, but he'd go along with the game she played. Just maybe, she was starting to realize Nerak wasn't so perfect after all.

She bent down to look at a train as it rolled around the track, then moved to the dolls and became transfixed with the babies.

"This is what's inside Becca," she whispered, her façade slipping again.

"Surely you have babies on Nerak. You don't come fully grown."

"No, but we're in instruction until it's time to go to our family."

A woman and a little girl of about six or seven came into the store.

"We leave instruction when we are her age." She watched the interaction between mother and daughter.

Nick knew she saw the exchange of love between the two. The way the woman lightly touched her daughter's hair, smoothing it back, caressing the golden strands. The smile on the little girl's face when she looked at her mother. Her laughter and her excitement.

As he observed Kia, he saw the sadness in her eyes. She'd never have children. Was she regretting living in a world without men?

Damn, he'd wanted to make her happy, show her some of his town, but he'd only managed to make her sad.

"Come on, there's lots more to see." He grabbed her hand and tugged her out of the store.

She read the different signs. "What's a pet store?"

He shrugged. "Animals."

Her eyes grew wide. "Animals? I have never seen an animal."

The sadness surrounding her was gone. If it would make her happy, then they'd go in and she could see an animal.

As soon as they walked inside, Nick realized his mistake. He'd forgotten about the puppies.

Kia hesitantly walked to the cage that was more like a playpen. Great marketing. It was close to the door. If anyone so much as put one foot inside the store, they would see the Shi-Tzu puppies. There were four of them . . . and they were at the playful stage.

"Now, Kia, it's okay to look, but we can't . . ."

She tentatively stuck out her hand to touch one of the furry black-and-white pups. It did the unthinkable. What Nick had dreaded.

One of them licked her finger and the other three bounced over to see what was happening. They couldn't just walk over, or cower in the corner. No, they had to bounce over.

Kia laughed and scooped one of them up in her arms. It immediately began to lick her face.

"Nick, what is it?" She cuddled the puppy close to her face. Pastel lights began to glow above them.

Not good. Damn, he needed to get her out of the store fast, before other people noticed the lights.

"It's a dog—a puppy. A Shi-Tzu."

"It's so soft and it smells wonderful."

"That's puppy smell. It can knock someone to the ground and make them act silly with just one whiff."

"I think you're making a joke. I like the puppy smell."

One of the puppies growled and barked. A tiny little *ruff*. A sound meant to do as much damage as the puppy smell.

It worked.

Kia put the one she held back in the pen and scooped up the one that had barked.

This wasn't good. Nick didn't need a crystal ball to tell him he was in trouble.

"Kia, why don't we go to the show now? I hear there's a Johnny Depp movie playing. You know, with swashbuckling pirates. Enough to make any normal woman swoon and feel all gooey inside and . . ."

Had she even heard him? This wasn't the way he'd imagined spending the evening.

"I'm sorry," a man said as he hurried from the back, hitching up pants that hung on his wiry frame. As soon as he saw Kia cuddling the merchandise, he came to an abrupt stop. "We don't allow people to pick up the puppies, ma'am." He pointed to a sign on the cage that read, "Due to health hazards, please do not pick up the puppies."

But when Kia turned and looked at him, he practically melted into a puddle at her feet. What power did she seem to have over men? As if Nick didn't know the answer to that. There was something about her that captivated the male of the species. She was sexy as hell, but there was more to it than that. Something in her eyes that drew the unsuspecting person in and then refused to let go. Apparently, the clerk was no different.

"I guess you can hold it for a minute." He blushed all the way up to his hairline. "You don't look like you would give them any kind of disease or anything."

"What do you do with the puppies?" she asked.

"She's not from America," Nick quickly explained. Then he turned to Kia. "They sell puppies and other animals."

As soon as her eyebrows shot upward, Nick knew he'd screwed up again.

She reached into her coat pocket and brought out a wad of bills. "Will this be enough?" She shoved the money into his hands.

"Kia, we can't . . . what will we do . . . my apartment has rules and puppies aren't included in my contract . . ."

Why did she have to look at him like that?

"But you have the book: *Where The Red Fern Grows*. You said it was about dogs. You do like dogs, don't you?"

"Well, yeah . . ."

The clerk grinned from ear to ear as he finished counting the money. "That's enough to buy all four of them."

Nick's pulse began to race. If he had a heart attack, would they know to dial 911? He was a goner for sure. "Kia, we can't. Not all four."

When she sighed, he let out his breath. He'd won. He didn't have a clue what the hell he was going to do with a puppy, but he'd try to figure something out.

The clerk looked disappointed. "I really hate to split them up. Two brothers and two sisters. It almost seems a shame to break the family apart."

"Family? They're a family."

Ah, no. Not the family sales pitch. He glared at the clerk, who refused to meet his gaze. Yeah, he knew better. "Kia . . ."

They left the pet store an hour later armed with puppy piddle pads, puppy carriers, puppy sweaters, puppy chew toys, puppy food, puppy dishes, puppy collars, puppy leashes, and four wiggling, squirming puppies.

"Shi-Tzu puppies," he grumbled as the clerk helped him load everything into his car. "They're not even manly dogs. Not even close." Damn it, he didn't want a bunch of flea-bitten dogs. He didn't want a commitment of any kind—including dogs.

And yeah, he liked dogs.

He'd often wished he had room for a German shepherd or maybe a Doberman. Now, those were dogs a man could take out for a walk.

He glanced at the pups. Cute and cuddly. That was the only way to describe them. He could just see himself with the four on leashes, walking them in the park. A tough undercover cop with four cutesy puppies.

As soon as everything was loaded and the clerk had left, Kia turned toward Nick. "This is purely for research, of course."

"Of course." Research. Yeah, right.

Kia suddenly threw her arms around his neck and hugged him tight.

It only took a second for him to wrap his arms around her and pull her even closer. Maybe it was her smell that made him give in to her every desire. Soft, seductive, and all woman.

And just as deadly as the puppy smell.

Chapter 19

It took three trips to sneak the puppies and all their supplies up to the apartment. Nick just thought he was paranoid before. As they made the last trip up, he could feel someone watching them. Ridiculous, of course.

He'd kept the dog carriers partially covered, and thankfully, the pups had remained quiet. He was almost certain they were in the clear as he shut the door behind them and leaned against it. He closed his eyes and tried to relax, letting out a deep sigh of relief.

"You're not sorry we brought the animals home, are you?" Kia asked.

Sorry? Why should he be sorry? Not when all he could picture were *101 Dalmatians*. Except in his mind's eye, he saw 101 Shi-Tzus with their flat little faces. He could clearly see wall-to-wall piddle pads . . . and chewed furniture . . . and puppy poop.

He opened his eyes and looked at her. "Sorry? Of course not. They're cute." What the hell was he supposed to tell her when she looked at him like she was holding her breath, waiting for his answer?

"Good. I was afraid when we were driving back to the apartment that you might have regretted your decision." She sat down on the floor and opened the carriers one at a time.

His decision? When had it become his?

The puppies bounced out of the carriers and right into Kia's outstretched arms.

"Are you hungry?" Anything to get her mind off the little monsters that were taking over his living room. What would be next? First a puppy, then a . . . a baby?

That thought was enough to knock the wind out of anyone's sails. He really liked Kia a lot, but he and babies didn't mix. He had no desire to be a father. Or get married. At least not for another ten years, if then.

"I'd rather play with the puppies," she said. "Clearly for research, of course. I'd like to observe how these animals behave."

It was worse than he thought if the puppies took precedence over food, and he didn't *even* buy this research crap. Nope, the puppy smell was getting really strong.

He hated being the bearer of bad news, but it was something he had to do. "What are you going to do when you leave? You said there were no animals on your planet."

Her hands stilled for the briefest of moments, then she returned to petting. "I don't have a plan." She glanced up, looking confused. "You'll take care of them for me?" Her eyes pleaded with him.

Why the hell did she have to look at him like that?

"Yeah, sure." It shouldn't be too hard finding them good homes.

That seemed to satisfy her even if she didn't look thrilled with the idea of giving the pups away. He had a feeling she regretted her decision to bring the dogs home just because she'd get attached to them. He certainly didn't buy that she'd only wanted to observe them.

Two hours later, they had the pups behind a makeshift barrier in the kitchen and it looked like they'd settled down for the night. He pulled Kia closer to him as they sat on the sofa. He liked feeling her softness pressed against him and he couldn't stay ticked off forever.

"Did your parents know you were going to be an enforcer when you were created?" she asked.

He lightly ran his fingers up and down her arms. "On Earth, we each have a choice what we want to be or what we want to do with our life. That's not the way it is on Nerak?"

She shook her head and snuggled closer. "We're each given specific characteristics. I was given warrior qualities. All warriors are similar in appearance."

"But your sisters aren't warriors?"

"No, they were given other characteristics. Lara is a gentle soul, a healer. Theora reads minds. I have many sisters. We're connected with one isolated gene. With Mala, the gene was split and she became our cousin. She reads emotions and can feel others'pain."

"But you have no choice what you want to be?"

"The Elders are wise. Our planet doesn't have too many people doing the same job."

"Yet, since there are no wars, your job is obsolete."

She stiffened in his arms. "I'm a warrior. Have no doubts, Earthling."

"That's not what I meant." Damn, that came out all wrong. "What I meant was that you are a trained warrior but you can't use your skills. Am I wrong?"

"No. That's why Mala left," she finally answered, her body relaxing against his. "Why Lara is curious to know more about your planet. Not that my sister would ever leave." She hesitated. "But we have things that Earth doesn't. We don't have wars, or disease. Our air is clean and pure."

"It's perfect," he said.

"Yes, it's perfect."

Silence filled the room. He wondered what she was thinking.

"If you can be anything, that means you don't have to continue in the same job," she said, breaking the quiet. "You can change? If it's your desire."

"That's right."

"Have you ever wanted to change?"

How many times? "Yeah," he told her. "Someday I'm going to open a bar. On a beach maybe. Get away from the city. I've always liked the ocean."

"You have oceans?" She sat up, looking at him.

"More than one."

"Earth does have some good qualities," she admitted and he felt as if he'd won something very important. She snuggled against him again. "What's a bar?"

He grinned. "A place where people go to relax, to unwind. Toss back a few drinks."

"Damn, that sounds nice."

His grin widened. He had a feeling when she did leave, she would be taking a lot of stuff back with her that might irritate the Elders. Maybe they'd get pissed and send her back. He liked having her around. That was an idea. Then again, they might vaporize him for being such a bad influence.

"You don't like being an enforcer, then?" she asked.

"I've been doing it for as long as I can remember. I joined the force when I was twenty-five, about ten years ago. Seeing what I've seen can make you old in a hurry."

She turned in his arms, raising her lips. "Then have sex with me and we can enjoy each other before you get any older."

He chuckled, but his laughter died when he gazed into her eyes and felt himself falling deeper and deeper into a place he'd never been before. "With you, I don't think it's ever been just sex. No, when we make love it's like sweet music." He lowered his mouth, capturing her bottom lip with his teeth, gently sucking before his tongue delved inside her mouth.

The heat emanating from her seared him with passion. He turned until he faced her, placing his hands on her shoulders and drawing her closer. She moaned and leaned into him.

His dick throbbed with the need to be inside her. To plunge again and again into her moist heat, to feel her muscles contracting as she pulled him deeper and deeper inside her body. Damn, she was so frigging sweet that she made him ache.

He ended the kiss, his breathing ragged. Her body trembled in reaction. What the hell was she doing to him? What were they doing to each other? He had a feeling she was experiencing the same thing.

"I want you so badly I hurt deep down inside me," she confessed.

There was nothing coy about her. Maybe that's what made her so different from the other women he'd dated. Kia didn't play games. But then, she didn't have to.

"I feel the same way." He leaned back, brushing the hair out of her eyes. "But you know it wouldn't work between us. We're from two different worlds. I just don't want you to get hurt."

"Nor do I want you to be hurt when I leave. Have no doubts that I will leave Earth. My home is on

Nerak. But it doesn't mean we can't make the time count that we do have together."

He didn't need any more encouragement. Hell, he was about to bust out of his pants now. Yeah, he'd make it damn special. Something she wouldn't forget for a long time.

He unbuttoned her top and slipped it off first one shoulder, then the other, baring her to the waist. She had the most beautiful breasts. High-tipped, tight nipples, rosy areolas.

Her chest rose and fell. She arched her back. He knew what she wanted but rather than caress her breasts, he pushed her hair behind her ear, tugging on her earlobe, running his thumb over the fleshy part.

Kia closed her eyes and pursed her lips.

"Do you like that?" he asked.

She nodded, apparently not trusting herself to speak. She opened her eyes, her gaze moving to his shirt.

"Want me to take it off?"

She shook her head.

"No?" He hadn't thought she could surprise him.

A slow seductive smile curved her lips. "I want to take it off."

There for a second she'd had him worried. It would've taken more than a cold shower to relieve him of this pain.

She pushed the top button through the hole, then the next and the next, and when they were all unfastened, she pushed the edges away, scraping her fingernails lightly through the hairs on his chest.

"I like the way you feel. The planes and ridges. I like the hair on your chest."

"Better than your companion unit?" As soon as the words were out, he wanted to call them back. He wasn't in competition with some damned robot. "I'm sorry. I—"

She placed her fingers lightly against his lips. He captured them, kissing the tips.

"Adam-4 does exactly what I want—or what I thought I wanted. He was built for gratification and nothing more."

"Are they all like that?"

She nodded. "Most of them. It was my choice that he wouldn't think or feel anything. I didn't want the connection."

She leaned toward him, running her tongue over first one nipple, then the other. He gritted his teeth as fire swept through him, but before she could go very much further with her exploration of his body, he held her away from him. He had to know.

"Why didn't you want the emotional connection?"

She looked him directly in the eyes. "He was only a means for physical gratification. Emotionally, I didn't need him."

"And me? Is it different with me?" Why the hell should he even care? Isn't this what he wanted?

"Yes, it's different with you, but I'm not sure I like feeling this way."

"Let me see if I can remedy that." He knew they were playing with fire, but he just couldn't stop walking toward the flames.

He lowered his mouth to hers, cupping the back of her head as he tasted what she so freely gave. Damn, she was so sweet . . . so hot. He stroked her tongue, caught her soft moan.

When he ended the kiss, he was shaking. She did this to him. "I want you so badly I can hardly stand it," he told her.

"No more than I want you."

He stood and began stripping out of his clothes. She leaned against the back of the sofa and watched, not making a move to cover her naked breasts or to take the rest of her clothes off.

Not that he minded. There was something about knowing he would soon have her naked and spread before him that turned him on. Anticipation was a hell of an aphrodisiac.

He kicked out of his pants. When he hooked his thumbs into the waistband of his briefs, Kia's gaze became transfixed. He watched as her breathing became more rapid, her pupils dilating as she waited.

"What do you want?" he couldn't resist asking.

"To see all of you," she said in a breathy whisper. "Now, Nick," she pleaded.

His dick quivered as the material slid over it. His heart raced, the blood pounding inside him.

"Closer," she panted, scooting to the edge of the sofa. Her tongue slowly licked across her lips.

He shook his head even though it was an effort. He knew exactly what Kia had in mind, and it was killing him to refuse her. His dick throbbed with the need to feel her lips closing over his shaft and sucking him inside her mouth. What he had in mind would give them both pleasure.

"Stand up," he said.

She didn't question, but stood. Her top bunched around her waist, her breasts beckoning him to taste, to touch. He couldn't resist. He pulled her closer and lowered his head, taking one tight nipple in his mouth, his tongue flicking across the tip.

She whimpered and clutched his head, tugging him nearer. He moved to her other breast and repeated the motion.

He shoved her clothes down. They puddled at her

feet. When he stepped back, all she had on was a pair of skimpy panties. God, she looked sexy as hell.

"Lie on the floor," he said, his words raspy. She didn't hesitate but did as he asked, lying on her back, waiting for him. For just a moment, he stood above her, his gaze slowly traveling over her. He started at her face, moved over her breasts, taking in the dusky areolas before his gaze traveled farther down her luscious body and stopped at the dark blue wisp of material that covered the thatch of dark curls.

She arched her back and moaned as if he'd actually touched her, actually run his hands over her nearly naked body.

He knelt beside her, gliding his fingers over the silky material of her panties.

"Nick, please."

"That's my intention." He slid her panties down and removed them, uncovering her. This was what he wanted. "You're so damn beautiful." He feathered back the tight curls, exposing all of her to his view.

"I want you," she told him. "I want to taste you on my lips."

His dick jerked in response to her words. He moved until he straddled her, his knees on either side of her face, his face right above her sex. He couldn't stand it anymore. Wanting her, seeing her. He had to taste her, too.

He lowered his mouth, brushing across her sex with his tongue. She gasped when he sucked her inside his mouth and scraped his tongue up and down her clit.

But he wasn't so lost in giving her pleasure that he didn't know when she licked her tongue across the tip of his dick. White light exploded inside his head as she sucked him in deeper, the heat of her mouth closing around him.

He rolled to his side, taking her with him, moving her leg over his shoulder until his face nestled between her legs once again. Now that his hands were free, he was able to explore more of her body.

He began to massage her ass, bringing her passion-swollen sex closer to his lips, then pulling back just a little so he could nibble and lick.

It was all he could do to hold back his orgasm, but he wanted her to come, wanted to taste her juices on his lips. He wanted to know everything about her.

Her body began to tremble; she gasped and arched toward him. He sucked and licked even as she cried out, her body tightening against him. Ah, man, she tasted so frigging sweet. So much heat.

While she was still panting, he moved her onto her back and grabbed a condom, quickly sliding it over his aching erection. He spread her legs open, staring down at her sex before he slid deep inside her.

Her passion-glazed eyes met his as she raised her hips up to meet his thrusts. His ass clenched as she sucked him deeper into her wet, moist heat. When he thought it couldn't get better than this, she wrapped her legs around his waist and he sank inside her a little more.

He began to thrust harder, stroking her on the inside, her body contracting around his. He plunged faster and faster until his own release exploded from him. It took him a second to realize the low growl came from him. He didn't care. He wanted Kia to know what she did to him. How she made him feel.

It was all he could do to take a decent breath. He collapsed to the carpet, rolling to his side, attempting to fill his lungs with precious air.

When he could take a halfway normal breath, he looked at her. "You okay?"

She shook her head. "I think it's going to be very

difficult to leave this behind." She opened her eyes and looked at him.

She'd conceded a little more. But he knew exactly what she was talking about. It wouldn't be easy letting go.

Chapter 20

"Explain why you started a barroom brawl during a drug bust." The Internal Affairs investigator leaned forward, her elbows on the desk, brown eyes narrowed as she unflinchingly stared him down.

At least, she attempted to. Candace Burke was the department investigator in charge of everything from employee complaints to drug deals gone wrong. Her promotion had gone through about a month ago.

She'd commandeered a room not much bigger than a closet and had installed a bright light in the center over the scarred and chipped table. The lady watched way too many old movies, if you asked him.

Nick leaned back in his chair, stretching his legs in front of him and crossing them at the ankles. He returned her stare. She wasn't bad looking, but it was as if she intentionally tried to make herself look plain.

Her dark brown hair was scraped back from her face and squeezed into a tight little bun at the base of her neck. Collar buttoned up high enough to choke a giraffe, lips pinched tighter than a miser's wallet, and glasses that would make Buddy Holly sigh with envy. She would've made a great schoolmarm during the horse-and-buggy days.

"Are you having trouble answering the question, Officer?" Her eyebrows rose to her hairline.

"Do you ever relax?"

The look she gave him could've frozen hell over.

Okay, that might not have been the best thing for him to ask, especially since it was his balls on the chopping block. She really needed to loosen up—get laid or something. Not that he thought it best to mention that right now either.

Maybe he should try to fix her up with Weldon. He really needed to get laid, too. Come to think of it, Nick had noticed they seemed to look at each other a lot when they thought the other one wasn't watching. Maybe there was a little bit of an attraction going on. That might be something to file away in case he needed the information later.

"Yes, I relax, just not on the job. This is an investigation, Officer Scericino. I'd suggest you remember that." She steepled her fingers, her gaze losing none of the chill.

"Since I've been forced to take vacation time, I don't think I'll forget."

"The brawl? Why did you start it? Was it a cover for something else?" She slapped the palms of her hands down on the table, making a sound much like the crack of a whip.

She probably didn't have much of a social life. Yeah, that was it. Or maybe he should introduce her to the mayor's niece. She'd be able to tell Candace how great it felt to loosen up. He let his gaze sweep over her once again.

Nah, that might be stretching the realms of even his imagination. She looked as stiff as the crisply starched suit she wore. He couldn't really see her swinging from a pole wearing only a thong.

"The guy was late," he finally said. "I doubted he was going to show."

"But you didn't know that for sure, did you?"

"Positively?" He shook his head. "No." Damn, now he was starting to sound like Kia.

"Scericino. That's Italian, isn't it?"

"German."

Her lips pursed. "Don't get funny."

He sighed. "Yes, it's Italian. Do you have a problem with my ancestors? My mother is Irish, if that makes you feel any better."

Ah, crap. Her look turned calculating. He really hoped she wasn't going to bring up the Godfather movies. If she did, he might be forced to stick cotton in his mouth and talk funny.

"Why did you start the fight?" she asked, switching gears without blinking an eye.

Yep, she'd watched way too many old movies. "Who says I did?"

She leaned back in her chair, looking more relaxed than Nick had seen her since he'd sat down. She wasn't too bad at playing cat and mouse, he'd give her that.

"The man whose nose you busted. He said there was a woman in the bar that night. Dark hair, blue eyes—dressed better than the drudges that usually hang out there."

He shrugged, but he could feel his pulse pick up. "Some guy was bothering her. I told him that he might want to keep his hands to himself. He had an attitude problem—I did a little adjusting."

"And the girl?"

"I gave her a place to stay for the night."

"A regular Good Samaritan."

"So I'm told."

"Are you involved with the Russian mafia?" She abruptly sat forward again, the front legs of her chair slapping the concrete floor. "Maybe the Italians and the Russians have put their heads together."

"You're joking, right?"

She opened her hands. "It could generate a lot of money if they combined forces."

Give me a fucking break!

He leaned forward in his chair. "And what if I talk—tell you everything." He lowered his voice, making the words raspy as he relied heavily on a long-unused Italian accent. "You gonna make me an offer I can't refuse?"

"If you think you're being cute, you're not." She drew in a deep breath. "I'm keeping you on suspension pending the outcome of this investigation."

"Ah, come on, Candy. You know damn well I'm not on the take." Hell, she'd known him long enough to know better than this.

She stood. "My name is Candace, not Candy. Maybe the time off will help you gain a little respect for the position I hold."

"The only way you can get respect is if you earn it." He didn't know if she'd heard him or not. She was already walking out of the room.

Well, hell. Why didn't she just slap his wrist and let him get back to work? Candy knew damn well that he wouldn't jeopardize the badge or his integrity. *Some people shouldn't be put in charge of anything.*

The one good thing about being on leave was that he might be able to get Kia home. That odd rumbling in his gut started again when he thought about her leaving, but he quickly told himself that she had to go sometime. Forever was something they would never have.

He pushed away from the table and walked out of the room.

"Spsssss."

Nick's eyebrows drew together. What the hell? Was there a gas leak somewhere? He turned around. He should've guessed—Weldon.

"What?" he asked.

Weldon looked from side to side, then over his shoulder. "We need to talk."

"Okay, talk."

Weldom vigorously shook his head. If the guy wasn't careful, his head was going to come loose and go rolling off behind him.

"No, not here. In my office."

Whatever. He followed as Weldon covertly made his way down the hallway. Weldon and Candy *should* get together. They'd make a pretty good team—sort of. Maybe they wouldn't be so damn uptight.

As soon as they stepped into Weldon's small office, he shut the door and tuned the lock. Nick's eyebrows rose. "You mind explaining just what you're doing?"

"It works," he whispered.

"Well, I'm glad for you. Who's the lucky girl?"

He looked confused, then it was as if a light went on in his head.

"Get your mind out of the gutter." He frowned. "The locator, I fixed it."

Nick felt as if the floor had just dropped out from under him.

Sam marked another name off the list of Hanks, then glanced through the pages. Half the names had red lines through them.

Kia frowned as she laid down the phone.

"What?" he asked.

She glanced in his direction. "He said he wouldn't mind standing in for the other Hank. I don't think I liked his tone of voice. It was very inappropriate."

"There are a lot of jerks out there."

"Jerks?"

He kept forgetting she didn't know some of the slang. "People you would just as soon not know."

She nodded. "Jerks. Yes, I think he was a jerk."

She stretched her back. Guilt washed over him. They'd been calling since Nick left for the station. He should've realized she would need a break.

"Why don't you grab us something to drink. A soda maybe. Walk around a bit and stretch your legs."

"That sounds good." But still, she hesitated.

"Did you want something?"

"You've been friends with Nick a long time?"

He dropped the papers on the coffee table and leaned back against the sofa. Maybe he needed a break, too. "Yeah, I've known him since the fourth grade." When her forehead furrowed, he explained. "School. We learn stuff: history, arithmetic, English."

"We learn on Nerak, too."

"Do you miss it?"

"Nerak? Yes. It's my home. My family are there. I would miss them if I were never to see them again."

"Yet, your cousin apparently decided to stay."

Kia straightened. "She will be ready to return when I locate her."

"Are you sure?"

She picked at the fibers on the sofa, not meeting his gaze. "No, I'm not."

"Then what will you do?"

She must've realized what she was doing because her fingers stilled. She raised her chin, meeting his gaze. "I am a warrior. I will convince her it is time to return home. She won't have a choice."

"Will you be able to leave Nick?" He threw the question at her, wanting to see her reaction.

For a moment, her mask dropped and he saw the stricken look on her face. But it was gone just as quickly, making him almost wonder if he'd imagined her wounded expression. But he was a good cop and he knew he hadn't imagined a damn thing.

He'd been afraid of this. He'd known Nick a long time and knew he sabotaged every one of his relationships. All because his dad had walked out when he was sixteen. Nick denied that was the reason, but Sam knew differently. He didn't want to see him hurt. Hell, he didn't want to see Kia hurt, either.

"What I feel doesn't matter," she continued. "Would you leave Earth to spend the rest of your life in a strange land? Even for love?"

He wasn't sure he would. "I don't know," he truthfully answered.

"I didn't want to hurt anyone. Only find Mala. Maybe that should be as soon as possible."

"I'll do what I can."

She stood, going into the kitchen. After she brought him a soda, she went back to the kitchen and brought the puppies out to play.

It was worse than he could've imagined. Why else would Nick let her bring the pups home? His friend was sinking fast and he didn't know if he could save him.

He picked up the phone and dialed the next Hank on the list. No answer. He went to the next one. Busy. He took a drink of the soda and dialed the next one on the list.

"Hank's Mule Barn, head ass speaking." Guffaws came over the phone.

"Is this the Hank that picked up the woman and brought her to Dallas?"

Silence.

Sam's pulse skipped a beat. "You let her out in front of a bar."

"I didn't do nothin' to her. I swear. I just gave her a lift. That's all. Said she was goin' to that ranch that

J.R. lived at. I took her as far as I could, even though she wasn't very nice."

Sam scooted to the edge of the sofa and grabbed a pencil. "Where did you pick her up?"

"Do I need a lawyer?"

He gritted his teeth. The guy might need a body bag if he didn't start talking. "You're not in trouble. I just need to know the location where you picked her up. That's all."

"Swear?"

He took a deep breath, then expelled it. "Nothing will happen after I hang up the phone. I only need the location."

Hank hesitated. "Okay, but you better be telling the truth."

"The location?" Sam prodded.

"Devil's Bend."

He gripped the phone. "And that's where?"

As Hank began telling him the exact location, he jotted down the directions. Hank abruptly hung up the phone before Sam could ask any more questions. When Sam redialed, no one answered.

Great, what if this turned out to be a wild goose chase? Lots of truckers picked up women, and they probably dropped them off at bars. It was a well-known fact hookers worked the highways.

Hank hadn't told him anything specific. He glanced down at the directions before making a quick decision. He had some time coming. Why not check it out? It could be nothing. One thing was for certain—Nick was too close to Kia to think rationally.

He crossed out the Hank he'd just talked to, then folded the piece of paper with the directions and stuck it into his pocket. He knew Mala was on a ranch, Nick had told him that much, and he had the area. That was all he needed.

One of the puppies ran toward him, stopped, sat on his butt, and barked. If you wanted to call it a bark. It was more like a squeak. What the hell was Nick going to do with four puppies? Sam snorted. Nick better not look in his direction, because he damn sure didn't want one. And besides, they were girly dogs.

The pup growled and barked, then bounced on its front legs.

"Think you're tough, huh?" He scooped the pup up in his hands and brought it close to his face. "You don't even have a nose, hardly."

The pup licked his face.

"Ugh! Did you have to do that?" He wiped the back of his hand across his face.

The pup was kind of soft, though. He set it in his lap. Probably didn't weigh more than a few pounds. He chuckled when he thought about Nick out walking the mutts. It would serve him right for letting Kia talk him into getting all four.

"I wondered where the other one had gone." Kia spoke from the doorway. She glided across the room, the other three puppies following behind her, tripping over their own feet. "I have been . . . observing them."

"Observing?"

"For research. Nothing more."

"It looked to me like you were playing with them."

She cocked an eyebrow. A woman with attitude. He bet Nick was having a hell of a time with her.

"I'm a warrior. I do not *play* with puppies. I was merely observing their reactions."

"To petting and cuddling?"

Some of her stiffness vanished, but she managed to hold herself together. She had spirit, he'd give her that. But he could tell she was upset about something.

"You'll help Nick take care of them after I'm gone?"

Damn, now he could see how Nick had gotten himself in this mess. "Yeah, I'll help him."

She smiled. "Good, then I won't worry about them. Nick will need the company after I leave so he won't miss me so much. I don't want him to be lonely."

"I doubt Nick will be lonely for long," he blurted.

She squared her shoulders. "And what exactly do you mean by that?"

Open mouth and insert foot. "Nothing, nothing at all. Just that he'll have the puppies for company."

She didn't look like she quite believed him, but she let the matter drop. He sighed with relief. That was a close one. The sooner he found Mala, the better off they would be.

Chapter 21

Uncle Yuri scared the hell out of Darla. He wasn't that big, only about five-ten. Everything about him was dark, though: dark skin, dark hair, and dark bushy eyebrows.

When those same eyebrows formed a vee, you knew you were in deep shit. At the moment, they were one sharp slash straight across his forehead. He was in a good mood.

He still scared the hell out of her.

"Tell me about the stones," Yuri said, his words gravelly, scraping over her skin like shards of glass. It wasn't a question. It was a demand.

She swallowed past the lump in her throat. Maybe this hadn't been the best idea she'd ever come up with.

Suddenly, she remembered a story Slava had once told her about a man who'd crossed the mafia leader. It wasn't pretty. Slava had told her the man's voice had become very high pitched and he was performing at a bar that catered to transvestites.

"I . . . I . . ." Sweat ran down her face as she quickly looked at the two brawny Russians who stood silently on either side of Yuri, then at the man himself. He sat in an ornate, high-backed chair behind a desk that was polished to a high sheen.

Ah, God, she'd be surprised if she didn't crap her britches.

"You are here. My stupid nephew said you wanted to talk; yet you don't talk? You are scared of Yuri?"

He laughed, a cross between a chuckle and a hacking cough. When he had his breath back, he took a long draw off his smelly cigar, then laid it back in the ashtray and blew a cloud of smoke, aimed right at her.

She squared her shoulders, a little of her bravado returning, and tried not to inhale the noxious cigar smell. As it was, her eyes were starting to water.

"No, I'm not scared of you."

His eyebrows veed. "Then you are very stupid. You should be scared, very scared. Now, enough chatter—talk!"

Her confidence puddled at her feet. At least, she hoped that's all that had puddled. She took a deep breath and could smell her own damn fear.

"I saw the stones." She related the story to him about the princess, about her shopping extravaganza, Ms. Big, the Ming vase, the carriers the princess and the cop had taken upstairs to his apartment. And in her telling, she grew more confident.

"Slava, did you see these stones?"

He shook his head. He was pale and sweating more than her. Like he needed to be afraid of anything. Slava had once told her that his mother had been Yuri's little sister and she'd made her brother swear he would take care of Slava. A deathbed promise. Darla had a feeling Yuri regretted it.

"I saw the stones," she told him again, chin raised.

"Are you willing to bet your life?" Yuri asked, his wheezing breath much like that of a hissing snake.

This was a horrible idea. Bad, bad, bad! But damn it, she had seen the stones.

"Yes." She was going to puke. Vomit all over his spotlessly clean desk.

Get hold of yourself!

"What do you want for this information?"

"Fif . . ." She cleared her throat. "Forty percent."

He smiled. It wasn't a happy smile. Not even close.

"Ten percent," he countered.

"Twenty-five." Oh, Lord, did she just open her mouth and utter those words?

He laughed. "I like a woman with balls. Okay, twenty-five percent."

She relaxed.

"But just remember, I don't mind cutting off a woman's balls, either. Don't cross me."

"I'm not stupid."

He was thoughtful. "No, I think you know exactly what you want."

Stupid? No, she was a fucking idiot. What the hell had she expected to accomplish? Yuri was going to cut her up into tiny pieces and feed her to the fish.

No, if nothing else, the stones were real. She'd seen them with her very own eyes. The stones alone would keep her alive. She could do this.

Nick reached into his coat pocket for the tenth time and felt the cold metal of Kia's locator. Damn, he wasn't ready for this.

Weldon, on the other hand, had practically gone ballistic. He'd adjusted a chip, then used a drop of his blood. The locator had given him specific directions to his office.

Great. Fantastic.

Kia could use Mala's sample and she would immediately find her cousin. And Kia would leave. He'd

have four squirming mutts to deal with, to find homes
for and . . .

He drew in a deep breath.

She couldn't stay. They'd both known that from the
very start. Well, almost from the start. Close enough.

The elevator doors opened and he stepped out.
His footsteps were heavy as he walked to his apartment. He could do this. No problem. Hell, he'd finally
be able to get his life back in order. Kia had stepped
in and turned it completely upside down. He was ready
to get his life back. No commitments, that was his
motto.

When was the last time he'd even thought about
his bar? It would be nice to have the time to concentrate on his dream. His hand stilled on the doorknob
as he closed his eyes for just a minute and envisioned
an island, the deep blue waters surrounding it.

The tension left his body. He could see himself in
a hammock, a tall icy drink in his hand and a beautiful woman strolling toward him. Windswept black hair,
her hand raising to brush glossy strands out of her
eyes. Ah, man, those deep blue eyes that he could lose
himself in.

"Kia," he breathed.

He shook away the image. Man, she was killing
him. But even as he opened the door, he knew death
had never tasted sweeter.

"How'd it go?" Sam asked.

"Candy really likes her new title." He shrugged.
"I'll live, but I'm still on vacation."

Sam stood. "Speaking of which, I'll be out of town
for a few days."

Damn, Nick was kind of hoping for a little help—
not that he needed it anymore. Moral support
would've been nice. Man, he needed to just get over

it. Kia was going to leave—end of story. It was time everything went back to normal.

Sometimes he forgot Sam actually had a life. His friend was all business most of the time.

"Sure," he said. "We can handle this."

Sam's forehead puckered. "You okay?"

He nodded. "I'm fine." He looked around at all the papers, knew they wouldn't need them anymore. "Thanks for everything."

"Things will turn out for the best. Don't worry."

"Nick." Kia swept into the room.

"I'll give you a call when I get back," Sam said.

Nick nodded, barely hearing the door close when Sam left. Kia had all his attention. He didn't think he'd ever seen a more beautiful woman.

"We didn't find Hank," she told him with a worried look. "I wonder if I'll ever track Mala down."

"Would that be such a bad thing?" he asked.

She squared her shoulders. "My home is on Nerak. My family is there."

He reached in his pocket and gripped the locator. No! It wasn't right that she would up and leave him. Why had she even come into his life?

Ah, hell, life really sucked sometimes. He pulled the locator out of his pocket at the same time the phone rang. His grip tightened. It rang again.

"Your communicator, Nick."

He answered the phone. "Yeah?"

"Becca's in labor. We just got to the hospital," Becca's husband said, his voice shaky.

"I'll be there in ten minutes. Tell her I love her." As Nick hung up the phone, he slipped the locator back in his pocket. He'd tell Kia later. He couldn't handle giving it to her right now.

"Nick?"

He looked at her, knew he wanted her with him. "Becca is having her baby. Will you come with me?"

"Her baby," Kia breathed, the warrior disappearing and the woman inside her making an entrance.

"I'd like you there with me."

"You honor me just by asking. Of course I will go. It will be a great research opportunity."

Nick helped her put the puppies behind their barrier. When one licked his hand, he chuckled and scratched him behind the ear. Lord help him, they were starting to grow on him.

They grabbed their coats and were out the door and on the way to the hospital in just a few minutes. Damn, his palms were sweating.

"You're nervous?"

He glanced at her before returning his gaze to the road. Man, why the hell was traffic moving so blasted slow?

"Does it show?" he asked.

"Yes. Will Becca be all right?"

"Women have babies every day. Of course she'll be okay." He cleared his throat. "My mom will be there."

"I understand, low profile." On the outside, Kia knew she appeared calm, except she was anything but. His mother had given birth to him and Becca. She had known the joy of holding her children.

Emptiness filled her.

Just as suddenly, she thought of Lara and her other sisters. The Elders, the princesses. Their world didn't have wars. No one died before her time. Disease was a thing of the past.

Suddenly, she felt as if she were being pulled apart. This wasn't good. Not good at all. Damn, she didn't like this feeling.

"And your father?" she asked since he hadn't

mentioned him. She saw his grip tighten again and sensed his anxiety.

"He probably won't be there. He lives out of state."

"Your parents don't live together?"

"They're divorced."

"And this upsets you?" She wished she knew more about the family structures on Earth.

"They haven't lived together for many years. He has a new family."

She decided the more Nick talked about his father, the more upset he became, so she dropped the subject and concentrated on the heavy traffic, the way Nick expertly maneuvered through the streets until soon they pulled into a parking area and went inside a building.

"This is the hospital," Nick explained. "People come here when they're sick. Do you have hospitals?"

She shook her head. "We have smoothies."

"I guess if it works." He took her hand as they went inside the box that would transport them to a different level.

When they stepped off, Nick led them to an area where there were places to sit. As soon as they entered the room, an older woman with red hair came to her feet.

"The doctor shooed us out," the woman said with a wide smile on her face.

Doctor. Kia knew this word. It meant the same thing as healer.

Nick enfolded the woman in an embrace. "Everything all right?"

"I'm sure it is. Women have been giving birth for a long time and we're pretty tough." There was just the slightest tremble in her words. The mother worried for her child.

Kia hung back, observing. This was one of Nick's

parents. The woman hugged him tight, then when she stepped back, Nick's mother brushed his hair from his face much like the woman had for her daughter in the toy store.

Kia moved back a step more, not wanting to intrude on their greeting but suddenly feeling more like an alien on Earth than she'd felt since her arrival.

She shouldn't be here. This wasn't her family unit. She knew nothing about this kind of connection. Just when she would've turned and hurried away, Nick reached for her hand and pulled her forward.

"This is Kia."

She was no longer on the outside looking in. The warmth of his family enveloped her until she felt as if she were a part of it.

"Kia," his mother said.

Nick's mother wrapped Kia in the warmth of her embrace. The feeling was even better than when she held the puppies. She could've stayed in this woman's arms forever and her life would've been content.

But she was a warrior and this shouldn't be happening to her. She straightened, putting space between her and Nick's mother.

She'd never met a real mother before. It was important she show her the respect due someone who'd borne children. She bowed slightly. "It is a great honor to meet the mother of Nick."

Nick slipped his arm around her shoulder and pulled her close. "Kia isn't from America."

His mother looked from one to the other. "So Becca told me." Her gaze stopped on Kia. "Welcome to my country . . . and my family. We don't have to be formal. Call me Letty."

Kia's pulse sped up. What would it feel like to be a part of these people? No, she couldn't think like that. "Thank you. Is Becca okay?" Maybe the focus should move back to the daughter.

"Becca is fine. We'll go in to see her as soon as the doctor has checked her," the mother said, then moved to the side. "This is Nick's brother, Tony."

Tony took Kia's hand in his. "I have to say my brother's taste in women has improved."

"Just make sure you keep your distance." Nick grinned.

Another child from the mother. She must be very happy to have borne three babies.

"Jack?" Nick asked.

"In with Becca." His mother motioned for them to take a seat. "They let us see her for a few minutes before the doctor made us leave so he could check her." Tears shone in her eyes. "She seemed to be doing well."

Tony reached over and patted her hand. "You'll have to excuse Mom. She gets emotional at weddings, funerals, and babies being born."

"And what if I do? It's a privilege I've earned," she scoffed.

He chuckled. "You're right."

A voice inside Kia's head began to chant. *You'll never have this . . . you'll never have this . . .*

Stop!

"You okay?" Nick asked close to her ear so that only she heard.

She nodded. "I like your family."

Her stomach rumbled. She liked them a little too much.

A woman wearing loose green pants that tied at the waist and a matching top came into the room with a worried look on her face.

"We have a slight complication," she said. "The doctor is taking Becca into the O.R."

Chapter 22

O.R.? Kia looked around the room. This O.R. must not be good, from the expressions on everyone's faces. Tingles of apprehension ran through her.

Letty had drawn in a sharp breath. Tony came to his feet with a worried scowl on his face and Nick was holding tightly to her hand. Her heart began to race. What was happening to Becca and her baby?

"What kind of complication?" Nick asked the authority figure.

"The baby isn't positioned correctly. This happens sometimes. The baby is in some distress. The doctor doesn't want to take any chances by waiting. They're setting up for a C-section. We'll keep everyone updated."

"Can I see my daughter?" Letty stood.

"I'm sorry. There isn't time." The woman hurried from the room before any more questions could be asked.

Complications? Kia looked at Nick. His face had lost some of its color. Fear stabbed through her. Fear for this woman she barely knew, fear for the unborn child, and fear that Nick would be hurt if anything happened to his sister.

"What does this mean?" she asked.

"I don't know for sure. The baby is supposed to

position itself as the time draws near for delivery," Nick attempted to explain. "Sometimes it doesn't turn correctly and they have to surgically remove it."

"And how is that done?"

He cast a worried look in his mother's direction. Letty rubbed her forehead. Tony tried to comfort his mother, but he was looking haggard himself.

"They cut her abdomen open and take the baby that way," he mumbled, his attention clearly not on her. "Mom, I'm going to get some coffee. I'll bring some back for you and Tony. Becca will be okay." But he didn't sound positive.

Kia only shook her head when he looked at her to see if she wanted anything. He left the room.

She concentrated on what he'd told her. They were going to take a knife and cut Becca open. A picture formed in her mind of Becca strapped to a table screaming as they came closer and closer to her with the knife.

A shudder ripped through her.

It would kill Becca. Probably the baby, too.

Letty glanced her way. "She'll be fine. This seems to happen a lot in our family."

"You were cut open, too?"

She nodded.

This was a great woman, a strong female!

"And you survived," she spoke with awe.

"That's where my Irish stock comes in handy. We can handle just about anything that's thrown our way."

That must be why Nick was such a great warrior. He had inherited some of this Irish strength from his mother.

But she didn't have this kind of strength. Her life had been relatively easy, now that she thought about it. Would she be able to survive her stomach being cut open? She didn't think so. The trauma of the experience would kill her.

For a moment, she had wondered what it would be like to stay on Earth. For a moment, she had let a fantasy envelop her. For a moment, she had pictured an idyllic life with just her and Nick. They'd make love all night and during the day they would work together as code enforcers.

Now she could see how foolish her thoughts had been. She wanted no part of Earth now that she knew just how primitive it was. She'd kick someone's ass if they came toward her with a knife.

"I shall return." She abruptly stood, leaving the small waiting area. She needed to walk around, gather her thoughts.

She went down the hall and around a corner. At the end was a set of double doors. She continued forward, hoping it would lead to an outside area where she could get some air.

But when she pushed the double doors open, she saw men and women who wore the same uniform as the woman who'd given them the information on Becca.

This was apparently the place where they took the mothers-to-be. She stopped at the first open door and looked inside.

"Tell the doctor I want drugs, damn it! Screw your beliefs." She glared at the man who stood beside the bed patting her hand. The woman's expression was wild. The hair sticking out around her face didn't help her ferocious appearance.

"Now, honey. You know we decided that we wanted to do natural childbirth," he spoke in a soothing voice, a placating smile turning up the corners of his mouth.

The woman grabbed him by the crotch. The man grunted as his face screwed up in pain.

"If you don't want me to stretch your dick out and wrap it around your fucking neck, then you'll go get me a nurse or a doctor right now!"

"Yes, dear. Just please let go," he said with a high-pitched squeak.

"I don't even like your stupid religion," she continued. "In fact, I don't like your mother, either! And the next time she bitches about the way I clean house, I'm going to tell her to go fuck herself! Now . . . get . . . me . . . some . . . drugs!"

"Yes, dear. Anything you want. I'm going right now." He hurried toward the door.

Kia couldn't back out of the room fast enough. She ran toward the double doors, not looking back. Her palms were sweating and it was hard to catch her breath.

The woman had clearly been in horrific pain. This wasn't good. No wonder the Elders had stopped childbirth. They were very wise. They had seen all these horrors and taken away the pain for all Nerak.

Yes, there were some things about Nerak that might not be perfect, but the Elders didn't let anyone suffer needlessly.

Kia went back to the waiting area and took her seat, thinking about what she needed to do to get home. They would finish calling the names on the list of Hanks and they would find the Hank who had brought her to the bar. Soon she would be back on Nerak and all this would be a bad dream.

Nick returned a while later carrying cups with dark liquid. By then, she'd composed herself as best she could. She watched as he handed his mother the coffee. Maybe not all of her stay would be a bad dream. No, some of it had been good. It just wasn't what she wanted.

"Any word?" he asked.

"Not yet," she told him as he sat in the chair next to her.

He gave her a funny look. "You okay?"

Before she could answer, the woman in green returned. This time she was smiling when she looked at Becca's mother.

"You have a grandson. The doctor had to do a C-section, but mother and baby are doing fine." She smiled. "The verdict is still out on the father, but we think he'll be okay, too."

"Can we see them?" Nick asked.

"They'll be in recovery for a while, but the baby will be in the nursery soon. If you'd like to wait at the window, you can have front row."

"I knew she'd come through this." Letty beamed. "Come on, let's go see my grandson."

They all started walking toward the elevator. Kia hung back.

"Would you like to see him?" Nick asked.

"They will permit this?"

"Sure. We'll be on the other side of the glass but we'll be able to see the baby."

A newborn child. Becca had almost died giving birth to this baby.

Kia had never seen an infant. Would it be like the puppies and attempt to capture her heart? Did a baby hypnotize a woman into believing she could endure the pain of childbirth if in the end she would have a tiny baby?

She looked around. Becca's family seemed happy, cheerful. They were excited to welcome this new member into their family unit.

"I'll wait for you downstairs, I think. I'll see Becca and the baby later."

He gave her a funny look. "Are you sure?"

"I'm tired."

"My family won't mind that you're there." He smiled. "Mom would love showing off her first grandson."

"I need to get some air." *Please, Nick,* she silently beseeched.

Apparently, he read her thoughts. He squeezed her hand. "I'll meet you downstairs. Do you remember where we came in?"

She nodded.

"Okay, I won't be long."

Kia got on the elevator with Nick and they rode it up one floor. His family had already left, anxious to see the newborn. When he got off, she stayed on, smiling and saying she would see him soon.

It was a relief when she was once again by herself. She pushed the button for the floor they had come in on and realized she had adapted quickly to her new environment. An insidious transformation that had begun to suck her in, until she'd realized just how imperfect Earth was.

Halfway down, the elevator stopped and two men wearing the same uniform of authority got on, except these were blue in color.

They looked her way. One of the men closed one eye when he met her gaze. She did not know this custom, but when she returned the gesture, he grinned. The other man was older and didn't pay much attention to their exchange.

The elevator stopped and the older man got off but the younger one stayed. As soon as the doors closed, he turned toward her.

"I'm John."

She warily eyed him. There was something about him she didn't like, but she would refrain from judging him.

"I'm called Kia."

His gaze slithered over her, lingering in all the wrong places.

"Not from around here, are you?"

"No."

He straightened, puffing out his chest. "I'm a doctor."

"A doctor?"

"Yeah, at least I will be as soon as this year is up. I'm still an intern, but that's all about to change. As soon as I finish I'll be a surgeon. That's where all the money is, you know. I plan on being a wealthy man. A mansion, maybe even a yacht."

He acted as if his words should have some meaning to her, but she had no idea what he was trying to imply. Apparently, being a surgeon carried some importance. Her curiosity was piqued. "What is a surgeon?"

He leaned back against the wall and grinned. "I cut people open, sweetheart. Slice and dice." He made a slashing motion with his hand.

She backed into the corner. He was the one who cut Becca open! "Stay away from me."

He reached into his pocket.

He was getting a knife! He was going to cut her open!

She grappled in her satchel and pulled out her phazer.

"Hey, sugar . . ."

She pushed the button.

Zappppp!

She leaned against the back wall, taking in deep breaths. He was gone. He wouldn't cut her open. Earth was a barbaric place. The sooner she was back on Nerak, the sooner she could forget this awful planet.

But as she walked out the front door, she knew there was someone she would still remember—Nick.

* * *

"I think Becca's delivery might have upset Kia," Letty told Nick as they stood in front of the glass looking at Jack Jr. "A lot of women are nervous if they haven't been around babies, and Becca said Kia acted as if she'd never seen a pregnant woman."

Nick was thoughtful. She did seem a little green around the gills.

His mother patted his hand. "You should give her a little time to digest everything. I'm sure she'll come around. She's a lovely woman."

And his mother was trying to marry him off. He spotted all the signs. He'd like to let his mother dream her dreams and not contradict her, but it wasn't fair not to tell her Kia wouldn't be around much longer.

"She's leaving soon," he told her. They were alone as they stood in front of the window. Tony had gone to the bathroom.

"And you're going to let her get away?"

What was it about him that people were always butting into his love life or lack thereof?

"You used to be a hopeless romantic, even when you were little," she continued. "What happened?"

He stiffened. "Dad pretty much opened my eyes when he walked out on us."

"Not all marriages are meant to be."

"You were together twenty-two years."

"But they weren't happy years. We settled. That's all."

"Until he found someone else."

She drew in a sharp breath.

"Mom, I'm sorry." Damn it, why the hell did he have to remind her that his dad was a jerk?

"It's okay. I hear his fourth wife makes him toe the line. I still speak with your grandmother on a regular basis. She told me his wife . . ." Letty chuckled. "She doesn't call her new daughter-in-law by her name. Anyway, he can't even watch his football games because it disturbs the serenity of her home."

"Good."

His mother sobered. "I shouldn't laugh. I should feel sorry for him that his life is in such a mess."

"But you don't."

She sighed. "No, not even a little bit. I'll probably burn in hell."

He grinned. She didn't look as if she were too concerned. His attention was drawn back to the babies in their bassinets. Jack Jr. yawned and stretched, pushing his arms out of the blue blanket the nurse had swaddled him in.

"Look," he told his mother. "Jack is already giving the nurses hell."

His mother chuckled, touching her hand to the glass. "Yeah, kids are like that, but we love them anyway."

Two nurses came around the corner. They were laughing about something. As they drew nearer, Nick and Letty heard their conversation even though they kept their voices lowered.

"Can you believe he streaked through the hospital? I know these interns run on very little sleep, but I never expected this one to go off the deep end."

"It couldn't have happened to someone more deserving." The little blond nurse bobbed her head. "He cornered me in the elevator once and made some suggestions about what he could do for me. It was enough to turn my stomach, and after working in the emergency room and seeing mangled bodies all shift, it takes a hell of a lot to make me throw up." She rolled her eyes.

"Yeah, he was always winking at me." The other nurse grinned. "But after seeing him in the buff, I don't think he could do a whole lot for anyone. Give me a break!"

They both laughed and were quickly out of hearing range.

"Streaking." Letty shook her head. "This has been a strange night. There must be a full moon."

Streaking? That didn't sound good. If Kia had turned her phazer on the guy . . .

He looked at his watch. Damn, had he been away from her that long? Sometimes he forgot Kia wasn't from Earth.

"Hey, Mom, I think I'll drop by to see Becca in the morning. You were right about Kia not looking so good. Maybe I should get her home."

They said their good-byes and he hurried to the elevator. When he saw Kia downstairs, leaning against the waist-high wall, he breathed a sigh of relief. She turned and smiled after he called her name. Maybe she *had* just needed a little air. She looked better than she had upstairs.

"They're doing all right?"

"Fine. Are you ready to go back to the apartment?"

"Yes."

But she was silent on the way to the car. They got in and he started it up, turning the radio to a classical station. Maybe the soothing sounds of Chopin would relax her.

His mind stayed busy as he pulled into the steady flow of traffic. But as soon as he hit the expressway, he had a little more time to think about what he needed to do.

He had to tell Kia about her locator.

The car wasn't the place, though. As soon as they were in the apartment, he would tell her.

And she would probably leave.

He drew in a deep breath. What if . . . No, there

weren't any what ifs. They'd had fun together. But it was over now. His life would go on as before.

"The baby was really okay?"

Some of his tension eased.

"Nick?"

He glanced her way. "The baby has all the parts he's supposed to have. Becca and Jack will make great parents."

She was quiet for a moment. "Someday you'll have your own child. I think you will also make a good parent."

His gut tightened. "Someday." She was ending their relationship. The way she'd said he would make a good parent. Not *they* would make good parents. That told him everything he needed to know.

He wouldn't make the same mistake his parents had made and get serious about a doomed relationship. Maybe his way was better after all.

He pulled in the garage and parked, glad the conversation was over. He didn't want to think about getting married or having kids.

Silence reigned as they rode the elevator to his floor, each lost in their own thoughts. Nick felt as if he was walking toward the electric chair. All he needed was a priest to offer the last rites.

Chapter 23

As they went inside the apartment, *Nick knew it was the time to tell Kia. He shut the door and turned around.* His mouth opened, but the words wouldn't come as he watched her slip her coat off and lay it across the back of the sofa.

When she turned around, their gazes met and locked. Something he couldn't really describe passed between them. A need? A longing. Maybe she'd already sensed the time for her to leave was nearing because she moved toward him, wrapping her arms around his neck, pulling his face close to hers.

"Make love to me," she said.

For a moment, his brain clouded. A reprieve. He envisioned slowly stripping off her clothes and sinking deep inside her hot body.

It was an effort, but he managed to restrain himself. "I have to tell you something. Weldon . . ."

"Shh." She placed two fingers on his lips. "It'll wait until morning. I want you."

Maybe it would wait until morning.

He lowered his mouth to hers. God, she tasted so frigging sweet. Her tongue slid across his, sending spasms of heat down his body. He ran his hands through her hair, pulling her closer. The rain-forest fragrance of shampoo wafted to him, mixing with the scent of their need.

She slipped her hands beneath his shirt, touching, caressing his back, lightly scraping with her fingernails. Shivers of pleasure ran down his spine.

They were both panting when he ended the kiss and stepped back. "If I don't slow down I'm going to rip off your clothes and take you right here, right now."

Her eyes half closed. "Would that be a bad thing?"

He almost did exactly that, but stopped at the last second. "I want this night to last."

She turned and sauntered toward the bedroom. Now what was she up to? At the doorway, she turned and crooked her finger. Oh, yeah, she learned real fast.

He immediately followed.

Once inside the bedroom, she went to one of the bags from the clothing store and brought out the bottles she'd said Sherry the store clerk had talked her into purchasing. He'd forgotten about them. Apparently, Kia hadn't.

"She said to light the candles. They smell good." She innocently smiled. "You wanted to make the night last, make it special, right?"

"Every night with you is special." He took the candles and lit them. Their cinnamon fragrance soon filled the room, along with a soft warm glow. When he turned back around, Kia had set the bottles on the dresser.

He reached over and turned his CD player on. The music was something he'd picked up when he was in New Orleans on vacation a few years ago. It was a throbbing, sensual beat that touched deep down into a person's very soul. The kind of music that set a person's inhibitions free. The kind of music that made a person wild with sexual desire.

Kia began to sway to the music. He sat down on the bed, leaned back on his elbow, and watched her.

The top she wore had a front zipper. She slowly tugged it down and slipped it off. Again, she wasn't wearing a bra. His mouth watered. Her impromptu striptease was amateurish . . . and sexy as hell.

She raised her hands, running them through her hair, letting the silky tresses fall in disarray. Lights and shadows touched her, kissing her naked skin. Slowly she slid her hands over her breasts, tweaking the nipples, then moving her hands downward.

This would be a good time to breathe.

He slowly drew air into his lungs, not wanting to draw attention to himself. No, he wanted all the focus to be on Kia. The way she trailed her fingernails lightly over her abdomen. The way she swayed to the music, completely absorbed by the beat, the sound.

She pushed her slacks over her hips and down her legs in one smooth movement. When she straightened, all that was left was a black thong. A very skimpy black thong. His pulse quickened.

She looked at him, hooked her thumbs in the elastic, and slowly tugged the tiny scrap of silk downward, exposing the dark curls that covered her mound. His dick throbbed with the need to fill her body, enclosing him in a cocoon of intense heat.

As she closed the distance between them, he stood. Tugged his T-shirt over his head and tossed it to the side. He didn't waste time stripping out of his jeans and briefs. They landed on top of his shirt on her side of the bed.

While he was removing his clothes, she watched, not making a move to touch him. Hell, she didn't have to. Her eyes said it all. Telling him exactly how much she wanted him. It was a hell of a turn-on.

She picked up one of the bottles of oil. "What does it do?"

"Let's find out." He untwisted the cap, which he tossed on top of his dresser before pouring a little of the oil in the palm of his hand and setting the bottle back down.

"This is very exciting. I never had to oil Adam-4."

He frowned, not really liking the fact that she had a life-size vibrator waiting for her on Nerak, but it did make him think of something he'd been meaning to ask. "Why do you call him Adam-4?"

"Adam-1 got too close to an incinerating machine and melted into a shiny blob, Adam-2 overheated, and Adam-3 wore out. Now I have Adam-4."

"So are you going to get me overheated?"

Her gaze slid sensuously over him. "Yes, I think I will."

He grinned as he began to massage the oil onto her shoulders, making her skin slick. The more he massaged it in, the more it warmed on his hands.

"That feels good," she moaned, arching toward him. "It heats my skin, making me feel hot all over."

How could he resist her breasts when she pushed them right at him? He reached for the bottle again and slowly poured the oil down her front.

She gasped, her eyes flying open. "Now, what will I put on you?" She eyed the empty bottle.

"Oh, I think we can find a way to share it." He pulled her down onto the bed with him so that she landed on top.

She laughed, sliding up and kissing him on the lips. Cinnamon. Sweet and sassy.

"Are you having fun smearing me with oil?"

She nodded and began to slide lower. She flicked

her tongue across one nipple. It beaded to a nub. Her gaze met his. Her smile was more than a little wicked. He couldn't wait to see what she'd do next.

She moved up a few inches, rubbing her sex against his erection.

"Oh yeah, baby, just like that." Lights swirled above his head. Fiery reds, passionate blues, and hot pinks. Ah, yes, this was good.

She inched her way down his body, nipping and kissing his chest, his abdomen. He held his breath. She licked down his length before drawing him into her mouth. He arched his hips; the breath he'd been holding rushed out.

The lights danced above him. Heat spread through him like fire through dry brush. "Ah, man, that's it." She sucked him in deeper. "Right there. Ah, damn."

She nibbled and licked at him while massaging his balls at the same time. For a novice, she learned damned fast, but if he didn't stop her right now, the night would end a hell of a lot sooner than either one of them wanted.

"Baby, you have to stop."

"Don't want to."

She slid his foreskin down and licked coming back up. He drew in a sharp breath. His eyes fogged over.

"No, baby, you have to stop," he managed to say again, then tried another tactic. "I want to kiss your sex, run my tongue up and down your clit, and suck on you."

She paused—long enough for him to lean forward and slide her slick body up his. Damn, even then he almost lost it.

No, it wasn't going to end this soon. He wanted to taste every delicious inch of her body until she begged him to bury himself deep inside her.

When she was on Nerak and she looked around

for sexual relief, he wanted her to remember him. Damn it, he didn't want her to forget about this night. Not ever.

"I think you tricked me." She eyed him.

"I think you're right." He cupped her breast, massaging before tugging on her nipple with his thumb and forefinger.

"That feels nice," she moaned.

"Only nice? I guess I'll have to do better." He rolled her onto her back and licked across one nipple before sucking it inside his mouth. He continued to massage her other breast.

"I like the way you taste," he said as he pulled back. "Cinnamon was a good choice of the flavored oil." He palmed one breast. "And I like the way you feel. The way you moan when I do this." He tugged on her nipple again, rolling it between his fingers. She didn't disappoint. A moan escaped from between her parted lips.

He moved to his knees, staring down at her. Fucking fantastic. He moved to the end of the bed. "Open your legs for me. I want to taste you."

She spread her legs without hesitation. He started at her ankles, running his hands up her legs, up her thighs, then down again.

She whimpered.

"Soon," he breathed. "Just feel the sensations and know that I'll be tasting all of you."

He moved closer, resting his knees on the bed, between her legs. She was so damn sexy lying on the bed wide open. It was all he could do to keep from plunging into her hot body. She would have an orgasm, but he wasn't through looking at her, wasn't through tasting her.

He dragged his finger through her silky, oil-damp curls. She arched toward him.

"Please, Nick."

"Please what? This?" He lowered his mouth to her sex, running his tongue over the lips, then the fleshy middle. Sweet. Cinnamon . . . and Kia. A heady combination.

She whimpered. He knew she was getting close. No more torture. He sucked her inside his mouth, his hands sliding beneath her buttocks to bring her closer, to hold her tighter against his mouth.

She cried out, her body convulsing as the first wave hit her. He continued to taste her for a few seconds more, then grabbed a condom and slipped it on.

He thrust inside her once, twice. She wrapped her legs around him and he sank deeper inside her heat. Their ragged breathing filled the room. Lights flashed, candles flickered. Again and again he thrust. Harder and harder.

She arched her back. He watched the expression on her face when she came. Saw the rapture and then the air around him seemed to explode as his orgasm grasped him.

He collapsed to the bed with a low groan.

When his world righted itself there was only one thought running through his mind. How the hell was he ever going to be able to watch her walk away?

The next morning Kia rolled to her back and stretched. Sex with Nick got better each time. No, he was right. It wasn't just sex. They'd made love and created a bond.

But now it was time to break it.

The room swayed, then righted itself at the thought of leaving him. She closed her eyes tight against the pain. Never in all her years had she felt anything that hurt this badly.

But she could never be what Nick needed in a life mate, and he deserved the best. And she'd figured out that when he used protection, it stopped her from having a baby. It was for the best but it left an emptiness inside her.

Small barks reminded her the puppies would want out to play. She glanced at Nick. He was still sleeping. She eased from the bed, trying to be as quiet as she could, trying to pretend her heart wasn't breaking.

But as soon as she stood, Kia planted her foot on Nick's pants and whatever he had in his pocket. When she moved his pants out of the way, the object slipped out.

Her locator.

She could feel the color drain from her face. She thought they would at least have a few days together. Leaning over, she picked the device up and flipped it open. The screen came on. So Weldon had fixed it. It would seem they only had hours left.

A spurt of anger burned through her, making her wonder if it was because he hadn't told her or because it was time for her to return home.

"I was going to tell you when I got home from the station." Nick spoke quietly, as if he'd read her thoughts.

Her anger evaporated at the sound of apology in his voice. "But Becca had her baby," she said, filling in what he'd left unsaid.

"And when we got back to the apartment . . ."

". . . I wanted to make love."

"You're not angry?"

How could she be? Not when they had precious little time together. She shook her head. To be angry would be to dismiss what they'd shared last night, and she would never do that.

"I'll insert Mala's DNA." She stood, going to the other room and retrieving her satchel. It only took a few seconds to process.

Nick joined her in the next room.

"Do you know these coordinates?" She handed him the locator.

He took the locator and went to his desk. "I have a map here somewhere." He searched in several drawers before he brought one out. After looking once more at the locator, he scanned the map. "That's going to be close to San Antonio. About four hours from here." His expression was solemn.

The time frame would be close. "You can take me there?"

He nodded. "I'll shower and get dressed." Just as he reached the door, he turned. "Don't go. Stay here. With me."

His words startled her. For a moment, she imagined spending the rest of her life on Earth, living with Nick, loving Nick—having his children.

Fear ran through her quick and deep. She wasn't nearly the warrior Earth women were. "I can't." She drew in a shaky breath.

He left the room without saying another word.

She went in the kitchen. The puppies immediately began to bark and bounce around. She picked one up, holding it close to her face, breathing the puppy smell.

Life on Earth was painful. But she would never regret leaving Nerak and knowing Nick.

She put the puppy on the floor and lifted the others out. They ran around her feet a few times, then set off exploring the apartment. They were getting bolder. They resembled each other, yet each one had its own personality. She wondered what they would be like when they got older.

Thinking about it would only make it worse, but it was so hard not to.

Chapter 24

Sam booked a small motel room for the night in the town nearest to the area where Hank said he'd picked up Kia. Washboard was just a small dot on the Texas map, but it had a motel. He still didn't know exactly what he was doing there.

What if this was a wild goose chase? He shook off his dark premonitions. Nick wasn't the only one with a gut instinct. Sam just didn't trust his like he should. He'd always preferred to look at the facts—go by the book.

For the first time in his life, he didn't have a plan. He wouldn't say that scared the hell out of him, but it made him feel a tad uncomfortable.

If he did find Mala, then he didn't know exactly what he was going to do. He only knew he had to help Nick. Sometimes a person just had to take a leap of faith.

He stepped from his room, tugged his coat a little closer to his body, and headed toward the small café the manager of the motel had recommended last night. As long as they had a pot of strong coffee, he didn't care what they had in the way of food. He needed caffeine and lots of it.

But as soon as he walked inside, he knew he'd be

ordering something to eat, too. The smells were just too tantalizing. He grabbed a stool at the counter and picked up a menu.

"I bet you'll be wanting coffee," the waitress said as she carried a glass carafe over. She wore a warm smile and a starched white uniform.

"You guessed right." He turned over the cup that was in front of him and she filled it. The rich flavor wafted to his nose. He closed his eyes, inhaling the full-flavored aroma. He was addicted to coffee. He knew it and he didn't care. Hell, it wasn't like he had that many vices.

After adding cream and sugar, he took a drink. Good wake-up coffee. He returned her smile with one of his own. "This is the best coffee I've ever tasted."

Her grin only got wider. "We have the best biscuits and gravy you'll ever eat, too. Add a couple of slices of our hickory-smoked slab bacon and fresh eggs and you'll think you've died and gone to heaven."

How could he resist?

While she turned in his order, he looked around. Two men wearing overalls and heavy coats came in arguing about the rising price of gas.

They stopped talking long enough for the waitress to pour their coffee and take their order.

A couple of cowboys were perched on stools farther down talking about the dance they were at last night. Sam wondered if he should ask them if they knew a woman around here by the name of Mala. It wasn't a name one heard every day. If she was here, he'd know it by the end of the day.

"So, where you headed, mister?"

He glanced at the waitress's nametag. Matilda. "I'm actually sticking around for a few days."

"Business?"

"Personal."

"In Washboard?" Her eyebrows rose almost to her hairline.

It was a small town. Matilda probably knew everyone. "I'm looking for someone."

Her eyes narrowed. "You a cop?"

"Yeah, you going to hold it against me?"

"Depends."

"The person I'm looking for isn't in any kind of trouble. Her cousin is searching for her. I'm only trying to help out a friend."

"So who's the woman you're hunting?"

"Order up!"

"Hold that thought." She went to the window where the cook had placed a plate of food and brought it over to him.

Before he could ask her about Mala, a group of people came into the diner. By the time he'd finished his breakfast, customers had filled almost every booth and table. He had a feeling he wouldn't get a very warm reception if he started asking questions. He knew how small-town people reacted to strangers asking questions.

He stood, dropped a tip on the counter, then went to the cashier. A young girl stood behind the cash register taking money. No one else was around. He handed her the ticket Matilda had slid toward him.

"Was everything okay?" she asked.

"It was very good."

She smiled as she handed him the change. He pocketed it, but at the last minute asked, "Can you tell me where Mala lives?"

Confusion spread across her face. "Sorry, my family just moved here."

"No problem." Damn, he was hoping she might've been able to tell him. If he didn't find Mala by afternoon, he'd drop back by and talk to Matilda.

As he stepped outside, he glanced down Main Street. There wasn't much to the place. It looked like most small Texas towns. A few shops with the family name emblazoned on the window or hanging from a wooden sign, a couple of closed stores. Probably gone out of business because of the superstores.

And a boutique.

Kia had been drawn to the store in Dallas. Maybe Mala frequented this one. He'd give it a shot.

He wandered down to the store, stopping at the window display before he went inside. Candles, a dress on a mannequin, fancy perfume bottles. Not exactly the type of store a man would go into. Maybe he'd tell the clerk he was looking for a gift.

He pushed the door open, and a bell tinkled above his head as he went inside. Sweet-smelling candles and potpourri assaulted his senses as he glanced around at all the frilly doodads. He suddenly felt like a bull in a china shop.

A curtain at the back opened and a man came toward him.

"Hello, I'm Barton. How can I help you?"

The last thing Sam had expected was a man. He quickly assessed him. Every hair in place, not a wrinkle in his suit. Some women would probably say he was good looking. He had a feeling the guy leaned toward the other side of the fence. Whatever floated his boat. He needed information. That was all.

"Yeah, maybe you can. I'm looking for a woman who goes by the name of Mala. You know her?"

"I tell you, they're making their move," Darla told Slava.

"Don't get too close or they'll know we're tailing

them." He shifted in the passenger seat, scooted it back, then stretched his feet out as best he could in Darla's little blue compact.

Darla gripped the steering wheel. He acted as if he was in charge. Yeah, right, that'd be the day. Why the hell had Yuri insisted Slava stay with her every second? She wasn't a damn baby-sitter.

Crap, that was probably it. Yuri needed someone to watch Slava so he'd stay out of trouble. Things were not going as planned. Now she had to give Yuri a cut of anything she got. Dumb idea bringing Slava's uncle into the equation. Now she was hung in the middle.

"You're getting too close again."

She ground her teeth together. "And you're getting my floor mats filthy. You couldn't have cleaned the bottom of your boots?" She sniffed, her nose wrinkling as a foul odor worked its way up to her nose. "And it smells like you stepped in dog crap."

"Sorry. Had beans for supper last night." He shifted again. "I didn't think you'd notice."

Ugh! Gross! She hit the button and rolled down the window on his side.

"Hey, it's cold."

"Live with it," she growled.

Was this what her life had come to? Tailing a cop and a princess with the gassy nephew of a Russian mafia leader? She must have really pissed off someone in her last life. Her next one better be a whole lot better.

Candace picked up her recorder and held it close to her mouth. "They're rolling down the window." She'd been tailing the man and woman for an hour now. They were probably doing drugs. If they threw a reefer out the window, she'd stop and pick it up. DNA.

She'd started out tailing Nick and his woman friend. She hadn't planned on it, but when she'd dropped by his apartment to conduct an impromptu home investigation and saw Nick and the woman hauling carriers down to his car and loading them in the backseat, she knew something was up.

Ha! Did they think she'd be fooled into believing there were dogs in the carriers? Four of them? No one was stupid enough to own four dogs and live in a tiny apartment. Nope, she wasn't born yesterday.

And that was why she was an Internal Affairs investigator. She knew a criminal when she saw one. Yeah, she'd suspected Nick for a long time. Ever since he'd brushed off her advances in the early days of her career, she'd known something was wrong with him.

What she hadn't expected was for Nick and the woman to leave town. Something was up. She'd stake her career on it. Hell, she *was* staking her career on it. Surely, the captain would understand why she had to miss work this afternoon.

This was big.

It hadn't taken her long to realize someone else was tailing Nick and his lady friend.

She'd hung back and let them get between her car and Nick's. As they passed, she covertly glanced at the woman. A very familiar woman from her days working as a street cop. She'd arrested Darla a few times. Mostly small stuff: prostitution, breaking and entering. Never anything really big.

Now that she thought about it, Darla had some kind of tie to the Russian mafia. She occasionally ran with some slob whose uncle was reported to be one of the higher-ups, if not Mr. Big himself.

Very interesting.

She could almost smell a promotion in the air.

She grabbed the recorder again. "They're rolling up the window. I don't know what the significance of rolling it down was, but I plan to sniff out every little detail."

Weldon's hands were sweating. What was he doing? He should be at his desk working. But no, he was running after the alien.

And apparently, so were a lot of other people. It had taken him well over an hour to figure it out. Nick and Kia were in the first car. After them was some woman and a man. And right in front of him was another woman. He knew they were following Nick and Kia because they never passed them. When Nick had stopped at a gas station, so had the other two vehicles. He hadn't gotten a good enough look to see who they were.

Why were they following them?

Not that Kia wasn't worth following. It didn't matter that she was an alien. Her looks were enough to tempt any man. Weldon's sigh was long and deep. He didn't stand a chance. It was obvious she was attracted to Nick, and why wouldn't she be? Nick was a nice-looking guy.

He jerked upright in the seat. Not that he teetered on the fence or anything. He knew exactly which side of the yard he was on.

Just as quickly, his shoulders slumped. But a lot of people at the station probably thought he wasn't interested in girls. He didn't date, not that he wouldn't if he had the chance.

With one finger, he shoved his glasses higher up the bridge of his nose.

He would date Kia in a heartbeat. That's why he'd gone back to Nick's apartment. He wanted to see her again, even if he didn't stand a chance. She was an alien, for Pete's sake. How many chances did one get in their lifetime to actually meet a visitor from another planet?

As soon as he got back to his apartment after meeting Kia, he'd sat down and made a long list of things he wanted to ask her. When he wasn't at work, he'd fiddled around with the locator. It took him longer to get the damn thing apart than it had anything. But it was a magnificent piece of technology. What he wouldn't give to travel to her planet.

"You're a fool," he muttered.

It had taken a few hours to realize as soon as he gave Nick the locator, Nick would in turn give it to Kia. Kia would then find this cousin of hers and they'd zip back to their planet.

What he was planning was pretty idiotic, but then, what kind of life did he have on Earth? It couldn't be any worse on Nerak. He only had to figure out how he could stow away on Kia's spaceship without being discovered.

Chapter 25

Kia watched the passing scenery: the gently rolling hills, the trees. When had the landscape changed? Had they been traveling that long? She looked up and saw how far Earth's sun had traveled across the blue sky.

Time was slipping away.

Her gaze moved to Nick. He'd barely spoken a word the whole trip. She hadn't meant to hurt him, but she couldn't stay. How would she survive on Earth? She was a warrior in name only. She'd never fought any battles. The one in the bar didn't really count.

No, Nick needed someone stronger.

"I think we must be getting close." He nodded toward the illuminated dial on his instrument panel. "We've been traveling almost four hours."

As his words sank in, she found it hard to take a deep breath. She would never see him again.

"You okay?" he asked.

She nodded as she reached for her locator. "I'm fine." But she wasn't. She didn't think she'd ever be fine again. But this was a sacrifice she had to make.

"You haven't changed your mind, have you?"

Was that hope in his voice or wishful thinking on her part? Had Nick thought about their relationship and realized she was right about it being time for her to go?

She frowned. He hadn't even mentioned her staying again. Only that one time. He could have argued a little more. At least tried to convince her to stay. Begging would've been nice. It might have at least convinced her that he cared.

She was so pathetic. It must be the influence of having lived on Earth. Even more of a reason for her to return.

Besides, her skills might one day be needed on Nerak. She wasn't as experienced as Nick, but she had displayed proficiency in other areas more suited to her training.

A thread of fear trembled through her. Having someone slice open your abdomen with a knife to remove a baby was not part of her job description.

They passed a sign that had Washboard written across it. She sat straighter in her seat and glanced at her locator. "We're getting close."

Soon she would be with Mala, and that was all that should matter to her.

But it didn't. She squeezed her eyes closed. She had no choice. She only wished it didn't have to hurt so damn much.

"This must be the town where they're going to make the drop," Darla said as she slowed, taking the same turn Nick and the woman had taken. She'd been careful not to stay on his bumper, letting other cars get between them. Now she'd have to be even more careful. Washboard was small, easier to notice if someone was tailing you.

"There's a place to eat," Slava pointed out. "I'm hungry. Can we stop?"

Idiot! She took a couple of slow, deep breaths and reminded herself that Slava's uncle would probably torture and kill her if something happened to his precious nephew. "If we stop, we'll lose them."

"Oh, yeah."

He reached into his backpack, but rather than pull out a candy bar or something else to eat, he brought out a gun.

"Look what my uncle gave me." He swung the barrel toward her.

She swerved, almost hitting a parked car. "Jesus! Put that damn thing away." Her hands shook as she aimed the car straight down the road again. "What the hell did you bring that for?"

His eyebrows slanted down and for a moment he looked a hell of a lot like his uncle. Ah crap, now she'd made him mad. This wasn't good. When he was riled he'd just as soon shoot a person as look at them. And since he was the one holding the gun . . .

"Why you always treating me like this?" he asked. "Haven't I always been there for you?"

No, he hadn't, but she wasn't about to tell him that. "You just startled me, that's all. I didn't know your uncle had given you a gun."

He shrugged. "Isn't much. Only a twenty-two, but if you shoot a person just right you can kill them."

"We might need it, but for now let's keep it put up. Okay?"

"Sure, Darla. You know I'd do anything for you."

Except get a brain. Slava had the IQ of a wood chip.

She glanced in her rearview mirror. There were two cars behind her. For a country road, this one seemed to have a lot of traffic. Odd. Maybe she'd missed a garage sale sign along the way or something.

The car in front of her slowed, then turned down

a private road. This was it. They'd reached their destination. She continued past the road, not wanting to draw attention to herself, and took the next right. The two cars behind her didn't even slow down.

As soon as they passed, she turned around and went back out to the main road. She glanced to the right and then the left, making sure it was clear before turning down the same road Nick had taken.

She set her foot on the brake, easing around a corner, then slammed her foot down when she saw the small house. Nick and his lady friend had stopped right in front of it and were getting out.

This was it—the drop!

She quickly backed up. There were trees she could hide the car behind. As soon as she was parked where no one could spot them, she glanced at Slava. He probably wouldn't stay behind even if she told him it was to guard the car. Then again, his muscle might come in handy.

"We're going to sneak up to the house," she told him.

"Covertly."

She raised an eyebrow.

"I heard that on the cartoon station when I was watching *Commando*. It means real quiet-like."

"Yes, I know what it means." She started to get out, but at the last minute hesitated. "Bring your backpack." She only hoped she was making the right decision. The gun might come in handy, but she'd have to make sure she was the one holding it.

Candace pulled to the shoulder, letting the car behind her pass. This stretch of road seemed awfully popular. Coincidence? Maybe. The car behind her had kept going, though. Damn, she'd been so concerned with the vehicles in front of her that she'd never thought about making sure she wasn't being tailed.

A mud-caked pickup came lumbering down the road. When it was even with her, it came to a gear-grinding halt and a man rolled down the window.

"You having trouble, lady?"

"Just stretching my legs," she lied. She nodded toward the road Nick had turned down. "Who lives down that road?"

The old farmer looked behind him. "That would be the sheriff and his wife. You in some kind of trouble?"

"No, I was just curious. I might want to buy some land in the area."

"Might as well get your eye off that ranch. It's been in his family for a long time. I don't think he'll ever sell it. He'd do whatever he had to, to keep it."

"I see."

"Now Jenkins has his place up for sale. Check with the real estate office back in Washboard. It's a right nice piece of property."

"Thanks, I'll do that."

As he drove off, Candy looked toward the road that ran to the sheriff's ranch. *He'd do anything to keep it in his family. Hmm, interesting.* And if he fell on hard times? Then what would he do? Surely the sheriff of a small town couldn't bring in much money. Not enough to run a ranch. Just how many bad cops would turn up in this investigation?

She climbed back into her car, wondering if she should call someone. But who? Suddenly, she realized she might just be out of her depth. Not to mention out of her jurisdiction. She'd come too far to turn back now, though.

She started her car and made a U-turn. She'd find a place to conceal her vehicle and at least see what was going on. Suddenly, proving herself didn't seem all that damn important.

She drew in a deep breath.

But bringing a bad cop to justice did.

Weldon waited until the farmer passed, then turned around and went back the way he'd come. When he was close to where Nick had turned in, he pulled off to the side of the road.

From what he could figure out, there were two other vehicles between him and Nick. Had they found out about Kia? Maybe they were reporters looking for a story. Whoever they were, he didn't like the feeling he was getting.

After cutting off the ignition, he got out of the car, making sure the doors were locked.

Did Nick even know he was being tailed? It was times like this when Weldon wished he knew how to use a gun. The basics were all he could muster—as in aim and pull the trigger. He doubted he could even hit the broad side of a barn.

Now wasn't the time to berate himself about enjoying the workings of a computer much better than firing guns. He wasn't like Nick and he never would be.

He stumbled across the rusty metal pipes of a cattle guard, hanging on to the side so he didn't slip between the cracks, and wondered again why he'd followed them this far. The ones tailing them were probably up to no good—and he wasn't hero material.

Crouching down, he made his way to the cover of trees . . . and almost ran into one of the cars that had been tailing Nick and Kia.

Sweat broke out on his forehead. *Oh, crap, why*

*would they hide their car if they were just out for a
drive or something?* His legs began to shake.

"Hands above your head," a voice commanded
from behind him.

He jerked his hands above his head and squeezed
his eyes shut. *Please, please don't kill me!* But the
words wouldn't come out of his mouth. He hated the
sight of blood—especially his own. "Don't . . . don't
shoot me," he finally managed to squeeze out between his stiff lips.

"I will if you don't keep your voice down."

The rustle of underbrush told him she'd moved
in front of him. He opened one eye.

Huh?

"Candace?"

Her eyes narrowed. "Weldon?"

What was the woman he'd been lusting after ever
since he joined the department doing out here?

"Weldon Cooper, yes."

Her eyes widened. "You look different. You're the
computer guru, right?"

She remembered. "Yeah." And he guessed he did
look a little different. He'd worn a pair of jeans, a ca-
sual shirt, and a blue baseball cap. Gone was the white
lab coat he usually wore.

He started to lower his arms, but she grabbed her
gun with both hands.

"Keep those arms up."

The way she stood with her legs slightly apart and
pointing the gun at him—damn if it didn't give him
a hard-on. He always did have a thing for tough females.

"I'm one of the good guys," he said.

"Then why are you here?" Her eyes narrowed on
him.

He swallowed past the lump in his throat. "I was following Nick and Kia. She's not from here . . . and I wanted to ask her questions about her . . . country." That sounded so lame. There was no way she was going to buy his story.

"Russia?"

"Huh? No, not Russia."

"Do you know anything about drugs?" She pushed her glasses up higher on the bridge of her nose.

Why would she ask that? "Yeah, a little. You pick up stuff when you work at a police station."

"That's not what I meant. Nick . . . drugs . . . Russian mafia? How is he tied in with them?"

His eyes widened and his mouth dropped open, then snapped shut. He would've laughed at the absurdity of it all except he made it a policy never to laugh when a woman was holding a gun. At least he was going to make it one now.

"He isn't tied to the mafia. Is that why you're here? You think he's a crooked cop?"

"Yeah, I think he's guilty as charged. Why else would they be tailing him if he didn't have something they wanted?"

His gaze swung up the road. "That's who's been following them? Ah, shit."

"You didn't know?"

He shook his head.

She relaxed her stance, studying him. "Don't ask me why, but I believe you. Maybe because you've never had any complaints against you."

He sighed with relief and lowered his arms.

"But that doesn't mean I trust you."

He jerked his arms back up in the air.

She rolled her eyes. "Lower your arms. But don't try anything funny."

He nodded, then thought of something. "Aren't you out of your jurisdiction?"

"Don't remind me." She holstered her gun.

Weldon couldn't resist reaching forward and brushing a leaf from her hair. When she jerked her hand up, their fingers touched. Her face took on a rosy hue.

"You had a leaf stuck in your hair."

His glance lowered and he saw the way her nipples were poking against her shirt. Oh, Lord, he'd made her nipples hard. Had he ever made a woman's nipples hard? He didn't think so. His experiences with sex weren't always the stuff movies were made of.

"Would you like to go out when we get back home?" he blurted out. Had he really asked her out on a date? Some of Nick must've rubbed off on him. Which wasn't such a bad thing.

"I have a job to do." She whirled around and started through the trees.

"You didn't answer my question," he said as he followed.

"I'm trying to get proof Nick is a dirty cop. What part of *working* don't you understand?"

He'd blown any chance he had with Candace. *Way to go, dummy*. Had he really thought a sexy, vibrant woman like her would go out with him?

"Yes."

He looked up. "What?"

"Yes, I'll go out with you."

He grinned.

He followed her through the brush and around trees as they made their way toward the house. He suddenly felt like he could do anything he set his mind to.

Oh, yeah, he was the man!

Chapter 26

Kia barely managed to lift her feet as she followed Nick up the steps. Her heart was pounding inside her chest so hard that she barely heard him tap on the door.

He studied her for a moment. "This is your cousin. You don't have to be worried or afraid. Everything will be fine." He squeezed her hand.

Is that what he thought? That she was worried and afraid? Suddenly, the truth hit her.

I am worried and afraid.

He was right, but she refused to let him witness her weakness. She squared her shoulders and looked him right in the eye. "I am a warrior. I fear nothing."

Yet when the door opened, she stepped behind him and held her breath.

"I didn't hear anyone drive up. I was in the back. Can I help you?"

For a moment Kia couldn't do anything, couldn't have moved even if her life depended on it. This wasn't her cousin! Or was it?

The woman standing at the door looked like her cousin. She sounded like her cousin. But she was different. Kia's gaze moved slowly over the woman. She had her hair cut in a short, bouncy style and she wore the jeans that Nick seemed to favor and a wrinkled red T-shirt.

Kia tentatively stepped from behind Nick, not feeling at all warriorlike.

"Mala?"

"Kia?" Mala's face drained of color.

Kia could only nod. Yes, this was Mala. This was her best friend, her cousin, and she'd missed her terribly and she didn't care what she wore. It was as if a band squeezed her heart. This was good!

Mala pushed the door open the rest of the way and threw her arms around Kia. Kia held her close, closing her eyes and relishing what had been missing in her life.

It was as if they hadn't seen each other in eons—it was as if they'd never parted.

"Come in, don't stand out there in the cold." Mala wiped the tears out of her eyes. "You have to tell me everything. How did you manage to get off Nerak? I thought you said you would never leave." She sniffed. "I didn't think I would ever see you again."

Kia's eyes were also damp. She had to blink really fast so she could see and not stumble in the house. Oh, but it was so good to have found Mala.

"I came the same way as you—in one of the older-model crafts. It was the worst experience of my life. I thought it was going to burn up when I entered Earth's atmosphere, but all I did was crash into a tree. I followed your coordinates exactly."

"Then it was the same tree I crashed into."

"I admit, I didn't think much of you after I landed. I was quite shaken by the experience."

Mala chuckled. "Yes, I remember my own landing."

The euphoria of the initial meeting was wearing

off. Kia tried to tell herself it was just the excitement winding down, but as she glanced around the room, she felt like a stranger, like she was once again on the outside of the circle looking in.

What was happening? What was different between them?

Mala's home was warm and cozy and it smelled like the cinnamon candles she and Nick had used. Everything looked inviting, but something just wasn't right.

Nick helped her off with her coat, then removed his and laid them across a chair.

"This is Nick," she introduced. For some strange reason she wanted to put off telling Mala that she was here to take her home. Mala seemed so . . . so comfortable in her surroundings.

"Hello, Nick."

"Hi, Mala, I've heard a lot about you."

"I swear none of it's true." She laughed.

Was this really Mala? She talked like someone from Earth. Her cousin had changed. She practically glowed. Realization dawned. Mala was gone. In her place was an earthling.

The truth hit Kia hard.

Mala wasn't going back to Nerak. Sadness and pain ripped through her like the sharp, biting wind outside the door.

"What happened?" she asked. "You've changed so much."

"I found what I was looking for." Mala's face shone with more than the general contentment that was on the faces of Nerakian women.

"Sheriff?"

She nodded. "Yes, and he gave me something very precious. Follow me and I'll show you."

They walked to another room. In it were two tiny

beds with bars. Kia tentatively stepped farther inside, then peered over the top rail. She jumped back as soon as she saw the baby.

"*You* had this baby?" Kia asked.

Mala grinned, pointing toward the other bed. "And this one. Twin boys."

The two babies were a part of Mala, born from her womb. Kia eased forward again, hesitantly reaching her hand forward and touching the baby's head. So warm! And his hair was soft and silky.

Suddenly, the baby stretched and yawned, then smiled. The tiniest little curve upward of his lips. Then he burped.

Carbonation.

She stepped to the other bed and peered over the rail. The baby opened his eyes and looked right at her, and then he smiled! Her heart swelled. Oh, the baby frowned and his bottom lip puckered. His arms waved in the air.

"I don't think this one is happy." Kia looked at Mala.

"He's probably wanting his pacifier."

She started forward but an object moved quickly across the bed and popped into his mouth.

"Telekinetic." Mala bit her bottom lip. "I think that might cause some problems when he gets older."

"You have done well, cousin," Kia said with much awe.

"My family is very precious to me."

"Did they . . ." She swallowed past the lump in her throat. "Did they cut open your stomach?" How had Mala survived? She didn't have the strength a warrior had. And yet, she still lived. Kia's self-esteem plummeted.

Mala frowned. "They gave me medication for the

pain. It wasn't so bad. And no, they didn't cut me open. Ugh! That sounds barbaric! Who told you that's how it was done?"

And that's the moment Nick realized what Kia had been thinking. Of course she would take him literally. Damn, she must've been horrified.

"Becca didn't feel when they cut her open." He looked at Mala. "Becca's my sister and she just had a baby."

"They didn't tie her down and cut her open?" Kia asked, some of the color returning to her face.

"No, sweetheart. They gave her something so she wouldn't feel a thing."

"But I thought . . ."

"I'm sorry you were so scared." He pulled her into his arms and held her close. No wonder she wanted to return as soon as possible.

Mala raised her eyebrows and looked first at Kia, then Nick, with more than a little speculation shining in her eyes. He didn't care what she thought. Or maybe he did, but it didn't matter. This was probably the last time he would get to hold Kia in his arms.

"I wasn't scared," Kia told him as she stepped from his arms and the warmth he'd felt seconds earlier was suddenly gone. "I'm a warrior and we don't get scared." She quickly looked at Mala.

"It's okay, even I've had the crap scared out of me a time or two," Nick told her.

She straightened, raising one eyebrow. "I assure you I've never lost control of any bodily functions."

He chuckled. "I didn't mean that literally."

She frowned. "Oh."

"You still haven't told me why you traveled to Earth," Mala said. "Or how you met Nick."

Kia took a deep breath. "Nick helped me to find you, and I'm here to bring you home."

Mala worried her bottom lip. "Kia, I . . ." She looked at Nick.

There was a knock on the door. "Mala, you home?" a female called out.

Nick followed the two women out of the room, knowing Kia was never going to be able to convince Mala to return with her. He had a feeling Kia already knew that, though.

Damn, he'd been afraid of this. He hated that Kia was going to be hurt and disappointed. He knew exactly how that felt.

It didn't change a thing, either. Kia would still leave with or without Mala. And she'd stick him with four pups. Hell, what was he going to do with them? They didn't even have names. He could probably call them shithead and they'd come bouncing over.

That reminded him, he'd better get them inside where it was a little warmer.

When they entered the living room, there was a man and a woman he'd never seen before and . . . "Sam?"

Sam looked at his feet, then back up. "You found the right Hank, I see."

Nick glanced at the two strangers, choosing his words carefully. "Weldon was able to fix Kia's . . . GPS device. It led us to this ranch."

"I didn't count on that," Sam admitted.

"So what are you doing here?" Nick could've sworn Sam said he was going to take a vacation.

"I thought if I found Mala, then Kia might go ahead and leave and then . . ." He looked around the room. "I could see you were falling for her and I thought it would be easier if she left sooner than later."

Nick thought of a smart-assed remark about how he didn't know Sam cared so much, but it died on his lips. Sam was watching his back—just like he always did.

"Thanks, I really appreciate it."

"Hello, Kia." The man beside Sam spoke. "You look much the same as the last time I saw you."

The man acted as if he knew Kia. Nick froze. Who the hell was this guy? And how did he know her?

"Hello, Barton," she spoke dryly. "It would seem Earth suits you."

"I thought there weren't any men on Nerak?" Sam said before Nick had a chance.

"There aren't." Mala and Kia spoke at the same time.

"I'm his wife, Carol, and I beg to differ." The short, red-haired woman spoke. "Barton is my husband, and I'd say he's all man—and then some."

Barton smiled. "Thank you."

"That's not what I meant," Mala said. She looked around the room at each person. "Barton is a companion unit."

"With an attitude chip that I notice wasn't damaged on his way to Earth," Kia said sarcastically. "How the hell did you get married? You're not supposed to marry." She was frowning when she looked at Mala. "I warned you about that blasted chip."

"I didn't need him," Mala said. "Carol did. She was having . . . a problem with her ex-husband, and Barton took care of it. I guess they needed each other. They married and now he helps her run the boutique."

"Wait a minute." Nick looked a little closer at Barton. Most women would probably drool over the guy. His frown deepened when he swung his gaze to Kia. "This is what a companion unit looks like?"

She shrugged. "Yeah, pretty much."

"I thought they'd be like a . . . a robot. You know, shiny chrome and . . . and . . ."

"Puhleese . . ." Barton straightened to his full height of six feet. "The earlier models might have been like that, but I assure you I can do everything that you can do—except better." He raised a sardonic eyebrow.

"That's telling them, sweetie," Carol chimed in.

Sam's face lost some of its color. "You're not going to try to make me believe I've spent half the day with a machine and didn't know it?"

"I like to think of myself as technically enabled," Barton told him.

"Don't change the subject." Nick wanted some answers and he wanted them right now. "You never mentioned companion units looked like . . . like . . ." He waved his arm toward the . . . thing. "Like him."

Kia shrugged. "I told you Nerak was far more advanced than Earth. The models you're talking about haven't been around for centuries."

"How the hell are you going to miss me if you have something that looks like . . . like . . ."

"Barton," he said, bowing slightly at the waist.

"Would anyone like something to drink?" Mala looked nervously at everyone. "And I have chocolate, too."

"Chocolate?" Kia chimed in.

"No, we don't want chocolate. We want an explanation." Nick's hands curled into fists, his mouth set in a grim line. "That's why you're in such a hurry to return to Nerak? You want to get back to Adam-4. That's why you asked me if I could vibrate that first time." He nodded toward Barton. "He vibrates, doesn't he?"

He didn't wait for her answer. Why should he? Her answer was written on her face.

"I should've guessed."

Man, how could he be such a fool? She was just like his father. She drained him dry and was ready to move on. No cares, no worries.

Kia stiffened her spine and glared at him. "Adam-4 isn't like Barton. Barton is special."

Barton smiled. "I didn't know you cared."

"I've had enough." Nick really hadn't seen this one coming.

He pushed past Sam and headed out the door, ignoring Kia calling him back. He heard Sam reassure her and heavy footsteps behind him.

"You think you might be making a mistake?" Sam asked, shutting the door behind them.

"Yeah, well, you wanted her gone, so what's the big deal? She'll be out of here before you know it."

"Maybe I was wrong."

"Yeah, you and me both."

"That's not what I meant."

Nick opened the car's back door and reached in for the carriers. "And you can give her the mutts. She bought them, let her deal with them."

But when he brought two of the carriers out, he did so carefully, telling himself it wasn't the pups' fault.

He could feel Sam studying him, assessing. Sam did that a lot, he always had. It was as if he weighed all the information.

"You love her and you know it," Sam finally told him.

Nick looked at his friend. Boy, was he ever wrong this time. "She's an alien. You were the one who kept warning me not to get too close. Okay, I'm ending it."

"No, you're running away."

"My father ran away. I'm just facing the inevitable. How the hell could I ever compete with the perfect man? *Or* the perfect world? I wouldn't stand a chance."

Sam grabbed the carriers Nick had placed on the ground and started toward the house. "I never thought you were one to give up."

Nick reached for the other two carriers but his hand stilled and he looked at Sam's back. "I'm not giving up. I'd already let her go. This makes it final, that's all."

"If that's what you want to keep telling yourself."

His eyes narrowed. He knew exactly what kind of game Sam was playing. Reverse psychology. Hell, he'd used it more than once when he wanted to get information out of a criminal.

It wouldn't work. Kia was leaving for Nerak whether Mala went with her or not. Her mind was already made up, and he damn sure wasn't going to beg her to stay.

Like that would even work.

His thoughts flew back in time. To the day he'd come home to find his father had moved out. His mother was in tears. He'd called his grandmother and she'd given him a number where his dad could be reached.

He'd gone to Sam's and called so his mother wouldn't overhear. A woman had answered the phone and said he wasn't there. Nick had been angry and refused to talk to him for six months.

Maybe if he had figured it out sooner, he wouldn't have begged his father to come home when he did finally speak to him. He might not have made a fool out of himself. He hadn't understood about the other woman until later—after his father had married Cherrie. Damn, she hadn't been much older than Nick. Barely legal. Something inside him clenched tight and squeezed.

"Kia's made up her mind," he told Sam. "She's leaving and there's nothing I can do to stop her."

"No, but I bet we can." A woman spoke as she stepped from around the side of the house.

Nick spun around and saw a gun was pointed right at him.

Chapter 27

Nick clenched his teeth. How could he let some-one get the drop on him? He scanned the area: cedar, pecan, and oak trees, rolling hills.

How?

The middle of nowhere, great cover, and they'd come out of the woodwork.

That's how.

"Who the hell are you?"

The woman was tall and thin and looked only marginally more intelligent than the guy with her.

"She's Darla," the ape said.

"No names, you idiot!" For just a second, she pointed the gun at ape-man, then quickly turned it back on Nick and Sam.

The ape downed his head and kicked at a clod of dirt. "I didn't tell them *my* name."

She stomped her foot. "Slava! There, now they know both our names."

"Slobber?" Nick asked with a raised eyebrow.

"Why, you—" Slava started forward but the woman grabbed his arm.

"He wants you to make a mistake," she hissed. "If you rush him, you'll put yourself in front of the gun. The other one will make a grab for it and that'll be the end of us."

"You're smarter than you look," Sam said.

"Thank you, but flattery will get you nowhere."

They were being held at gunpoint by idiots! Nick was already mad because Kia had failed to mention *companion units* looked like frigging movie stars. His gaze narrowed on the barrel of the twenty-two. Now he was really pissed. It wasn't even a manly gun that had him rooted to the spot. No, it was a little girly pistol.

Darla's gray eyes turned steely. "Inside, both of you, and take the carriers with you. We don't want to leave such precious cargo outside, now do we?"

Dognappers? The pups *did* have their papers. Wouldn't it have been easier to go to a pet store and buy a dog?

Nick eyed her one more time before he started up the steps. He didn't care if she did have a gun, he wasn't letting her get her greedy hands on the pups.

He could take them if the right chance came along. She didn't look too smart, and he didn't think her sidekick even had a brain. Slobber might intimidate some people, but big and ugly didn't mean a thing to Nick.

Sam went inside first, Nick right behind him. He thought about slamming the door in Darla's face but he didn't want to take a chance Slobber would push his way inside and Darla would start shooting.

He glanced around the room, assessing how many people were in danger. Mala was sitting beside Kia on the sofa. Kia stiffened, Mala's eye narrowed, but that was the only indication they knew something was wrong. Barton and Carol were probably in the kitchen. Good, maybe they would stay put and out of harm's way.

"Nick, it's not what you think. I . . ." Kia's words

trailed off when Darla and Slobber walked in behind him.

"It would seem we have company." He watched as Kia's eyes took on a calculating gleam. He could almost hear what she was thinking—could she take them?

He gave an almost imperceptible shake of his head, warning her to hold tight and not do anything. When she nodded her understanding, he breathed a sigh of relief. "This is Slava and Darla. Apparently we have something they want."

"We want what's in those carriers. Open them up." She waved the gun. "Do it now or I shoot your little girlfriend."

Kia's eyes widened as she came to her feet. "No, you can't have them!"

Slobber took a menacing step toward Kia. "You better be quiet. We can do whatever we want."

"Leave her alone!" Mala said.

"You want some of me?" Slava raised his arm, shaking a meaty fist toward Mala.

"Touch one of them and you're dead, buddy," Nick advised with deadly calm.

Slobber hesitated, looking at Darla, then Nick. "I wouldn't really hit a woman. But they need to be good." He frowned. "I only hit men."

"Let's just do as they say," Sam said, trying to bring calm back to the situation. He bent over. "Look, we're opening the carriers."

"Smart man." Darla stepped closer, practically rubbing her hands together.

The first pup bounced out, then the second carrier was opened and the next pup came out and tackled the first one.

"What the hell is this?" Darla waved the gun. "Stop jacking around and open the other two!"

Nick did as she ordered and two more pups came out. One immediately squatted and made a puddle on the floor, and the other ran over to sniff it.

"Those are puppies." Slava looked at Darla. "Can I play with them?"

She stomped her foot. "We're here to find out about your illegal operation." Her eyes narrowed as she looked at each person in the room. "I know all about it."

"Our operation?" Nick had no idea what the crazy broad was talking about.

"Yeah, your operation." She pointed her gun at Kia. "I saw the jewels you flashed when you were shopping that day. Damn near bought out the whole store, so don't try to tell me they weren't real. I wasn't born yesterday."

Kia opened her mouth, but Nick gave her a warning look. She snapped it shut. He breathed a sigh of relief and turned his attention back to Darla. The last thing he wanted Kia to do was agree with Darla that she wasn't young.

He remembered all too well what had happened at the Bountiful Earth offices when she'd told the assistant to the operations manager that she didn't look as if she were born yesterday. The woman had been furious enough to say she was calling security. Kia ended up zapping . . .

His gaze snapped back to Kia. He raised his eyebrows and pretended to push a button. She frowned. He made a pushing motion again and tugged at his shirt. She immediately glanced around the room until her gaze landed on her satchel. Disappointment flitted across her face when she spotted it across the room.

Okay, scratch that idea. Her phazer was too far away.

"And I saw you go in the Bountiful Earth offices and come out with all those papers. When I sneaked inside after you left, I overheard Ms. Big talking on the phone."

Huh? Where the hell was this lady from, outer space? Maybe not outer space, but he'd almost bet she called the state hospital home.

"I followed her and saw the handoff to another lady. When I tailed that one, she unwrapped the Ming vase."

"Ming vase?" *Do what?*

"Yeah, Ming vase," Slobber said, puffing out his chest. "Uncle Yuri put a tail on her. He's the top man. No one messes with him."

"And the carriers? What were they supposed to be?" Nick asked.

Darla shifted from one foot to the other. Her face turned a deep shade of red. "I was wrong about the carriers. Who in their right mind has four mutts in an apartment?" She waved the gun. "But I'm not wrong about the jewels or Ms. Big."

"Yeah, you are wrong about her. There is no Ms. Big," Nick told her.

Slava turned to Darla. "Uncle Yuri isn't going to like that. He's going to be real mad." He brightened. "But he'll be mad at you, not me."

"Shut up! Once he sees the jewels he won't be mad at anyone. It doesn't matter if I was wrong about a *few* things."

"Why don't you turn around and walk back out the door," Sam told her. "We'll forget all about this."

Darla didn't make a move. Not that Nick thought she would.

"I want those jewels. They've got to be worth a fortune. Hand 'em over."

"They're in my satchel," Kia quickly spoke up.

Nick looked across the room. For a moment, he couldn't breathe. What if they suspected she was going after more than the jewels?

What if . . . he stopped worrying so much?

Kia was a warrior. This was what she'd been trained for. She could do this.

"Get the gems," Darla said. "And don't try anything funny or someone will get hurt."

"Of course." Kia stood and started across the room.

"Where are you going?" Darla demanded.

Kia stopped, cocking an eyebrow. "I thought you wanted the jewels. They're in my bag."

Aw, man, don't cop an attitude, babe. Just get the phazer out of your satchel and zap these jerks. Except she wasn't looking at him so she couldn't see his expression that warned her not to push her luck.

"You think you're so smart," Darla sneered. "Well, I know you're not some foreign princess. We're the same, you and me—criminals. You might have everyone else fooled but you can't con me for a minute."

"She sure is pretty, though," Slava said.

Nick bristled. Gorilla-man better not get any ideas about Kia. Slobber might be big and ugly, but Nick would turn his lights off in a heartbeat if he laid a hand on Kia.

"Shut up, Slava. Try to remember why we're here."

With Darla's attention on the brute, Nick inched closer to her. If he could get a little nearer he could . . .

"Don't move!" Darla warned, swinging the gun in his direction, then backing closer to the door.

The door suddenly swung open, banging against the wall.

"Freeze!" Candy yelled as she stormed into the room, gun drawn.

Darla screamed.

Barton stepped from the kitchen.

Nick dove toward Kia to shield her.

He barely heard the sound of the gun as it fired twice.

But he felt the searing pain in his side. He hit the floor with a hard thud, landing on his wound. He gritted his teeth and hoped like hell he didn't pass out.

Concentrate! He had to concentrate.

As if in slow motion, he watched as Kia scrambled inside her satchel, then jerked the phazer out of her bag. She aimed it at Darla and pushed the button. There was a popping noise and Darla was gone.

"What'd you do to Darla?" Slava swung to the right, then the left looking for her. "Darla!"

"Law enforcement, hands up!" Candy spoke from the doorway.

What the hell was Candy doing here? And Weldon stood behind her.

Maybe Nick was hallucinating. He looked at Kia, smiled when he saw she was okay even if she was a little out of focus. Apparently realizing the situation was under control, she quickly slipped her phazer back into her purse. His gaze swept over her again just to be sure she hadn't been hurt. Yeah, she looked better than good.

Damn, he felt like crap, though.

"Okay, where'd the woman go?" Candy swung her gaze around the room.

Nick didn't think he wanted to try to explain how Kia had zapped her. Then he'd have to tell Candy not to worry because Darla would show up in about nineteen minutes or so—minus her clothes.

"Sir, are you okay?" Candy was looking toward the kitchen.

He swiveled his gaze in that direction, feeling as if he'd drunk one too many beers. Barton stood in the doorway, a small hole in the center of his chest with green fluid seeping out. Antifreeze? *Don't let their parts freeze up? Keep the companion units nice and hot.*

Maybe the bullet had been more than a graze. He was losing it.

"I'mperfectlyfinethankyou," Barton said.

Nick blinked several times as he tried to decipher what Barton had just rattled off. He hadn't thought anyone could talk that fast.

"What . . . I . . . meant . . . to . . . say wasssssss . . ."

"Barton, you're not okay. Sit down." Carol led him to the sofa.

"The babies," Mala said and started toward the kitchen.

"Sleeping," Carol told her. "I was in there when the shooting started. They didn't even blink."

Candy tossed her handcuffs to Sam. "Cuff him. I'm going to look for the woman." As soon as Slava was cuffed, she hurried through the house.

"Candy doesn't know she's a . . . a you-know-what," Weldon assured Nick, then quickly looked around, but he didn't have to worry about Slava hearing. He was sitting in a chair against the far wall talking to the puppies that crowded around his feet.

Nick pushed up on one elbow, but couldn't quite make it off the floor.

"He's hurt," Kia said, rushing over. "Nick, are you all right?"

He vaguely heard her words. The room was getting darker and it was getting harder to hear. He made an effort to stay focused. "'Course I'm okay. It's just a scratch, but I might need help getting up." His words slurred.

Slurring words wasn't a good sign. Crap, he was going to be really ticked off if Darla had killed him with her blasted girly gun. He'd like to taste Kia's lips one more time, feel the heat of her body close to his.

"Why didn't you say something?" She knelt beside him, gently pushing him to his back so she could see the extent of his injury.

"Just a flesh wound. It's not the first time I've been shot."

Sam knelt down beside him and did a quick examination. "You're right, a flesh wound. I need a towel or something." He met Nick's gaze. "You're getting blood on Mala's floor."

This was the sympathy he got? He was lying here on the floor dying and his longtime friend and partner was afraid he'd stain the floor?

"It hurts." He glared at Sam. Okay, maybe he was feeling a *little* better. He'd still been shot!

Mala hurried out of the room and came back a few minutes later with a white towel, handing it to Sam.

He applied pressure to the wound. "We need to get you to a hospital, buddy. A Band-aid won't quite do it. Maybe a couple of stitches."

A couple of stitches? It felt as if his whole side had been ripped open!

"I called Mason, Mala's husband, when we were still in the kitchen and told him what was happening," Carol said. "He'll be bringing backup. The ambulance will be on standby, ready to transport," Carol told him.

"Are you sure he's going to live? His lifeblood is draining." Kia worried her bottom lip.

Nick reached out and squeezed her hand. "I'll be . . ." He grimaced. "I'll be fine."

Sam opened his mouth, apparently noticed Nick's warning look, and rolled his eyes as if to say, "give me a break."

Nick's soon-to-be ex-friend wasn't a doctor. What did he know? And maybe he wasn't dying, but Kia didn't know that. He liked the attention she was giving him.

"Promise me your lifeblood won't drain away," Kia whispered.

"As long as you stay with me." As soon as he said the words, it hit him. Aw, hell, when had he fallen in love with her? He closed his eyes for a second, thought back. He remembered the exact moment. It was when she'd walked inside the smoke-filled bar.

"A robot," Weldon breathed, stepping closer to Barton.

Nick opened his eyes. Great, he was lying on the floor, possibly dying, and Weldon was drooling over the fact there was a robot in the room.

"Can you help him?" Carol asked Mala, wringing her hands.

Mala shook her head. "My knowledge only goes so far, and this is beyond my scope. I'm so sorry."

"I can fix him," Weldon said. "I may not be able to fight, or fire a gun . . ." He stood taller. "But I know computers." He knelt beside Barton and opened his shirt. "How do I get inside him?"

Oh, yeah, fix the robot and I'll just lie here at death's door. Hey people, he wanted to shout, *I'm the human with a bullet wound.* But he didn't. Maybe because Barton looked a little too human.

"I'm an Internal Affairs investigator!" Candy yelled from outside.

"Mason is here." Mala looked around the room. "We'd better move Barton to another room. I don't think Earth is ready for him yet, and there will be other people arriving." She hurried to the front door. "I'll make sure Mason doesn't shoot anyone, and tell him to send the ambulance people inside."

"Where's Darla?" Slava asked when she hurried past.

"Just stay where you are," Sam warned.

"Okay, the puppies are cute."

"You promise you're going to be all right?" Kia asked Nick amidst all the confusion.

"I promise."

Mala went outside. A few seconds later a tall, dark man came inside. *Must be the husband*, Nick thought to himself.

"The ambulance is coming. I had them standing by at the gate just in case," Mason said, looking at Nick. "Mala said you'd been shot."

"Just a scratch," Sam said.

Nick glared at him. Couldn't he see as long as Kia thought he was dying, she might stick around? At least until he could convince her to stay.

"Francine." Mason spoke into his radio.

"Yeah, Sheriff?" a woman's voice answered.

"Call Doc Lambert and have him stand by for a gunshot wound. Nothing serious, but he'll still want to take a look."

Could he not get a break from anyone?

"Yes, Sheriff. I'll be sure to explain the ominous nature of the situation."

Ominous nature? Had he been transported to the Twilight Zone?

Mason shrugged. "Francine's word of the day."

Two paramedics pushing a stretcher hurried inside. One started an IV while the other took Nick's blood pressure.

"Allergic to anything?"

"No."

"Are you hurting?"

"Yeah, it burns a little . . ." He saw the worry leave Kia's face. "I mean a lot. The pain is excruciating."

Actually, the pain had eased considerably. He gave
Kia a wobbly smile, focusing on her and not what was
going on around him. It was kind of nice having her
fawn over him.

Maybe Sam was right. It was only a scratch. Hell,
he probably didn't even need to go to the hospital.
And he couldn't let Kia go back to Nerak.

Nick took a deep breath. He'd . . . he'd beg her to
stay and take a chance she would.

"I'm giving you something for the pain, pard,"
one of the paramedics said.

Nick jerked his gaze toward the medic and the
needle he'd inserted into the IV port. For a second
he couldn't move, only watch as the medic pushed
on the barrel, injecting the painkiller into the IV.

No, he couldn't!

The room began to swim.

"He has a strange reaction to meds," Sam said
from the other side of a very long tunnel.

"It's only twenty-five of Demerol."

Oh, God, it might as well have been a hundred
milligrams. Pain medication always made him loopy,
even in small doses.

"No, I don'tttt . . ." The world began to spin. He
started to get up but only managed a few inches.

"Where are they taking him?" Kia asked from far,
far away.

"To the hospital. He'll be okay," Sam reassured
her.

"Kia . . ." He blinked, then everything started getting dark. *Don't go.* But the words didn't come out
of his mouth. Ah, no. He would never see her again . . .

Chapter 28

"**Y**ou finally decided to wake up." A woman's soft voice wrapped around him.

Kia.

Nick smiled and pulled the pillow closer as he fought the last dregs of sleep. Man, he'd slept like a baby. Kia did that to him. Ah, sweet Kia. He dragged his eyes open and looked into the face of a woman . . . but it wasn't Kia.

Bad dream!

He closed his eyes tight.

Ah, man, I didn't do something stupid last night, did I?

Like go on a beer-drinking binge and talk this woman into going home with him. She wasn't as bad looking as the last one, but she damn sure wasn't Kia.

He opened one eye. "Who are you?"

She came into focus again. Ah, crap, she was old enough to be his . . . his . . .

A lot older than him.

Something glinted on her hand when the light above his bed hit it.

How could he? The woman was married. He had to get the hell out of here right now. He started to sit up but she pushed him back down. *Easily* pushed him back down. Wow, that was some binge.

His eyes came into focus. He frowned. Not his apartment, either. Hers?

"Uh, where am I?" he asked.

She turned and gave him a friendly smile. "In the hospital."

Hospital? Had her husband come in and beat the hell out of him? Not that he would blame him. This was the guy's wife.

"You were shot," she continued in a whispery voice, then pointed to the drawn curtain on the other side of his bed where there was apparently another patient, then put a finger to her lips.

Her husband shot him?

Being shot didn't sound good. "Am I dying?" he asked, keeping his voice low so he wouldn't wake the other patient.

She chuckled. "No, it was very superficial. Dr. Lambert only Steri-stripped it."

"Then why am I in the hospital?"

"The paramedics gave you Demerol. It completely knocked you out. We've never seen anything like it, especially such a small dosage. The doctor wanted to keep you overnight just to be on the safe side. Your friend Sam dropped by to check on you late last night, but you were still out of it."

Sam? Everything came back in a rush. The dognappers who turned out to be jewel thieves. Barton was a robot. And Candy was way out of her jurisdiction. This woman was a nurse . . . He sucked in a deep breath.

And Kia . . . Nerak . . .

The nurse raised the blinds, flooding the room with morning light.

He blinked past the sudden brightness that blinded him. It was too late. Kia would be gone by now. Back on Nerak, and there was no way he could reach her.

He didn't even get the chance to beg her to stay or to say good-bye.

Just like when his father had walked out. And the same feelings were there, emptiness and betrayal.

"Are you okay? You look a little pale."

"I'm fine." He'd never be fine again.

"I'll get your vitals, then remove the IV so you won't feel quite so tied down."

"Yeah, okay." Whatever. It didn't matter. Nothing mattered anymore.

She went about her job and when she had the IV out, she covered the site with a cotton ball and piece of tape, then had him bend his arm.

"If you need anything, the call button is on the rail. The doctor will be around to see you in a while and probably release you."

He nodded and looked out the window. Had Kia made it home safely?

"Hey, buddy." Sam spoke in low tones as he came around the curtained side. "How are you feeling?"

"As if I just came off a week-long drunk." He frowned. "And my side is sore," he added so Sam would feel guilty he'd taken the injury so lightly.

Sam chuckled. "You're always such a wimp when it comes to getting shot or stabbed."

"What happened to Darla and Slava?" He put off asking what he wanted to know most of all. A pain worse than the bullet ripped through him. He didn't want to hear when or how Kia had left.

"Yeah, I owe you one for that." Sam wore a sour expression. "Darla with clothes on was bad enough, but naked was enough to give a dead person cold chills. I'll have nightmares for years to come." He made himself comfortable half sitting on the end of the bed. "Right now, she's sitting in jail still wondering what the hell happened."

"And Slava?"

Sam chuckled. "The guy can sing, and the song was all about his uncle Yuri. In case you've forgotten him, he's the head of the Russian mafia in our area. All we had to do was promise to put Slava in the witness protection plan and give him a puppy."

"Not one of mine." Nick glowered. No way was Slava getting one of his pups.

"Nah, we'll get him one from the pound. It does seem like he has a way with dogs, though. I think it'll work out all the way around."

Nick glanced out the window. He guessed with Kia gone he could get his life back in order. It was a dismal thought.

"And Weldon was able to fix Barton," Sam continued. "Did you know Weldon and Candy have a thing for each other? Which is good for you. She said she was dropping the case and you can return to work when you feel better."

"Yeah, everything is great."

Nick closed his eyes. It might have been better if the bullet had killed him, then he wouldn't feel as if he were already dead.

But he had to know. "Did Kia leave? I mean, did everything look okay when she took off?"

"She didn't leave."

Nick's eyes flew open. "What do you mean, 'she didn't leave'?" Hope sprang inside him. He still had a chance.

"Just what I said. She didn't leave."

He flung the covers back and stood. A wave of dizziness rushed over him, forcing him to grab the bed until it was gone. Damn pain med would probably linger all morning, but it wasn't about to stop him. "Get my clothes. I have to get to her before she takes off. I have to beg her to stay."

"Slow down, buddy." Sam pushed the curtain open, revealing Kia sleeping in the other bed. "She's been here all night."

Nick's heart began to pound. "Why didn't she go?"

"I told her if she left, you'd die." He shrugged. "I figured no one would be able to be around you if she left, so I told a little white lie to save us all a lot of heartache."

Nick swallowed past the lump in his throat. He should've known Sam would be watching his back— just like always.

Kia yawned and stretched.

"I think you can handle it from here," Sam said as he watched Kia stirring awake. He was grinning as he left the room.

Kia opened her eyes, then blinked past the sunshine. She smiled when she saw that Nick looked much improved. Her gaze swept over him and she noticed the back of his gown was open. Now that had interesting possibilities.

"You didn't leave," he said.

She shook her head as she got out of her bed and moved to his, then patted the other side for him to get in next to her.

"How could I when you were hurt?"

He took her hand, bringing it to his lips and kissing it. Warm tingles made their way up her arm.

"But I'm okay now." He looked into her eyes. "Please, don't leave me."

"I tried. After you left in the ambulance. I tried but I couldn't. Not now, not ever. I love you."

When she'd seen he was wounded, she'd thought . . . No, this wasn't the time to think about her fear. Nick was alive and they were together.

He covered her lips with his and she felt whole

again. The heat from his kiss seared into her, a promise they would be together forever.

He ended the kiss and she snuggled closer to him.

"What about Lara?" he hesitantly asked.

"Breaking a promise is serious, but there's no other way. I love my sister and I shall miss her horribly. She'll probably never forgive me for leaving and not returning."

"No regrets?"

"No. My love for you is strong enough to help me past the sadness of knowing I'll never return to Nerak. Lara would truly understand. My place is with you."

"I love you."

"Of course," she stated and lowered her lips to his again.

Nick's love, her puppies, and chocolate—who could ask for anything more? Unless it was sex.

Hmmm . . . she wondered . . .

Can't get enough of Karen Kelley's sexy aliens?
Try the rest of the series!

CLOSE ENCOUNTERS OF THE SEXY KIND

Beam me up, hottie . . .

Sex with the perfect man is overrated, especially if your Mr. Perfect is a robot, and you know there's something better out there. Can Mala help it if "out there" is *way* out there? Her grandmother, an intergalactic traveler, left a diary behind describing the exceptional lovemaking talents of Earth men. So Mala decides to head for Earth and see what the fuss is about . . .

When the local conspiracy theorist insists he's seen a UFO land out near Devil's Bend, Sheriff Mason McKinley rides out to investigate. But instead of little green men, he finds the sexiest woman he's ever laid eyes on. Though Mala's odd behavior—an obsession with the naked channel, straightforward offers of sex—might have something to do with amnesia, what red-blooded American male wouldn't feel lucky? Still, Mason doesn't want to take advantage of a lost soul . . . however much she wants to be taken advantage of . . .

"Would you like something to eat?"

Eat? She'd had two food capsules prior to leaving her planet, which was enough nutrition for one rotation, but she was curious about the food on Earth. Her grandmother had mentioned it was almost as good as sex. She just couldn't imagine that.

"Yes, food would be nice."

"Why don't you sit on the sofa and rest while I throw us something together." He picked up a black object. "Here's the remote. I have a satellite dish so you should be able to find something to entertain yourself while I rustle us up some food."

She nodded and took the remote, then watched him leave the room and go into another. The remote felt warm in her hand. A transferal of body heat? Tingles spread up and down her arm. The light above her head flickered.

She glanced up. Now that was odd. But then, she *was* on Earth.

Her attention returned to the remote.

Very primitive. The history books on her planet had spoken about remote controls in the old days. You pointed it at the object it was programmed to work with so you wouldn't have to leave your seat.

She pointed it toward the door and pushed the power button. The door didn't open. She tried different objects around the room without success. Finally she pointed it toward a black box.

The screen immediately became a picture. Of course—television. She made herself comfortable on the lounging sofa and began clicking different channels. Everything interested her, but what she found most fascinating was a channel called Sensual Heat.

She tossed the remote to a small table and curled her feet under her, hugging the sofa pillow, her gaze glued to the screen. A naked man walked across the set, his tanned butt clenching and unclenching with every step he took. When he faced her, the man's erection stood tall, hypnotizing her. It was so large she couldn't take her gaze off it.

A naked woman appeared behind him. She slipped her arms around him, her hands splayed over his chest. Slowly, she began to move her hands over his body, inching them downward, ever closer.

Mala held her breath.

"I want you," the woman whispered. "I want to take you into my mouth, my tongue swirling around your hard cock."

The man groaned.

Mala leaned forward, biting her bottom lip as the man's hands snaked behind him and grabbed the woman's butt. In one swift movement, he turned around. "Damn, you make me hard with just your words."

"And I love when you talk dirty to me."

"So, you want me to tell you what I want to do to your body?"

The woman nodded.

He grinned, then began talking again. "I want to squeeze your breasts and rub my thumbs over your hard nipples." His actions followed his words. "You like that?"

"Yes!" She flung her head back, arching toward the man.

Mala leaned forward, her mouth dry, her body tingling with excitement. Yes! She wanted this, too!

"Do you like French bread, or white bread?" Mason asked, walking into the room.

She dragged her gaze from the television. Bred. That was what humans called copulating. Getting bred. Her nipples ached. "Yes, can we breed now?" She stood and began slipping her clothes off.

"No! That's not what I meant." He hurried forward and grabbed her dress as it slipped off one shoulder, quickly putting it back in place. Damn, what did Doc give her? This was one hell of a side effect.

"You don't want to copulate?" Her forehead wrinkled, causing her to wince and raise her hand to the bump on her head. "Do you find that I'm not to your liking?"

"Yes, I like you."

"But you do not wish to . . ." She bit her bottom lip as if searching for the right words. "To have sex?"

His hand rested lightly on her shoulder as he met her gaze. "Of course I'd like to . . . uh . . ." He marveled at how soft the fabric felt. His fingers brushed her skin, thinking it felt just as soft. What would she taste like? His gaze moved to her lips. Soft . . . full lips. Kissable.

He jerked his hand away from her shoulder. Anyone watching would think he'd been burned . . . and maybe he had, because he certainly felt hot.

He cleared his throat, his gaze not able to meet those innocent, sensuous turquoise eyes. He felt like such a heel. He'd invited her to his home and all he could think about was having hot sex.

THE BAD BOYS GUIDE TO THE GALAXY

Take me to your leader. Come to think of it, just take me.

Planet Nerak was perfect—no disease, no darkness, no hunger—until an expedition to Earth brought back an unwanted guest. Enter one talented Nerakian named Lara, sent on a special fact-finding mission in the vast region called Texas. Fortunately, a warrior (he calls himself a "cop") named Sam Jones has offered to help. Unfortunately, Sam's skill at sex is quite distracting—as are plenty other earthly delights, like the dangerously addictive substance called chocolate. Temptations such as these could seriously compromise Lara's—ahem—research . . .

Crazy, that's what Sam is. What sane man would voluntarily isolate himself in the Texas woods with an alien, not to mention a female one with a superiority complex, legs that won't quit, and a penchant for walking around buck naked? Between bragging about her home planet and levitating, Lara wastes no time getting on Sam's last nerve . . . and even less time getting into his bed. Talk about going where no man has gone before. Of course, when you're from Texas, nothing—not even an entire planet—is going to stop you from getting what you want.

"Where's your dress . . ." He waved a finger around—"thingy . . . robe, whatchamacallit?" He finally pointed toward her.

She raised an eyebrow. He didn't seem to notice the clean floor. Disappointment filled her. She'd hoped for more. Silly, she knew. After all, he was an earthman, and she shouldn't care what he thought.

"My robe was getting dirty along the hem, so I removed it."

Her gaze traveled slowly over him, noting the bulge below his waist. It was quite large. Odd. She mentally shook her head.

"Your clothes are quite dirty. Once again, I've proven that I'm superior in my way of thinking," she told him.

"You're naked."

She glanced down. "You're very observant," she said, using his earlier words. "Did you know there's a slight breeze outside? It made my nipples tingle and felt quite pleasant. Not that I would be tempted to stay on Earth because of a breeze."

"You . . . you . . . can't . . ."

She frowned. "There's something wrong with your speech. Are you ill? If you'd like, I can retrieve my diagnostic tool and examine you." He was sweating.

Not good. She only hoped she didn't catch what he had.

"You can't go around without clothes," he sputtered. "And I'm not sick."

"Then what are you?"

"Horny!" He marched to the other room, returning in a few minutes with her robe. "You can't go around naked."

"Why not?" She slipped her arms into the robe and belted it.

"It causes a certain reaction inside men."

"What kind of a reaction?" What an interesting topic. She wanted to know more. Maybe they would be able to have a scientific conversation.

Kia had only talked about battles, and Mala had talked about exploration of other planets, but Sam was actually speaking about something to do with the body. It was a very stimulating discussion.

He ran a hand through his hair. "I'm going to kill Nick," he grumbled. "No one said anything about having to explain the birds and bees."

"And what's so important about these birds and bees?"

He drew in a deep breath. "When a man sees a naked woman, it causes certain reactions inside him."

"Like the bulge in your pants? It wasn't there before."

"Ah, Lord."

"Did my nakedness do that?"

"You're very beautiful."

"But I'm not supposed to think so."

"No, we're not talking about that right now."

She was so confused. Sam wasn't making sense. "Then please explain what we are talking about."

"Sex," he blurted. "When a man sees a beautiful

and very sexy naked woman, it causes him to think about having sex with her."

He looked relieved to finally have said so much. She thought about his words for a moment. A companion unit did not have these reactions unless buttons were pushed, and even then, their response would be generic. This was very unusual. But also exciting that her nakedness would make him want to copulate. She felt quite powerful.

And she was also horny now that she knew what the word meant. She untied her robe and opened it. "Then we will join."

He made a strangled sound and coughed again and jerked her robe closed. "No, it's not done like that. Dammit, I'm not a companion unit to perform whenever you decide you need sex."

"But don't you want sex?"

"There are emotions that need to be involved. I'm not one of those guys who jump on top of a woman, gets his jollies, and then goes his own way."

"You want me on top?" She'd never been on top, but she thought she could manage.

He firmly tied her robe, then raised her chin until her gaze met his.

"When I make love with a woman, I want her to know damn well who she's with, and there won't be anything clinical about it." He lowered his mouth to hers.

He was touching her again. She should remind him that it was forbidden to touch a healer. But there was something about his lips against hers, the way he brushed his tongue over them, then delved inside that made her body ache, made her want to lean in closer, made her want to have sex other than just to relieve herself of stress.

And don't miss Karen's latest,
HOW TO SEDUCE A TEXAN,
available now from Brava . . .

She topped a rise and slammed on the brakes, the car fishtailed, spewing a thick cloud of dust behind her. Her heart felt as if it had taken residence in her throat. She skidded to a stop, barely missing the cow that languidly stood in the middle of the road looking unconcerned that it had almost been splattered across her windshield.

Nikki's heart pounded inside her chest and her hands shook. She closed her eyes and took a deep breath. When she opened them again, the black and white cow looked at her with total unconcern. This was so not how she wanted to start her vacation slash investigative reporting.

"I almost wrecked because of you." She glared at the cow with her cold-eyed, steely glare that she'd perfected over the years. If it had been a person rather than a dumb animal, it would've been frozen to the spot.

The cow opened its mouth and bellowed a low, meandering, I-was-here-first moo.

She didn't think the cow cared one little bit that it had almost become hamburger. Damned country. She'd take city life and dirty politicians any day.

"Move!" She clapped her hands.

The cow didn't get in any hurry as it lumbered to

the side of the narrow road and lowered its head. The four-legged beast chomped down on a bunch of grass, then slowly began to chew.

She shifted into park, then waved her arms. "Shoo!"

Nothing.

She honked the horn.

Nothing.

The hot sun beat down on her. A bead of sweat slid uncomfortably between her breasts. She judged the narrow road, wondering if she could maneuver around the cow without going into the ditch.

Before she decided to attempt it, another sound drew her attention. She glanced down the dirt road, shielding her eyes from the glare of the sun as a cloud of dust came toward her. The cloud of dust became a man on a horse.

Correction. A cowboy on a horse.

Hi-ho, Silver, the Lone Ranger, she thought sarcastically.

But the closer he got, the more her sarcasm faded. The Lone Ranger had nothing on this cowboy. Broad shoulders, black hat pulled low on his forehead . . .

Black hat. Bad guys wore black hats. Right? Things were looking up.

At least until he brought the horse to a grinding halt and dust swirled around her—again. She coughed and waved her hands in front of her face.

"Bessie, how the hell do you keep getting out?" he asked.

His slow, southern drawl drizzled over her like warmed honey, and she knew from experience warmed honey drizzling over her naked body could be very good. Sticky, but oh so sexy.

Did he look as good as he sounded?

She shaded her eyes again at the same time he pushed his hat higher on his forehead with one finger. Cal

Braxton's tanned face stared down at her. His cool, deep green eyes only made her body grow warmer with each passing second.

So this was the infamous playboy star football player. The man who had a pretty woman on his arm almost every night of the week—at least until Cynthia Cole had come into his life.

"I almost hit your cow," she told him as she slipped off one of her high heels and rubbed the insole with her other foot. It didn't stop the tingle of pleasure that was running up and down her legs. He could park his boots by her bed any day.

"Sorry about that. Bessie thinks the grass is greener on the other side of the fence."

He pulled a rolled-up rope off the saddle horn and swatted the end of it against Bessie's rump. The cow gave him a disgruntled look before ambling down the road.

His gaze returned to her . . . roaming over her . . . seducing her. "Are you lost?"

"On vacation."

He easily controlled the prancing horse beneath him. "Staying nearby?"

"At the Crystal Creek Dude Ranch."

His grin was slow. So, he did have all his teeth, and they were pearly white. She ran her tongue over her dry lips.

"My brother owns it," he said. "I'm helping him out. It looks like we might be seeing a lot of each other. Name's Cal—Cal Braxton."

His thumb idly stroked the rope. For a moment, she was mesmerized as she watched the hypnotic movement.

"You know, you shouldn't drive with the top down in this heat," he said.

She almost laughed. It wasn't the heat from the sun

that had momentarily stolen her wits. Cal was good. Ah, yes, he knew all the moves that made a woman yearn for him to caress her naked skin. And he made those moves very well.

Historical Romance from
Jo Beverley

An Arranged Marriage   0-8217-6401-2   **$6.99US/$9.99**CAN

An Unwilling Bride   0-8217-6724-0   **$6.99US/$9.99**CAN

Christmas Angel   0-8217-6843-3   **$6.99US/$9.99**CAN

Tempting Fortune   0-8217-7347-X   **$6.99US/$9.99**CAN

Forbidden Fruit   0-8217-7599-5   **$6.99US/$9.99**CAN

Dangerous Joy   0-8217-7346-1   **$6.99US/$9.99**CAN

The Shattered Rose   0-8217-7934-6   **$6.99US/$9.99**CAN

Available Wherever Books Are Sold!

Visit our website at **www.kensingtonbooks.com**.

Discover the Romances of

__Hig
__Hig
__Hig
__Hig
__Hig
__Hig
__Hig
__Hig
__Hig
__Hig
__Hig
__Hig
__Hig
__Hig

Available Wherever Books Are Sold!

Visit our website at **www.kensingtonbooks.com**